CU00923160

# THE HOUSE AT ANGEL'S BEACH

PHILLIPA NEFRI CLARK

Storm

Ebook ISBN: 978-1-80508-363-4
Paperback ISBN: 978-1-80508-365-8

Cover design: DB Cover Design
Cover images: iStock, Shutterstock

Published by Storm Publishing.
For further information, visit:
www.stormpublishing.co

ALSO BY PHILLIPA NEFRI CLARK

**Temple River**

*The Cottage at Whisper Lake*

*The Bookstore at Rivers End*

**Rivers End Romantic Women's Fiction**

*The Stationmaster's Cottage*

*Jasmine Sea*

*The Secrets of Palmerston House*

*The Christmas Key*

*Taming the Wind*

*Martha*

**Bindarra Creek Rural Fiction**

*A Perfect Danger*

*Tangled by Tinsel*

**Maple Gardens Matchmakers**

*The Heart Match*

*The Christmas Match*

*The Menu Match*

**Detective Liz Moorland Series**

*Lest We Forgive*

*Lest Bridges Burn*

*Last Known Contact*

*To Amanda and Matt. And to Emily G.*

# PROLOGUE

*2012*

The top of the steep driveway was the worst part.

The car struggled for traction, wheels spinning in the mud and the gears grinding as the driver's foot missed the clutch three times before making contact. First gear, then second, and with a jolt the front tyres reached the bitumen on the other side of the gate.

Rain and the dark made it impossible to see where the girl was. Which way she'd run.

But it made sense she'd be going home as fast as she could.

*I have to find her first. I have to explain everything so she understands.*

The car turned left onto the main road to Rivers End.

*Clutch, gear change. Again. Accelerate.*

So much water on the road. The wipers weren't working. A fumble for the dial turned on the radio instead. Old cars like this were next to useless. Nothing was automatic.

*How do I turn the stupid wipers on?*

Brilliant light flooded the car.

Headlights on the wrong side of the road.

Almost dead ahead.

With every ounce of strength the driver hauled the steering wheel away from the oncoming lights, sending the car sliding and spinning and then an almighty crash and glass breaking and the seat belt straining and then an abrupt, shuddering stop.

Silence.

Rain was coming through a broken window.

Gasping breaths.

*I'm alive. I missed the other car.*

The door wouldn't open but then someone was there, pulling until it groaned and relented.

Hands helping the driver out. Checking for injury.

'I'm fine. I missed them.'

But that wasn't true. Up the road a bit, in a ditch, a car was on its side. The headlights pointed toward the clifftop overlooking the sea.

'I almost died.'

'Why were you driving?' The voice was yelling. 'You were drinking all night.'

The other person ran to the second car, then back.

'We have to go.'

Someone else was there. Upset voices. Pointing and yelling. So much yelling, until the voices quieted.

The driver's arm was gripped. 'Come with me.'

'Where?'

*Shouldn't I be helping?*

There were other noises. Sirens grew louder and they walked faster.

*Where are we going?*

In a minute there were trees all around and the road was further away, but still, red and blue lights from a police car flashed through. The sirens cut out as vehicles surrounded the wrecks. Doors slammed and people shouted to each other.

Unforgettable words.

'Over here! I think she's dying. Hurry!'

# ONE

The ceiling was white, or would be once dust and water spots were removed. Paint peeled around the rather ugly chandelier. From the rose to the window, reminiscent of a lightning strike, a zigzagging crack was yet another sign of the decay of the room.

Of the whole house.

*And a mirror of my life.*

Ivy was bone-tired.

As dust motes danced in rays of early morning sunlight through the window near her makeshift bed – an old and lumpy sofa – Ivy had no interest in getting up. Discomfort was fitting for today. For here and now and what was to come. The only thing missing was the grey sky and endless rain she'd left in England only a few days ago. But this was springtime in Australia, with the promise of warm, bright days at her childhood home near the sea. The backdrop of waves whooshing onto the sand had been the one thing which had helped her get any sleep since arriving two days ago.

Jet lag was one reason she'd struggled to settle at night.

Being back at Fairview House was another.

And if she was completely honest, the arrival later today of her sister had more to do with it than anything else.

Rolling onto her side, Ivy squeezed her eyes shut. This day should be one of excitement and anticipation at seeing Jody again after four long years. A final flurry of cleaning and preparing a bedroom and bathroom for her to use during her stay, adding a vase of flowers from the garden, and planning a nice dinner together – perhaps a picnic on the beach.

Instead, she was hiding beneath a blanket and her stomach was churning.

Growing up they'd been inseparable.

*Things happen. People change.*

While true on the surface, it was a long way from the whole truth of the matter. The phone call a month ago, just before Jody's thirtieth birthday, had been out of the blue. Despite the divide between them since the fallout over Jody's wedding, Ivy always called on her birthday, careful to take the time zones into account between England and Australia – where Jody had settled. For the first time in ages, Jody made the call because she was about to inherit a share of Fairview. It was time, she'd said, for the two of them to make a united stand against the past and finally move forward.

Although reluctant to ever set foot in Fairview again, Ivy had finally agreed. They'd been apart far too long, with hurt feelings and harsh words a constant barrier. Mistakes and misunderstandings on both sides. So, Ivy had taken leave from her job and made arrangements for one final flight to Australia.

Hiding from the day wasn't helping and Ivy groaned dispro-portionately at the effort of getting up when an urge to visit the bathroom forced her into action.

Thanks to a broken hot-water system which put her off the idea of a shower, Ivy did her best with a cold face-wash which was less than pleasant. Someone was coming to look at the system today, thank goodness. Just a pity to spend money on the place when its future was in limbo. Back in the small, upstairs living room where she'd been sleeping, she donned shorts and T-shirt and then ran down the curved staircase, trying to ignore old memories of better days. They'd haunted her since she'd climbed off the bus at the top of the driveway a few days ago and every single one of them was unwanted.

In the kitchen, she filled the kettle she'd dug up from a cupboard and thoroughly cleaned. Ivy had bought some instant coffee, bottled water, and a few snacks as she'd waited in Melbourne for the bus. Before leaving the city she'd texted the woman who kept an eye on the place to ask for a few cleaning supplies to be dropped off and sure enough, a box filled with the items on her list, along with keys to all the doors on the property, was on the kitchen table on her arrival. And Mary had been extra thoughtful and cleaned and turned on the fridge, and left a couple of homemade meals.

The first sip of coffee was pure nectar and Ivy took the cup upstairs and into a bedroom in a corner of the old house. There were two windows, one overlooking the long and winding driveway and one facing the front of the property, with a view all the way to the sea. After opening both windows, Ivy sipped her coffee, her eyes drinking in the Southern Ocean. She and Jody used to share this bedroom as kids. And when Mum took them to live in England all those years ago, Dad kept this room set up for their summer visits. In almost two years before their first trip back, their life in the little seaside town had faded from their thoughts and it had been strange coming back to a father and a home they barely remembered.

'Until I stood here again.'

It had all come back to her then and she'd wept with joy when her feet hit the soft, warm sand for the first time again. Jody had been every bit as enamoured with the little beach, which always felt like their own private playground. An unexpected smile touched Ivy's lips.

*This isn't getting the rooms ready.*

She needed to get on with things. After her coffee.

Jody could have this as her room. She'd always loved it and wanted it for herself but back when Fairview House was thriving as a must-go destination hub for artists of all kinds, bedrooms were a precious commodity needed for guests and even as teens, the girls had shared. Ivy turned her attention to the other window. A memory hit her suddenly.

*Jody was running up the driveway. Rain bucketed down and she wasn't even wearing a raincoat. Where was she going so late at night?*

Ivy's heart jolted and she lurched back. Where had that come from? She blinked and looked out again, to brilliant sunshine and no sign of her sister. It wasn't a memory. Not hers, anyway. Jody *had* run up there the night of the car crash, but Ivy had been asleep. The house was playing games with her head.

Cleaning helped push away the nerves in her stomach and she worked through her list.

*Vacuum everything, including the walls and ceiling. Wash the walls with a solution of vinegar and water. Mop the timber floorboards with more of the same. Turn the mattress.*

She stared at the bed.

It was ten years since she'd been in this room. What a different life it was then. Jody had been in England, pursuing a performing arts degree. Ivy was living here, working at Fairview as well as undertaking her own studies. It was hard to believe she was back in her childhood bedroom. Now it was Jody living in Australia while Ivy had turned her back on the country she'd once loved so dearly.

*Not just Australia.*

The ringing of her phone kicked her brain back into the present and she answered without looking, expecting it to be one of the local tradespeople she'd left messages with yesterday.

'Ivy Ross speaking.'

'Are you at the house?'

'Hi Jody. Yes, I've been here for a couple of days.'

'For some reason I thought it was today you were arriving and I wondered why we didn't arrange for me to get you at the airport. Anyhow, I'm in Green Bay and was going to pick up some supplies. Unless you've been shopping?'

Ivy left the bedroom and followed the hallway to a large built-in linen cupboard.

'I've got everything for cleaning but almost nothing in the way of food. But the fridge is running, so it's probably safe to bring a few things.'

'Do you have a list?'

Jody sounded as vague as ever.

'No. Just pick up something for lunch and we can shop later.' She found a set of brand new sheets, still in their packaging, and took them to the bedroom. 'And milk if you want it in coffee.'

'Tea? I'll get some tea. Are there still cups and a kettle?'

'Yes. And I have tea. So just milk. And lunch. Bread rolls and cheese if that makes it easier.'

'Any type of cheese? What about some relish? There's some nice relish here.'

'Relish is fine. Any cheese. And milk. If you want it.'

'What about plates and a knife?'

Rolling her eyes, Ivy slid the sheets from their packaging. 'Most of the house is as it was left, so there are plates and knives and even fresh bedding. I'll see you in a bit.'

*Hang up now, Jody.*

'Yes. See you in a bit.'

The line went dead and Ivy sighed. At least Jody sounded like her old self, instead of being angry all the time. Or cold. If there was one positive of this time at Fairview, it was the chance to mend fences with her sister.

. . .

The bedroom as done as it was going to be in a hurry, Ivy repeated her cleaning efforts in the main upstairs bathroom. Later she'd work out her own sleeping arrangements because her back ached and it wasn't all from the scrubbing and vacuuming. Thirty-three years of age was too old to sleep on a lumpy sofa.

As she carried the bucket and mop downstairs, a flash of yellow went past the open front door and a car's motor ground to a halt. Leaving everything in the laundry, she took a second or two to calm sudden nerves, then went to greet her sister.

The Mini Cooper was a convertible and indeed, bright yellow.

And the woman climbing out was hardly the sister Ivy knew.

Had someone else arrived by coincidence?

Jody had always had long golden hair and carried a few extra kilos – just enough to make her curvy and get plenty of attention from young men. She wasn't one to worry about her dress code and preferred jeans to anything.

But this woman was thin. Not just slender, but underweight, to Ivy's trained eye. Her hair was cropped into a pixie cut and dyed in a fashionable silver colour. She was dressed in a body-hugging short dress and heels. Not noticing Ivy on the steps of the house, she closed the door of the car and leaned down to check herself in the side mirror.

So elegant and... perfect.

The woman straightened and saw Ivy and waved, the wide smile exactly the same as Jody's. She hurried around the car and Ivy met her halfway and they hugged as if they would never let go of each other again. Jody felt as thin as she looked and Ivy had the silly thought that if she squeezed too hard, she might break. But her sister hung on to her until more than a minute passed.

They both stepped back.

'Well, look at you.' Jody's eyes swept over Ivy. 'Did we switch bodies?'

'You've lost weight.'

'You've gained it.'

Ouch.

*The stress of running a Covid hospital ward for two years will do that.*

'Your car is rather... bright. And fancy.'

Jody laughed shortly. 'And more expensive than you'd expect for such a small thing. Bit like jewellery, I expect.'

And she wore plenty. Rings, earrings, two pendants. All were tasteful and looked costly.

'Shall we go in? Let's get your luggage.'

The Mini might look small but there was room for two suitcases, a computer bag, and a suit bag. Oh, and a bag of groceries, which Jody picked up, along with the clothing bag.

One by one, Ivy hauled out each suitcase, surprised at their weight.

'Good thing we're not flying, although with first class it probably doesn't matter so much,' Jody said.

*First class travel. Expensive jewellery. And car. Where is Jody?*

Between them they dragged the luggage up the couple of steps and through the front door before Jody returned to the car to put up the roof and lock it. About to remind her that they were in the middle of nowhere, Ivy kept the thought to herself. Her sister lived in the city and was used to keeping everything under lock and key.

Jody caught up, closing and locking the front behind her.

'Leave it open. The house is desperate to be aired.'

'Best to protect ourselves, don't you think? And our belongings.' Unfazed, Jody gazed around. 'It is a lot smaller than I remember.'

'It is a lot more run-down, for sure. I know Mary – the lady who used to work here – has come in a couple of times a year just to do a basic clean. Remove cobwebs. Open windows for a while. But there is so much to do, Jodes. So much.'

'Well if you get your way, a developer will bulldoze the lot.'

'I don't remember ever mentioning developers and bulldozers.'

Jody shrugged.

'Let's get the shopping in the fridge.' Ivy took the bag and led the way, talking over her shoulder. 'Rather than letting Fairview deteriorate further, the only options are to sell or else rebuild the business. And the latter is what Dad wants, I expect.'

In the kitchen Ivy unpacked quickly, putting the milk, cheese, and some tubs of Greek yoghurt into the fridge. 'Tea or coffee?'

'Tea.'

Jody stood in the doorway watching, her expression unreadable. Maybe it was the makeup. The false eyelashes. Perhaps Ivy just hadn't got used to the changes in her sister.

'Dad doesn't really get a say though. Not if you and I make a decision, because between us we own more of Fairview than he does. I'd think a developer would pay a lot more for this dump than a private buyer.'

'But you loved it here, Jodes.' Ivy topped up the kettle. 'This was always your happy place.'

Jody finally took a seat at the old kitchen table. 'Things changed, didn't they. Dad changed them.'

*He drove drunk and killed another driver. And I hate him for it.*

Ivy kept her dark thoughts private and her voice even. 'I

guess he's been paying for it in prison and deserves every minute he's in there.'

'You don't mean that. People make mistakes.'

'Mistakes?' Ivy's laugh was bitter. 'He lied about being the driver. For two years, he let us all believe the car was stolen to protect himself. I don't think I can forgive or trust anyone who lies to such a degree. Can you?'

Jody should be agreeing. They'd both been hurt and their lives turned upside-down. But there was a peculiar vulnerability in her sister's eyes when she softly spoke. 'Not everything in life is always as it seems on the surface, Ivy.'

The shrill whistle of the kettle stopped Ivy from asking what Jody meant. As she finished making the tea, she forced the anger down. Today wasn't about rehashing the choices their father made but finding a middle ground. Stepping stones back to each other. This rising tension was no good for either of them and although it was clear they had differing opinions about Dad, their own relationship was more important to her right now. She wanted to heal it. Somewhere under the new-look-sister who sat in the kitchen was the same girl Ivy had grown up with and loved with her whole heart. If there was one thing Ivy excelled at these days it was managing her emotions and wearing a cloak of composure.

No more angry laughs. No more debating Dad.

Ivy ignored the nagging voice in her head. The one which told her she didn't have a hope of keeping the cloak around her shoulders this time.

# TWO

After a lot of pulling and pushing, Ivy and Jody got the luggage upstairs and then there was a bit of complaining about the bed being a single rather than the king size she was now accustomed to at home. Ivy was happy to leave her to unpack while she made lunch.

Jody had been right to have them come here, as much as Ivy was uncomfortable back in Fairview House. Being in the same time zone again and face to face was the best chance they had to sort out the future of the property. It was deteriorating after a decade without residents and was a waste of the money being paid for insurance and land rates.

'I had to buy new clothes,' Jody said. She wandered into the kitchen, glancing at the plate Ivy had just put on the table piled with cheese and relish rolls. 'I never wear shorts and beach stuff and gave my old clothes away when I trimmed down. Any excuse to shop is a good one.' Her eyes rested on Ivy's waist. 'It was always harder to buy nice clothes when I was heavier.'

'Have some carbs. You look like you haven't had any in ages and lack of them can make people a bit... tactless.' Ivy pushed the plate toward her sister. 'I have gained exactly six kilos since you saw me four years ago.'

With a shrug, Jody picked up the plate. 'I noticed the bottled water in the fridge so bring a couple and we'll sit outside.'

She didn't wait for an answer.

Jody's idea of "outside" was to walk down to the beach.

A bottle in each hand, Ivy jogged to catch up, passing cottages on either side of the wide path. They settled under the last tree before the beach, on patchy grass where they'd sat hundreds of times. Sea air filled Ivy's senses. Her plans the last two days to go for a walk had come to nothing, being too busy and tired, and now she was struggling not to run into the waves and splash like a kid.

No sooner had they sat than several seagulls circled and then landed in anticipation of a feed.

Jody waggled a finger at them. 'No chippies here, fellas!'

Ivy laughed and Jody gave her a curious look.

'You used to say that all the time. Even when we had a whole packet of hot chips.'

'I did? Probably. The only gulls I see these days are the ones on the Melbourne Cricket Ground. Aaron's company has a corporate box there and no matter whether it is football, cricket, or even a rock concert, the seagulls make an appearance at some point.'

'How is Aaron? Sounds like the company is going well?'

Jody picked up a bread roll and gazed at it. 'Very well. Both him and the company. Cyber security is huge and his people are good. Really good. He's thinking of buying an apartment in Queensland, somewhere on the beach. Likes the idea of us zipping up there for a long weekend when the weather is freezing at home.' She took the top off the bun and tossed it to the seagulls, causing a riot as they jostled to tear pieces off.

'Oh, you know not to give them bread.'

'Better them than me.' Jody shrugged and bit into a slice of cheese.

They ate in silence, Jody only nibbling on the cheese with a bit of relish then downing the bottle of water. Ivy's appetite was poor but stress worked in funny ways on her. She either couldn't eat or couldn't stop and today was a couldn't eat day. There was still so much to do, but sitting here with the breeze ruffling her hair was a welcome break. The ocean was a pretty shade of blue-green under the clear sky, but the water might be deceptively cooler than it looked with springtime only partway through. Nothing had ever matched the velvety warmth of the summer sea here.

*It's been too long between visits.*

Ten years since she'd seen the waves roll onto the golden sand. Four years since a quick trip to Melbourne to support Jody when their father's attorney had secured an appeal against his sentence for vehicular manslaughter and other charges. Ivy wasn't needed as such, but Jody had heard the crash and been on the scene within a couple of minutes so her testimony mattered and although he hadn't walked free, Gabe's time left to serve was marginally reduced. The cost of reliving the experience for Jody was profound and she'd retreated to the long silences and copious tears from the past. Ivy had only come for her sister, because if it was left to her, their father could end his days behind bars.

After a week, Ivy had returned to England and resumed her nursing career.

Jody stayed and married the much-older Aaron, whom she'd met just before the hearing.

Ivy snuck a look at her sister. She'd never met Aaron but the changes in Jody were remarkable and it was too soon to decide if they were for the better.

'Stop staring. Is it because my hair is short?'

'The style really suits you.'

That seemed to surprise Jody and a faint smile appeared for a moment. 'I wasn't sure at first but I like it. Feel less like a hippy.'

'You were never a hippy, Jody. Just free-spirited and talented.'

'And look how far that got me.' The smile was gone. Jody got to her feet and brushed herself down although hardly any sand had touched her. 'Shall we do a walk-through and see what we're up against?'

They started with the main house. Jody collected her iPad.

'Better than pen and paper, Ivy. Look at this.' She turned the screen. 'I write by hand and the clever thing turns it into readable text which I can print out. Useful for committee meetings.'

'Committee meetings?'

'I'm sure I've told you.' Jody frowned. 'I'm CEO of the charity which Aaron's company started, plus I sit on the boards of several others. You *must* know.'

'I absolutely did not know.'

*But your acting career held such promise. Have you really stopped following your dreams for film and theatre?*

A small piece of Ivy's heart broke.

'How weird. We can talk about them later because it is just as weird being back here. In my head this looked different,' Jody said.

They were in the living room, which sprawled across several sitting areas with a massive fireplace.

'Different?'

'Warmer. Not in temperature but the feel of the room; now it is cold and sad.'

'There was always something happening in here. Music. People. Food.'

Ivy wandered to a grand piano which was covered in a dust sheet. She lifted the sheet but changed her mind. They weren't here to relive the past. Not even the good parts.

'How do you want to do this, Jodes? We each own one third of Fairview. You, me, and Dad. I think we need to have an accurate picture of the assets and property in order to make sound decisions, don't you? Shall we itemise the important things like the piano? And make a note of anything needing attention?'

Jody made a spluttering sound and Ivy grinned.

'Okay, I know it all needs work. What if we just mention each room and anything notable. Then later we can fill in any blanks.'

'Sure. One way or another, Dad will need money to live on once he's released next year, so even if we keep Fairview, we might need to sell some assets.'

'The grand piano is an asset. It came over from England decades ago and is worth a lot. Actually, can you make a note about checking the insurance? I know everything is kept up to date thanks to Dad's solicitor managing his affairs, but now we have interests, it's time for the two of us to be involved.'

Jody made a note. 'Done. So, I'll add the piano to my list of assets.'

*An evening filled with laughter and songs around the piano. Dad playing, his face alight with joy as a guest requested and then sang a tune along with him. Jody curled up in the corner of a sofa with a book. Ivy sitting cross-legged on the floor with a notepad, scribbling words about her impressions and sketching some of the people.*

'And the artwork in here?'

Ivy blinked and the music faded.

'Yes.'

Jody finished writing and left the room.

So much for not reminiscing. Something moved in Ivy's heart. Ghosts from the past. That was all it was.

The rest of the lower floor was straightforward. The dining room with its huge mahogany table and matching chairs and sideboards was able to seat sixteen. Dad's taste was eclectic and he'd kept a number of pieces which were in the house when he bought it almost fifty years ago. Georgian in style, the house had been owned by one family for generations before the last of them died and it became a deceased estate. And one at a bargain price, hidden away from the Great Ocean Road and more popular tourist spots. But perfect for his vision of a retreat for painters and poets and novelists and sculptors.

A formal lounge was much smaller and more intimate, and had another fireplace.

Despite appliances modern decades ago but desperately in need of replacing, the kitchen was a warm and welcoming room and always a favourite for family and guests.

And so it went.

Upstairs were six bedrooms and two of the three bathrooms. In addition, there was the second living room where Ivy had been sleeping, and a library.

Opening the door to the latter was a dreadful shock.

Ivy and Jody stood in silence, surveying the mess. Floor-to-ceiling bookcases lined three walls of the room, broken only by the window facing the back of the property. Beside the door was a long narrow table with two banker's lamps and two chairs. There'd once been a couple of armchairs beneath the window but they were gone.

'Last time I was in here, the bookshelves were filled. But look at them,' Ivy said.

Jody's mouth had dropped open and her eyes glistened.

They'd loved this room. No book was off-limits and they'd read far beyond their years since a young age. Many afternoons and evenings were passed in companionable silence broken only by the sharing of a passage or their father suggesting that bedtime was long past.

'The window is broken.'

Ivy stepped over piles of precious books which covered the floor. All but the top shelves on either side were empty, their contents unceremoniously dumped. Glass from the smashed window pane littered the floor, the lock was dangling, and the window was open by more than six inches. She carefully opened it further and put her head out.

'Oh my goodness.'

'Let me see.' Jody poked her head through. 'Huh? But why climb up a ladder to this window instead of breaking one downstairs?'

A long ladder was flat on the grass below.

'Why do this at all?'

Ivy straightened and surveyed the room.

'Do you think kids would do this as a lark?'

Jody picked up a copy of an Enid Blyton book, one they'd both read multiple times as children. 'Drag a huge and heavy ladder from one of the sheds? Then climb up it, break the glass and lock, lift an awkward window and wreck the place? As a *lark*?'

'A dare, maybe. Empty houses can attract all sorts of strange things.' Ivy gazed at the top shelves. 'Those are too high for anyone to reach. Didn't there used to be rolling ladders in here?'

'Yes, look the rails are still there. Anyway, we're going to have to clean this up.'

'We will, Jody. And we can add a new lock to our shopping list today.'

'And someone to replace it.'

'I can do that as well as board the window up until we can find a glazier.'

Raising both eyebrows, Jody placed the book onto a shelf.

'Don't look like that. I renovated my flat and there's not much I won't have a crack at doing.'

'See, that is all well and good if you are single, but Aaron would be horrified if I wanted to fix something or repaint our apartment. That's what tradespeople are for.'

'I doubt one's marital status has anything to do with it, because plenty of couples work on their houses. Together. And it's satisfying.' And not everyone had the money to hire professionals for every job. Had Jody become a bit snobby?

But Jody was already on her way out of the library.

This was the only room which had been trashed. Ivy's eyes were drawn, again, to those higher shelves. Had the person been looking for something rather than it being a prank? If so, had they found whatever had motivated them to cause such destruction?

'Or couldn't you reach?'

It must have been a recent break-in as Mary had assured Ivy the place was secure and had checked each room.

A shiver went up her spine.

Had the intruder been here when she arrived?

# THREE

'Do you really want the local police knowing we're here? You know what they think of us.' Jody opened the passenger door of her car and tossed the keys to Ivy, who was a few feet behind her.

'You want me to drive your canary car?'

'Well I can't see your car anywhere,' Jody said.

'I got a bus from Melbourne. No point me hiring a car when I don't know how long I'll be here.'

'And just how did you plan to get around?'

Ivy patted her stomach. 'Great opportunity to walk off these hundreds of kilos you think I'm carrying.'

'All the way to town?'

'All the way.'

Muttering something about being the sister of a madwoman, Jody climbed in. About to tease her about not wanting to drive, Ivy clamped her lips shut. The accident Dad caused had happened not far from here and although Jody had only been a witness to the carnage, unpleasant memories might be making her a bit nervous.

Once she'd worked out the instrument panel, Ivy nosed the

Mini along the driveway which wound around the front of the house then between a row of trees leading up to the road in a gradual rise. From the gate at the end of the long, narrow dirt road, it was impossible to see the house and cottages further down. The property was as secluded and private as any she'd ever come across. Jody jumped out to open and then close the old timber gate.

They turned left onto the road which connected Green Bay to Rivers End, and then would meet up with the Great Ocean Road a few kilometres past the town. They passed a right-hand turn leading to what was once a bustling train station, now abandoned, and a graveyard on the left, overlooking the sea. Both glanced at it then looked ahead in silence. That was where Jean Curry, the driver of the other car, was buried.

The road began to descend and the town of Rivers End appeared spread out before them.

'I'd forgotten how pretty it is,' Ivy said. 'And look at how much it has grown!'

'What's that big building near the old church?'

'Can't see. Watching the road.'

At the bottom of the hill, Temple Bridge crossed the river. As the car bumped over the old hardwood planks, Ivy took a quick look to her left, where the river flowed under an arch of sorts which was part of the limestone cliff, and then disappeared. She knew where it went. A lagoon on the beach. It was where the river met the sea.

Ten years was a long time to be away from a place but before then, she'd been here for more than twenty years. Not all the time, but almost every Australian summer. The few she'd missed, thanks to Mum being difficult about it, Ivy had longed for the long warm days and freedom to be here, in Rivers End. Since her parents' divorce when she was little, she'd racked up enough travel miles to rival any adult.

The road ahead hugged the back of the cliffs on its way to

Warrnambool but Ivy took a right turn to head into the small town.

'Oh, look at the inn! And don't tell me you can't see it right in front of you,' Jody said. 'That place always looked so run-down but someone is putting money into it.'

Construction was underway at the old inn, which Ivy had never been inside but knew was made up of only half a dozen basic guest rooms. From the look of things, a second row of accommodation was almost complete and there was a swimming pool and a big play area taking shape.

'Good for them. Do you remember Sadie, the daughter?'

Jody was silent, her attention on her mobile phone.

Ivy passed the shops and pulled up outside the police station, which was a converted house another block away. The Mini was fun to drive. Responsive and had bells and whistles miles ahead of her old Astra at home. But unlike Jody, she didn't have a wealthy husband and nursing wasn't going to provide an income to support a similar lifestyle. For that matter she didn't have *any* husband, and probably never would.

A sliver of pain cut into her heart. It was unexpected and she drew in a sharp breath.

'Hang on a sec. I'll only be a minute.' Jody was tapping fast on her phone.

Was it being back here which brought back memories so vivid she could almost see them? There'd been one great love in Ivy's life. It didn't work out. They'd broken up after her father's confession and Ivy had no trouble blaming her father for it. So far she hadn't met anyone who filled her heart with such joy and her days with laughter like Leo, despite genuine attempts to find a perfect someone. Easier to pour herself into her career than keep looking.

'Okay, I'm done. Aaron wanted to know I was here and I'd forgotten to phone.'

'That's nice that he wants to know you're safe.'

'Sure. Yes, it is. Why are we here?' Jody suddenly noticed the police station. 'I thought we decided not to bother reporting the break-in.'

'We did no such thing. Some person or persons damaged the property and if we don't make a report then what happens if they come back? Or we discover something else is damaged or missing and need to claim on insurance?'

Jody's face had paled. 'I'm sure it was only kids messing around. Let's go and shop. Please.' Her eyes pleaded with Ivy.

'Don't be upset,' Ivy said in her calm, no-nonsense nurse's voice. 'I'll go. Look, why don't you drive to the supermarket and start shopping and I'll walk over in a few minutes. It really won't take me long.'

After taking a deep breath, Jody climbed out, slinging her handbag over a shoulder. Ivy joined her, holding out the car keys but her sister shook her head. 'I'll walk. Just don't tell them anything apart from the broken window. Like, not about us staying there or being co-owners with Dad.'

She stalked away before Ivy could ask what on earth was going on. Jody had been a bigger part of the investigation than Ivy so it must be something about the police which was bothering her; probably nothing more than having to talk about that night yet again. There was no other reason Jody would fear the police, because she had done nothing wrong.


As it was, there was nobody at the police station and Ivy phoned the number on the front door. It rang out and she left a message with her phone number and a request for a call back about a break-in. This was a one-person station so probably only attended part of the time.

Ivy drove the short distance to the supermarket and parked not far from a new bookstore – at least, new since she'd been here last. It was one thing she and Jody had wished for on their visits and the lack of one in the town had encouraged their father to add children's and young adult books to the mix in his library.

She leaned back against the headrest and closed her eyes. For years she'd managed to hold the memories at bay, both the good and the awful. There were so many of the good in comparison and being back here, her second home, was chipping away at the barriers she'd so carefully constructed with the help of a good therapist.

'Look at the memories through a filter.' Her therapist had taught her some techniques which worked to a degree. 'They happened. The filter can be whatever you want or need, so if it is a good memory then the filter is love or joy. The difficult ones? Treat them as if you are watching from a distance. Simply an observer.'

She'd become an expert at watching from a distance – right until the moment she'd walked down the driveway to Fairview House, stopping at the curve which finally revealed the hidden homestead and the handful of cottages, and beyond them, the vast expanse of the Southern Ocean.

It was taking all of her learned skills and a lot of self-control to keep that distance and since Jody arrived it was becoming even harder.

Ivy opened her eyes to look at herself in the rear-vision mirror and whispered to her reflection. 'There is no way of knowing if you and Leo would have lasted.' Her eyes were wide in the mirror.

Dad might not have done anything to destroy her chance with Leo, not directly, but his choice to get behind the wheel had been his alone and the fallout...

Ivy opened the door. She'd had enough of her thoughts.

Inside the supermarket she stopped to get her bearings. This had changed too, and been extended with a whole different layout from her last time in here. Jody was easy to spot, as she stood in the fresh produce department holding the handle of an empty trolley.

'Oh there you are. I can't find anything.'

'I've been less than ten minutes and you walked, so you've been in here for what? Three, four minutes?'

'No need to be sarcastic. They've changed everything.'

'Okay, what if we start here and visit each aisle. Is there anything in particular you want?'

'Cheesecake,' Jody said. 'But I'll settle for a bunch of the kale over there.'

Shopping with Jody was interesting, to say the least. Their once-similar tastes in food had gone in different directions over the years. Jody was into organic food and low-carb, high-protein options. Ivy bought rice and pasta and pre-made sauces and a wide range of vegetables and fruit.

'Nothing else?' Ivy was sure they had enough to feed a crowd and hoped it wouldn't go to waste.

Jody directed the trolley to a small bottle shop which was part of the supermarket. She stopped at a stand where there was a special on red wine and transferred four bottles to the trolley.

'You do remember I don't drink?' Ivy asked.

'But I do.'

'Four bottles?'

'Good point.' Jody added two more. 'Not one word of judgement, Ivy. Not one.'

She pushed the trolley away, almost running into a woman who was exiting an aisle. They both said sorry and Jody headed for a checkout. The woman gazed after her, not moving. Ivy walked past, offering a small smile, and the woman's eyes met hers. She wore a black top with *Rivers End Bistro* emblazoned on a pocket and beneath it, a nametag. Tessa. An odd expression was on the woman's face and she didn't return the smile. Perhaps the near miss with the trolley had startled her.

At the checkout, Ivy glanced back. Tessa was still there, watching them.

Again, Ivy smiled and the woman abruptly turned and disappeared back down the same aisle.

For the second time today a shiver went up Ivy's spine.

# FOUR

All the way home from shopping, Jody tapped on her phone. Ivy figured that was the real reason she was driving and wondered if her sister still saw her as a chauffeur. With the age gap, Ivy had become very popular once she had her licence and she'd got used to driving her sister around both in England, and here when they visited Dad.

It would have been nice to have a conversation about the strange woman at the supermarket but Jody didn't stop tapping until she got out to open and close the gate. When she slid back in, she put the phone away. 'Did the hot-water person say when they are coming?'

'First thing tomorrow now.'

A text message from the company had been apologetic about the change of plans.

'We should fill some saucepans with water and boil them all and I can have a bath at least.'

'Go right ahead. Are you sure you want to carry pots of hot water upstairs?'

'Me?'

'You want a bath. There isn't one downstairs. Do I look like your maid, Jodes?'

'I'm not strong enough to carry them and you're used to lugging heavy things around.'

'What heavy things?'

'People. In the hospital.'

Unable to stop herself laughing, Ivy nosed the Mini back into its earlier spot. For a smart woman, Jody sometimes came up with the strangest stuff but that was also one of her most endearing features. She'd always been a little offbeat and Dad used to say it showed her artistic soul.

After opening the boot, Ivy lifted a couple of bags out.

'I'm going for a walk.'

'Well, give me a hand first... Jody?'

Her sister was already leaving. 'Back soon.'

Muttering a few uncomplimentary words beneath her breath, Ivy transferred the shopping to the kitchen in several trips. She considered leaving the bottles of wine in the car but even annoyed, she couldn't bring herself to leave the task incomplete.

As she unpacked, she kept an eye on the window. Jody hadn't gone far and was sitting on a bench under one of the trees. She was on the phone and even across the distance, seemed agitated. Deciding it was none of her business, Ivy finished what she was doing then sat at the table with her laptop and a notepad.

Their earlier inspection of the property had stopped after they'd discovered the damage in the library, which left them everything outside to check. The cottages, sheds, and the big garage, as well as the boundaries to see what condition the fencing was in. With only a couple of hours of daylight left, they'd need to decide which to tackle first.

The front door clicked shut and Jody hurried in, straight to the fridge. She dug around to find a bottle of water and opened it with her back to Ivy. After a few sips, she plonked down on the opposite side of the table. Her eyes were puffy and red and her makeup had streaks through it. She slid the notepad across to read it and then pushed it back, her eyes flicking to Ivy's.

'You've been crying. What's wrong, Jodes?'

'What could possibly be wrong, Saint Ives.'

Jody knew how much Ivy hated the nickname and only used it when she wanted to fight. Ivy reached out a hand to take one of Jody's.

She snatched it away. 'You knew I didn't want the police involved yet you had to go and tell them your name and number. Have they called yet?'

'No, but—'

'Just as well. And when they do, then tell them it was a mistake. We don't need them poking around here again.'

'We can't *not* report it.'

'Of course we can. Nothing was taken. You bought a replacement lock. We can pick up the books. There's no real harm done but the minute the police set foot here we might as well give up everything.'

'I think you are overreacting.'

Jody jumped to her feet and snatched the water bottle off the table.

*Go on, prove my point.*

Ivy kept her voice calmer than she felt. 'I'm sorry I upset you and I'll deal with the police report. What if we work on something from the list I made?'

'You've always been the clever one, so you sort it out. I'm going to freshen up.'

She was out of the door and thumping her way up the stairs before Ivy could find any words to stop her.

.  .  .

A patrol car drove past the front of the house, turned around, and stopped outside. Ivy had seen it come down the driveway from the bedroom she'd chosen for herself. She'd been cleaning the inside of the windows, needing to do something but not wanting to leave the house with Jody in such a mood.

She opened the front door just as the police officer was about to knock and he stepped back in surprise.

'Good afternoon. I saw you driving down.'

'I see. Ivy Sutherland?'

'Ivy Ross. I don't recall leaving my address when I phoned.'

'Lived here me whole life and know where to find a Sutherland and never heard of another Ivy. Besides, word gets around this town.'

Her heart sank.

'And you are?'

The officer was only a bit older than Ivy and there was something about his eyes, which she thought a bit shifty, that was familiar.

'Senior Constable Mick Hammond.'

*Ah. Now I know.*

'Would you like to see the damage? I'm keen to replace the lock on the window today if possible.' She stepped inside and held the door wide. 'Please, come in.'

'Always wanted to take a look around this place.' He stopped inside the door and glanced at the steep and narrow staircase. 'Library up there?'

'It is.'

'No need for me to look. You said lock on the window? That how they got in?'

'I was hoping you'd be able to confirm that, Senior Constable Hammond.'

'Mick. Call me Mick. How'd they get to the window?'

*Why did I bother calling you?*

A door closed upstairs. Mick's hand covered his holster.

'That's just my sister.'

'You sure?'

'Actually... would you mind taking a look, just in case?' She was impressed with how pathetic she'd made her voice sound.

He crossed his arms and stared at Ivy. 'The sister who was there that night?'

'I only have one sister. Now, shall I show you the ladder?' She wasn't waiting around for more of his potshots. Everyone thought they knew something about the Sutherland family but most had the good manners to keep it to themselves. This man had no filter. Ivy brushed past him and waited outside until he joined her. The minute he appeared she stalked around the corner. 'This way.'

To his credit, Mick took things more seriously after seeing the ladder.

He took a few photographs. 'I've got a fingerprint kit in the car. Might just dust the bits most likely to have been touched. Go ahead and replace the lock and phone me if you think the intruder returns.'

'I will. Have there been break-ins in town lately?'

'Nope. Not much crime now I'm on watch.'

Ivy turned away to hide a smile.

'Are you selling up or setting up again?'

Something made Ivy look up. Jody was at the window of the library watching them.

'Undecided. Jody and I have full lives elsewhere. We're taking stock first.'

Mick began plodding back toward his vehicle and Ivy walked with him. 'Do you need me to hang around?'

'Nah. I'll dust and then head off. Let you know if anything comes of it.'

At the patrol car he lifted the boot, then turned back to Ivy. 'For what it's worth, people turn into judge and jury without knowing the facts. My own family has had its share of pointing fingers. I wasn't a copper back when the car crash happened but if you want my opinion, something didn't add up. You sure your father was responsible?'

*Why say such a thing? Of course he was responsible.*

'He... he confessed.'

'People confess for odd reasons.' He began to rummage around in the boot.

Ivy watched for a minute then decided she'd had enough of speculation and bizarre theories. Perhaps Jody had been right and she should have left things alone.


Jody appeared as night fell and set to work preparing dinner alongside Ivy as though no harsh words were spoken earlier.

'I thought mushrooms in garlic and cream with some pasta... or if you prefer no pasta I can make some zucchini ribbons?' Ivy had been searching low-carb recipes on the internet.

Deftly slicing a pile of mushrooms into chunks, Jody glanced up. 'Pasta won't kill me this once.'

The concession was Jody's version of a peace offering. Ivy made one of her own. She found a wine glass in the cupboard then opened one of the bottles of red wine and poured a small glass. When she put it beside the chopping block, Jody looked up with an expression of surprise.

'Thanks. You won't join me?'

'Not on the wine. But I bought some cranberry juice.'

Jody went to the same cupboard and took out another wine glass. Then she opened the fridge. 'Did we really buy all of this?'

'We really did. Cranberry juice is in the door.'

'Ah.'

Once Jody had poured some of the dark crimson juice into the wine glass, she offered it to Ivy, then picked up her own. 'What on earth shall we toast to?'

'Right. Um... the beautiful colour of both our drinks?'

Jody giggled and tapped her glass to Ivy's. 'Cheers to that.'

They fell into a silence but it was free of tension and inter-spersed with the bubbling of the pasta pot and chopping and slicing as Jody moved on to creating a salad. The kitchen was filled with the aroma of garlic and herbs and Ivy gathered the moments in to remember and treasure. Time with her little sister. Quality time.

Once they'd eaten, Jody helped wash up. Her mood was better but whether two glasses of wine was behind that or her own desire to be in a better place, only she knew.

'I'm going to go to bed early,' Jody declared as she refilled her glass, this time almost to the top. 'Driving all the way from the city was exhausting and all the other stuff... anyway, goodnight.'

'Okay, goodnight. We can work on the list tomorrow?'

'Sure.'

Jody took her glass and her footsteps climbing the stairs were normal instead of the earlier stomping. This was better. Maybe her sister had needed to blow off some steam and now was feeling ready to deal with the house and all that came with it. Pity she needed a few glasses of wine to help her into that headspace.

Ivy turned off the lights and checked the house was locked before going to her room. She was every bit as tired. As worn. And unprepared for the emotional toll. Her mind kept bouncing around about selling Fairview.

Sitting cross-legged on the bed, Ivy opened a slim briefcase where she kept copies of paperwork attached to her co-owner-ship. Dad's solicitor – Mr Appleby – had provided a consider-able amount of information three years ago and Ivy assumed Jody would also have copies. She'd printed them from digital files to carry if she didn't want to use her computer. All of this was in addition to the paperwork from when Dad was training her to take over the management of the business.

She still had access to the different bank accounts associated with Fairview but there was chunks of information she didn't have. He'd been old-fashioned with his accounting practices and she had only a vague recollection of him keeping records in the safe. Nothing electronic.

There was a copy of the original title transfer to her father many years ago. He owned it outright with nothing owing other than land rates which were due very soon. She'd looked at that in the past and was still puzzled. How had a man in his mid-twenties, not wealthy, afforded a beachfront acreage, including a home which was probably eligible for heritage listing?

*I know so little about you, Dad.*

After putting the paperwork away, too tired to think about any of this right now, Ivy lay on her side and stared at the wallpaper.

From the next bedroom came soft whimpers. Jody was crying again.

# FIVE

'I might leave my husband and move in here. Imagine being able to look at that view for the rest of your life.'

Ivy and Jody were at the last of the cottages they'd been inspecting and before going inside, sat on the top step of the small front deck. Jody had a point. This one was the furthest from the main house and the closest to the beach, almost at the point where grass and sand met. High enough to avoid even a king tide, the cottage offered unlimited views to the horizon.

Sitting here was nice. Jody was in a better mood and Ivy had slept well.

'You'd give up your life in the city and your husband? The outlook is pretty, but still...' Ivy grinned.

'City life isn't really for me. I mean, there's perks, like great restaurants and easy access to the theatre and concerts, and great boutiques and beauty salons but apartment living doesn't match this.' Jody gestured to the water as it sparkled under the early morning sun. 'Aaron though? He's a keeper but I can't see him agreeing to downgrade his lifestyle to such a degree.'

'What a sweet turn of phrase. A keeper.'

Jody shrugged and checked her phone. 'He's a good man. Busy. Slightly odd at times. But good.'

'And you miss him. Is that why you were crying last night?'

'There's no reason for me to cry about Aaron. I was tired, that's all.'

'It's just that earlier, you seemed a bit upset on the phone. Under the tree.'

'The phone? Oh that. If you must know it was my PA and I was frustrated because someone who'd offered a decent donation changed their mind last minute. It happens sometimes, but then I worry about the impact on the foundation if money dries up.'

'I truly had no idea about your charity work.'

'It probably wasn't highest on my list of things to discuss with you. Not compared to my family's opposition to my wedding.'

'Do you want to talk about it? What happened back then about your wedding?'

'Why ruin a perfectly pleasant day?'

*Because you expect that we'll end up arguing about why your family didn't attend.*

Ivy had been in the wrong to take their mother's side about the whirlwind romance, she knew that now. But she'd wait until Jody was ready and do her best to make things right about that time.

Ivy opened her sketchpad to a drawing she'd done of the property. It was rough but gave a basic idea of where the boundaries were and included all the buildings. There were 'x's on most of the structures. 'Once we've done this one, that's all of the residential buildings. Then there's the garage and the stone hut left.'

'You can do those.'

'No, *we* can.'

'Well, I've given this some thought and realised you have

more to gain than me. You were going to take over from Dad. Fairview was always going to become yours which means whatever I think about its future won't matter.' Jody ran fingers through her hair and then smoothed it again. 'Maybe it was a mistake coming here because this place is nothing but bad memories. Aaron encouraged me to go to therapy but it took two years to get to the point where I could sleep all night.'

'You suffered for what, six years without getting help?'

'More like eight. Why? Did you see a shrink straight off? After Dad went to prison?'

'Not straight off.'

*Or often enough.*

Jody stared at the sea, seeming to have lost interest in the subject, and Ivy stood and stretched. 'Hot-water person will be here soon so let's try and finish this first. And you're wrong. Fairview was always going to belong to the both of us. Dad told me that years ago.'

Inside was a bright living area with a kitchenette plus a bathroom and one bedroom. As with the other cottages, the front was almost all glass, reinforced to protect against the weather. There were also roll-down shutters for winter and storms but none had been used in years. Ivy had tried to pull one down and didn't have the strength so assumed it had been in one position for too long.

There was a sofa and an armchair and coffee table plus a small bookcase with a selection of novels and non-fiction books. The kitchen was so pristine it might never have been used and really, why would it? Meals were readily available in the main house all day and evening, always. For someone here to write or paint or whatever, a full day of working on their project followed by drinks, dinner, and singing around the piano was a great way to unwind.

The sudden sound of running water... a torrent, startled Ivy and she glanced around. No Jody.

'Hey, Ivy?'

Jody was in the small bathroom, running the shower, her hand under the faucet and steam rising around her.

'Remember the cold showers we had this morning?'

'Oh my goodness, I completely forgot each cottage has its own hot-water unit.'

As Jody turned the tap off they both burst into laughter.

The hot-water system for the main house was beyond repair and a replacement would take a day or two to source from one of the bigger towns. While the service man was here, Ivy got him to check the unit on each cottage and they, at least, had a clean bill of health.

Ivy gave some thought to moving into the front cottage, deciding against it only because she didn't want to leave Jody alone in what was a large, rambling house. And if the intruder returned when her sister was on her own, she'd never forgive herself. But she decided to visit the little cottage at least once a day for a shower and to sit in the sun with a coffee.

Once the hot-water van trundled up the driveway, Ivy collected her sketchbook again and found Jody staring into the fridge.

'Shall we do this quickly then get an early lunch?' Ivy asked.

'I guess. I'm used to eating out most days. Making lunch feels a bit weird.'

*Buying lunch every day is weird. And expensive.*

Jody brought her iPad again and once they reached the garage, she tapped at it a few times. 'I really should go and plug it in before it goes flat.'

'I can write notes. Do you know which key opens this?'

They were at the side door of a garage large enough for at least eight cars and double the normal height of similar structures. Dad had only owned one car that Ivy remembered and that was totalled in the accident. She snuck a look at Jody, who was still tapping away on the screen and frowning. Was this why she was reluctant to go in here? Bad memories?

After working out which key herself, Ivy opened the door and stepped into a cold and musty space. She found a light switch and her mouth opened. There might not be any cars in here but there was a tractor, a ride-on mower, and something covered with a dust cloth. Something suspiciously like a motorcycle. 'Jody, come and see.'

'Just trying to fix this.'

'No, come here. Please.'

By the time Jody managed to find her way inside, Ivy was pulling the dust cloth off and they both let out a gasp.

'Isn't that one of those ones Dad always said he'd buy one day?'

Ivy walked around a Triumph Thunderbird. 'Um. Yes. How did we not know?'

'How could we?'

'Do you mean he bought it after the accident? In the time before he confessed?'

Jody ran a hand over the handlebars. 'He always wanted one. Do you remember him saying that the time would come when he'd leave the retreat with a manager and ride a motorbike around Australia?'

'I wish he'd done it earlier,' Ivy said. 'I was supposed to become that manager.'

Tears began to fall down Jody's cheeks although she didn't seem to be aware of them. She kept walking around the machine and then picked up the dust cloth and covered it again. 'Now he never will.'

Had Jody not been so sad, Ivy would have said something about him bringing it on himself. She was glad she kept quiet. It didn't help anyone for her to keep repeating the same words or

variations of them about their father. He'd had the courage to
confess even if it took a while, and that had to count for
something.

'Ivy, would you mind if I go back to the house? I might make
us something to eat.'

'I won't be too long. And thank you, that sounds good.'

With Jody gone, Ivy wandered around the garage making
notes of the main items. Apart from the tractor and ride-on
mower – which would be handy if it still worked – there was a
decent assortment of small machinery including two generators.
Everything looked in good condition and what couldn't be used
here might be saleable.

After closing and locking the door behind her, Ivy followed
a path past the garage to the last of the buildings. Her heart beat
a bit faster as glimpses of the stone hut – little more than a
couple of rooms built for the original groundskeeper almost two
centuries ago – appeared through the branches of bushes and
trees. It was up a slight incline and completely private. She and
Jody had always been curious about the hut but Dad had made
it off limits. Not that it stopped them sneaking up there now
and then, risking getting in trouble for little reward.

Ivy walked around the hut, half expecting her father to
appear. Why had they never been allowed inside when they
had the run of everywhere else on the property? Jody had been
particularly curious as she'd got into her mid-teens, coming up
with all kinds of stories. If it wasn't the final resting place of a
bushranger and therefore haunted, it was where Dad kept a
gold-filled treasure chest washed up from a wreck, and how he
paid for everything.

There might be merit in that idea because the money had to
have come from somewhere.

Although curious about it as a child, she'd also always had a
slightly uneasy feeling which returned as she stared at the door.
Ivy loved buildings with big windows, the opposite of this

which had only a couple of tiny ones high up on one wall. Other than those and the timber door there was nothing to break up the big slabs of stone.

Taking out the keys, Ivy easily found the one to this door. It was the only skeleton key and it took a few attempts and fair bit of force to make it turn.

The door was heavy and creaked and Ivy giggled a bit nervously. She'd almost closed it again and run back to the house and it wasn't in her nature to be easily spooked. She'd have a quick look and lock it up again.

Expecting to find either the remains of furniture from the long-gone resident groundskeeper or else a room full of gardening tools, Ivy had to blink to be sure of what she was looking at.

There was no electricity so Ivy opened the flashlight app on her phone, moving it around and casting peculiar shadows as it illuminated old-fashioned lanterns which were scattered around. An open doorway led to a kind of utility room with a sink and ancient washing machine and a row of long-dried up herbs hanging from the ceiling. Not even a bathroom, although there was a boarded-up outhouse a few metres from the building. Cobwebs dangled from random parts of the ceiling.

What was completely out of place was a four-poster bed. It was fairly modern in style and the soft lacy curtains gathered around each post were in good condition, if a bit dusty. On either side were low tables covered with candles in a selection of sizes and colours. And in the middle of one table was an empty bottle of wine and two glasses, covered with dust. Just behind these was a portable, battery powered CD player. Ivy popped it open. Inside was the *Greatest Love Songs from 1973*.

Ivy turned and ran out, locking the door and fleeing from the hut without a backward glance.

. . .

'You didn't tell me what the police officer said. Does he think it was a real break-in?'

Ivy put down her fork, not exactly loving the kale salad and having picked out the good bits. Walnuts, cheese, strawberries. She wasn't hungry anyway. Not after her bizarre discovery, which for now she was keeping to herself.

'He dusted for prints and will phone if anything comes up. Do you remember him? Mick Hammond?'

'Should I?'

'No. You probably hung around with a different group. His family had a dreadful reputation as criminals but it seems he went off and became a cop. I remember him as a mean boy but yesterday he wasn't too bad. He's mellowed or something.'

'Speaking of remembering people. Did you know Sadie Carson has moved back to Rivers End?'

'Jody, I mentioned her yesterday.'

With a puzzled look, Jody picked up a walnut with her fingers and put it in her mouth.

'When we were driving into town I asked if you remembered her. She was such a nice girl but always seemed sad. And then she left Rivers End and we lost touch.'

'Her name now is Sadie Forest. Did you know she became a documentary maker? All social welfare stuff in Sydney but her mother still lives here and runs the inn so it might be a bit of a problem.' Jody collected both plates and went to the sink. 'What if she decides to investigate us?'

Ivy didn't quite understand. She was impressed that her sister was making an effort to share the workload though.

'Are you even listening?' Jody asked.

'I am. There's no story here, so stop being paranoid.'

Running water stopped the conversation and Ivy took their glasses and cutlery across and collected a tea towel.

Jody added everything to the sink in one go, including the chopping board and knife.

'Do you have a housekeeper?' Ivy asked.

'Of course not.' Jody scrubbed at a plate which really didn't need such attention. 'We have a cleaner. She comes in every second day.'

How different their lives were, not only from their carefree childhoods, but from each other. Ivy lived alone in a small flat and did everything for herself on a budget. Not so her sister.

'You haven't said if you went inside. The hut.'

*I wish I hadn't.*

She'd run until she'd been struggling for breath and then sunk onto the ground in a heap. Finding what was obviously some type of love nest shocked her on so many levels and Ivy was nowhere near being able to dissect her response. It was silly, in hindsight, to allow the discovery to upset her so. But questions spun around her mind and little memories tried to force their way through.

'Ivy, are you ignoring me?'

Talking to Jody about the hut wasn't a good idea.

'Sorry. Miles away. Um, I got really hungry.'

Jody shot her a disbelieving look. 'Well, you didn't eat much. I don't think I'm *that* bad a cook.'

'It wasn't you. Kale really doesn't taste like anything to me but the rest was nice. What do you want to do this afternoon?'

'Swim.'

'The water does look inviting. But I meant about moving forward. Making decisions. What if we set aside a bit of time to work through it all?'

*And hopefully without tears and tantrums.*

# SIX

Jody refused to do a thing until she'd had a swim but Ivy fancied a walk around the rocks. Leaving Jody to squeal at cooler-than-expected water before finally diving in and confidently freestyling through the low waves, Ivy put on a pair of runners and headed for the other end of the beach.

With low tide, the flattish rocks were transformed into pools of varying sizes, alive with fish and seaweed and interesting shells. This had been as much the playground of two girls often left to their own devices and encouraged to explore as any other part of the property. Dad sometimes joined them, squatting to point out a particular species or warn about what should never be touched. But it was more fun when they were alone with a sand bucket to fill with empty shells, interesting sea drift, and even sea glass. The bucket would go back to the house for its contents to be transformed into parts of whatever work of art the girls were creating.

Ivy worked her way to the furthest edge of the rocks and stood with her toes wiggling over. The sea was lazy with little swell. There was almost no breeze and the air was warm and held promise of a hot summer ahead.

*I wish...*

One more summer here would be divine.

She could relive all the good memories and then create more to replace the bad ones. Spend her days watching the ocean change colour and walking and cooking and even try to write again. Growing up, Ivy had written stories almost as much as read books and later, part of her interest in managing Fairview was the opportunity to pursue her love of writing. Not poetry, like Dad, but sweeping sagas of family drama across generations.

Nobody understood why she gave up on her writing dream but she knew. Having real-life tragedy forced upon a person will do that, let alone losing the chance to have a future with someone who might be your soulmate.

Leo hadn't been the poor person who lost their life that night. She had to stop thinking like that because there were times when nightmares woke her in tears and terror after dreaming of looking everywhere for him and eventually finding him in the wreckage. He hadn't been in the crash, but his great-aunt Jean had. She'd been heading home to Green Bay after an evening with friends. They said she died instantly after the impact of Dad's much heavier car hitting hers, forcing it to roll twice before landing on its side.

Nobody had blamed Dad. Not then, while everyone believed his lies about his car being stolen. No, it was two years later with his shock confession that Leo and his family learned the truth and Ivy's world collapsed. Fingers were pointed at her and Jody, accusing them of knowing the truth. Abusive, anonymous phone calls to Fairview. Horrible words painted on the gate. Her own car sprayed with the word 'shame'. And she was overcome with that shame. She fled to England, abandoning Fairview and Rivers End. And Leo.

Ivy retreated from the edge and found a rock suitable to sit upon closer to the cliff face and out of the sun. Her heart was pounding and if she didn't get control soon she'd fall into despair or else panic. She hadn't felt this way in years. Certainly not out of the blue on a gorgeous day beside the ocean.

Her relationship with Leo had started on a day almost like today.

*A game of beach volleyball drew Ivy and Jody away from fishing on the end of the jetty. They rarely caught anything but when they did it was King George whiting and Dad would always make a big fuss about how clever they were and cook it on the barbeque.*

*A couple of families had set up the game and there was constant laughter and calling and people running back and forth. After packing up their fishing gear, the two of them watched from near the lagoon, wishing they could play. It looked like so much fun.*

*Ivy was twenty-one and Jody almost eighteen. It was two weeks after Christmas, which they'd spent in snow back home in England with Mum. She'd complained about them leaving again but the lure of sun and surf was too strong and they'd flown out on the second day of the new year. This time was different though because Ivy had a decision to make.*

*She'd finished school, travelled around Europe for ages and worked back in London for a year. Her future beckoned. There was an arts degree she liked the look of and it came down to applying in England or Australia. Having dual citizenship, she had options not available to many people and her leaning was toward moving here permanently. There was even a campus within driving distance from Rivers End if she wanted to live at the retreat. Dad had offered to pay her to learn how to manage Fairview and study at the same time.*

*The next few weeks would help her decide.*

*There was a shout to 'watch out!' and the volleyball came flying in Ivy's direction.*

*Her hands shot up and caught the ball.*

*Jody clapped and laughed and Ivy was pretty impressed with her quick reaction.*

*A young man, maybe a couple of years older than Ivy, jogged in their direction with an apologetic grin.*

*'That was some catch.'*

*His voice was deep for someone so young and held a gentle timbre which did something silly to Ivy's tummy. And when his grin turned into a wide smile as she tossed the ball to him, a million butterflies jiggled around in there.*

*'Would you both like to join in? Could use a player on my side who can catch.'*

*'Sure thing, you know I'm even better than Ivy.' Jody wasn't waiting for a second invitation and tore off toward the group.*

*'Hi, Ivy. My name is Leo. Leo Webb.'*

'Ivy, please don't make me walk to you with bare feet!'

Jody's voice was shrill and Ivy's head shot around. Her sister was on the sand where the rocks started, waving her arms.

'I'm coming,' Ivy called.

As the cloud of memories lifted, she pulled herself together. Leo was years ago and by now would have a family of his own.

When she reached the sand, Jody threw her arms around her in a quick hug then released her and stalked away.

Ivy jogged to catch up. 'How long were you calling for me?'

'Too long! I thought you'd had a heart attack sitting there so still, staring at the ground and not responding. Did you fall asleep?'

'Kind of. Sorry to worry you. Can we slow down?'

'I'm going to have a shower and then we can do this stuff you want. Is the cottage unlocked?'

It was and Ivy had been down earlier and stocked it with fresh towels, soap, and shampoo. She returned to the main house, hoping Jody would leave the bathroom tidy but expecting she wouldn't. Jody had never been good at tidy so why start now?

By the time Jody returned, wrapped in a sarong, her hair slicked back, and skin a bit pink from the sun, Ivy had made a pot of tea and had her laptop open on the kitchen table. Jody took her wet swimwear to the laundry and went straight to the fridge. She found a punnet of strawberries and rinsed them under the tap before tossing half into a bowl.

'These look fresh. Have some.'

'You enjoyed your swim.' Ivy was happy to see the change in her sister.

Jody's eyes were alight. 'Loved it so hard. We have use of a swimming pool and spa and stuff at our apartment building which is great and I use it a lot, but does anything compare to the open sea? And once you're in, the water warms up fast enough.'

'Yes, I noticed the squeals stopped after a bit but figured a shark might have taken you.'

'Hey!' Jody threw her half-eaten strawberry at Ivy, who ducked. It hit the ground with a splat. 'That was meant for your face so you can clean it up.'

Trying to control her laughter, Ivy got a piece of paper towel and scooped up the remains. 'This poor piece of fruit didn't deserve that.' She tossed them into a makeshift compost bin she'd made from an old chipped salad bowl.

'Why are you composting? When you looked at the vegetable garden earlier you said it wasn't worth bothering with.'

'I probably shouldn't have been so quick to dismiss them. I've sent you photos of mine at home? Balcony garden beds?' Ivy clicked on the laptop a couple of times to bring up her photo gallery and turned the screen so Jody could see. 'I've only got a small space but manage to grow quite a bit.' There were two raised garden beds on wheels against the rail. Each had two arches of polytube over them. 'I cover those with mesh when it's too cold or when I put in new seedlings, but once any begin to flower they come off to give the bees access.'

'Oh, are those herbs? Yes, they are herbs. I really do miss being able to go and pick my own food. Think of all the kale I could grow. Why don't you plant some when you go home?'

'Because, dear sister, I hate waste and as you've already seen, kale is wasted on me.'

After Ivy poured tea for them both, they got to work with a spreadsheet on Ivy's laptop. She set it up to list all the buildings, including any notes they'd made about contents and condition and soon it was populated with information.

'I've added a photo of the map of the property and found some aerial images from Google Maps.' Ivy opened one. 'It was only when I saw this one that the sheer size of the grounds were evident. I guess growing up here it just felt... normal.'

Jody peered at the screen.

The boundary ran from the road to the beach, narrowing closer to the water. On either side of the property the land looked unsuitable for homes, being rocky or too steep.

'It truly is unique,' Jody said. 'The closest houses are on the other side of the road and this looks like one of the few properties for miles between the road and sea. Do we know what Dad paid for it? It is a hectare, I think.'

'Sounds right. Um... I'll see if I have that on here. Have you not gone through all the paperwork from Mr Appleby?' Ivy opened more files until finding the copy of the original deed title. 'Hang on, this is odd.' She zoomed in a bit. 'The property changed hands from a Mr W. Bell in 1975. I think Dad had the retreat operating from 1976. It says unencumbered. I think that means there was no mortgage but that doesn't make sense. Dad was what – twenty-five or six?'

'It wasn't an inheritance? Dad's parents died a long time ago or maybe he had an uncle or grandparent who left it to him?'

Opening another document, Ivy pointed at the screen. 'Jodes, that's a receipt. One dollar. And look at the wording.'

'Transaction complete after satisfactory fulfilment of agreed terms.'

They sat back and looked at each other.

'That almost sounds as if Dad was given the property based on him finishing some kind of job for W. Bell, whoever that is. It would be one heck of a job to take full ownership of these grounds and all the buildings.'

'You've had access to all of this for three years, so why hadn't you seen this earlier?' Jody demanded.

'Because I've barely glanced at them. I didn't expect to be given a one-third share on my thirtieth birthday and quite honestly, I still don't know that I'm happy about it so I've hardly been curious about how Dad acquired Fairview.'

Jody bit her lip.

Ivy sighed. 'Go on. What do you want to say?'

'I know your life is in England. I know you don't forgive Dad for what he did. And like me, I know you had different plans for your future...'

'But?'

'But life's too short, Ivy.' Jody met her eyes. 'Have you even spoken to him recently?'

She hadn't. Not since a brief conversation following his appeal.

'I don't think I want us to sell Fairview.' There was a soft plea in Jody's voice. 'I know I said I might have made a mistake coming here but being back in the ocean... back here... I don't want to sell.'

'And I think I do,' Ivy said. She put her hand on Jody's arm.

'We'll figure it out but we need more information first. Even talk to local real estate agents and see if we can find out more about the history here and who was the man generous enough to gift an entire acreage to a young man. I don't feel ready to ask Dad about any of it so shall we do our own investigation together?'

'Sure. Tomorrow though. I should catch up on some work for the charities.'

'Okay. I might get into the library then and replace the lock. There's bound to be some timber board or something in the garage I can use in place of the glass.'

'Who will do dinner?' Jody put the rest of the strawberries back in the fridge after Ivy had grabbed a couple from the bowl.

'I can. Any requests?'

'Kale burgers?'

'You are so lucky that I won't waste a strawberry on you, young woman.'

# SEVEN

Rivers End Real Estate was one of four shops on the corners of the only real intersection in town. The others were the bookshop, a café, and a jewellers.

'Do you remember the man who owned the jewellery shop? Mr Campbell?' Jody had driven today and parked a couple more shops along from the gracious old building which she was talking about. 'He was so kind to us kids. Never minded us looking at all the sparkly things inside and always with a story about the town if he was sitting on the bench outside.'

The bench was still there, and when Ivy peeped in through one of the windows, so was George Campbell, sitting on a stool behind the counter, peering at a watch through a magnifying glass. 'Should we go and say hello once we're finished?'

Jody shook her head.

'Why ever not? I've noticed your expensive rings and earrings, so don't tell me you don't like sparkly things.'

'I'd love to buy one of his handmade creations, but do you think he'd really want us in there?'

She meant now. After the accident and infamy it brought to the town. Jody might be right.

'Only one way to find out. But first the real estate agents.'

They waited to cross the road.

'Doesn't the bookshop look nice?' Jody gazed in its direction.

'Another one to visit. And the café. Wasn't it more a bakery before, though?'

'Oh, yes it was. Do you remember Dad would give us a dollar and we'd get a sausage roll each and go to the lagoon and eat with our legs dangling in the water as we sat on the bank?'

They crossed over to the real estate agents. It had big windows filled with pictures of houses and land for sale on two sides. Beneath each window were planter boxes with flowers in a riot of colour which was quaint and fitting for the little town.

Ivy pushed the door open and they entered a bright and friendly space with a long counter, thick carpet, and tub chairs around a small table with brochures. Soft music played in the background and the aroma of coffee wafted from somewhere. A man, around thirty, was finishing a phone call on the other side of the counter and he smiled at them.

'Have you ever been in here?' Jody whispered.

'Never. But I thought it was owned by a much older couple.'

'Good morning, ladies. Interested in buying?' The man came around the corner and shook both their hands. 'I'm Xavier.'

Ivy and Jody introduced themselves.

'We were hoping you might be able to help us, but not with buying a property.'

'Selling? I have buyers ready to purchase.'

'Maybe. At present we're trying to gather some information about the history of our father's property. We have deeds and a receipt, neither of which quite make sense.'

Xavier frowned. 'I've only been in Rivers End for a couple of years so it depends on how historical you are talking about.'

'Mid 1970s.'

He laughed. 'Wasn't even born then.'

'Would you have any suggestions who we could ask?' Jody smiled widely and Ivy could have sworn she fluttered her eyelashes.

'I do. I'm not the owner here, not yet, but in the process. Normally the owner is travelling but he's back in Rivers End for a few weeks and although it was still a bit before his time, he knows everything about real estate in the region.' Xavier glanced at his watch. 'He should be here within half an hour.'

'We can come back,' Ivy said.

'Do you want to leave the documents? John can take a look and save you some time.'

Ivy tightened her grip on her bag. 'Thank you, no. So, about half an hour?'

'I'll let him know you'll be dropping in.' Xavier opened the door for them.


They sat outside the café with a coffee each. The sun was pleasantly warm and for once, Ivy allowed herself the luxury of doing nothing other than people-watch.

As soon as they'd settled at the table, Jody had begun scrolling on her phone.

Ivy had few social media connections and little interest in retreating into a device. Instead, her eyes roamed the street, taking in the changes since her last visit and the things which were the same. Rivers End was growing and the street was busier than she remembered. There were a couple of new restaurants. A new beauty salon. The bookshop. Yet it had kept the feel of a small country town.

*How idyllic this was growing up.*

A small pang of loss... or was it nostalgia... made Ivy sigh.

'Wishing you'd bought that apple slice you were eyeing off?' Jody didn't even look up from her screen.

'It did look nice and I'm contemplating buying a few goodies for later.'

George Campbell hobbled out of the jewellery store and settled onto the bench with a newspaper. He must be in his eighties now but was obviously still running his beautiful business.

'How long do you think the jewellery store has been open?'

Jody glanced across. 'Oh, there he is. Just like I remembered. No idea. I'll find out.' She typed something on her phone. 'Dad loved the place. And I think a few small sculptures made by Fairview guests went there to be sold. Okay, a long time. Since the beginning of the 1900s and it has been passed down through the family.'

'How wonderful is that? An inheritance worth more than money.'

'Then why contemplate selling Fairview? It was Dad's dream come true and you know he wanted us to be part of it – he wouldn't have given us equal shares in it otherwise. Or is it about the money for you?' Jody put her phone onto the table and leaned forward to stare at Ivy. Scrutinise her. 'I'm financially secure, but what does a nurse get paid in England?'

'Not nearly enough for what we do but that isn't the point. I don't want a cent of anything from our father.'

'Shuffle over into the shade, Ivy. The sun is messing with your brain, because Fairview is worth a lot.'

'Dad is still alive and will be released next year as far as we know and I don't think we should have to contribute to the upkeep and rates and stuff of a property for him to live in alone. He'll need money in the bank to secure his future because he's not going to be working ever again. He's seventy-four. Surely you don't believe he'll go back to his poems and make enough to live on?'

'If he reopened Fairview as an artist's retreat then he could pretty much retire. He could hire someone to manage the day-to-day and live out his days in the place he loves. *You* could come back and manage it.'

'Have you thought that through, Jody? Logically?'

'No need to get snippy,' Jody said.

'Sorry. But seriously, how would he cope? Imagine what he is walking back into. A property which needs a lot of work to make it habitable for guests. Work and money to get it up and running. More than that, Jody... who will even come?'

Jody's shoulders sagged as Ivy continued.

'The reputation he built was ruined the day he walked into the police station to confess. Do you really think people will come in droves to stay at a place of such tragedy and deception?' Ivy's heart raced. She hadn't meant to bring that up but it was true and needed to be understood clearly. It didn't matter that she was beginning to fall back in love with Fairview, because this was why selling was the only answer.

John Jones was balding, sixties, and had a ready smile. He welcomed Ivy and Jody into his office at the real estate agency after offering them refreshments.

'Now, you're quite sure you won't have a coffee? Daphne – that's my wife – left a plate of homemade cookies if you'd care for one?'

'That's kind, but we were only just at the café,' Ivy said. 'And thank you for giving us some of your time.'

'Oh, I love talking about real estate and particularly the history of it in our little town.' He took the documents Ivy held out. 'This is for Fairview House?' Over his glasses, he shot a look at first Jody, then Ivy. 'Gabe Sutherland's place?'

*Please don't make this hard.*

'And you are his daughters then? I remember you as chil-dren.' He smiled and returned to the documents.

Jody gave Ivy a sideways look. This was just as hard on her, the constant expectation of being met with anger, or hatred, or disgust. Living away from Rivers End was the only sure way of avoiding the scrutiny. The judgement.

'These old deeds are history in themselves. The first part of the deed is considerably older than Palmerston House, which is often incorrectly assumed to be the oldest large home in the region, being built in 1850. But the original family built the stone hut all the way back in 1835 and lived there while Fairview House was constructed. From memory, it was completed almost ten years later.'

'I had no idea it was so old. Being Georgian, I did wonder if it was more of a replica of the style,' Ivy said.

'No, it is old. It may be eligible for heritage listing.'

'Wouldn't that affect it being sold?' Jody was interested by this. 'For example, it couldn't simply be bulldozed if a developer buys the property?'

'Correct. All kinds of criteria need to be met both before and after listing, should it be eligible. I imagine a developer would be willing to keep the house itself intact if it meant getting hold of the remaining land, given its proximity to the beach.'

Jody leaned back in her chair, expression thoughtful.

'Now, the descendants of the original family occupied the house until the early 1970s when the last of them passed away, leaving it to a distant cousin in America, of all places. All a bit before my time. But according to this, Mr W. Bell purchased Fairview House in 1974 and then only one year later, he sold it to your father.'

'But did he sell it?'

John read the receipt then returned to the deed title. 'Yes and no. Gabe paid one dollar which made it a legal contract. But for all intents and purposes, it was a gift.'

'But why would he do such a thing?' Jody asked. 'Nobody just gives away a house.'

'Did Gabe work for Mr Bell?'

'No idea,' Ivy said.

'Was he an active member of the local church?'

That made Ivy laugh shortly. 'Sorry. No disrespect meant, but although Dad was born into a Catholic family he was a long way from practising.'

With a small smile, John handed the documents back. 'What a curious situation. Mr Bell is long deceased so we can't ask him, not that I would have recommended you do. He was private and not the man to cross, although he had much to do with our now-defunct Historical Society and was a senior and influential member of one of the churches in town.'

*Instead of answers, we have more questions.*

Ivy stood and slid the documents back into her bag. 'We won't keep you any longer, John. Thank you for being so helpful.'

'Are you going to sell Fairview?'

John led them along the hallway to the front door.

'No,' Jody said.

'It is undecided.'

Jody scowled and opened the door, stepping onto the pavement.

'If you do, please think of talking to Xavier. He's a fine agent and will look after the interests of your family.'

After shaking John's hand, Ivy joined Jody, who glared at her and then shoved her sunglasses on.

'I'm going to visit the bookshop.' Not waiting around for an argument or complaint, Ivy crossed the road.

# EIGHT

The bookshop put Jody back into a good mood... or what passed for one these days. Between them, the sisters bought five books, all recent releases. Outside, they paused at the display windows which were filled with ideas for springtime reading.

'A person could go broke in there,' Ivy said. 'Did you see the stand with the old books?'

'I did. Mind you, I imagine some of ours in the library would rival those for age and value.'

They wandered back to the car and stowed the books in the back.

'I spoke to the owner, she's called Harriet. She is interested in looking at any from Fairview we wish to sell. That might help Dad a bit more, if we can sell some books which won't matter so much to him,' Ivy said.

Jody didn't answer. She was at the driver's door but her attention was behind Ivy, on the far corner of the intersection. She took her sunglasses off, her eyes squinting as she stared. 'We know him, I think.'

'Who?'

'Forget it. Don't bother looking.'

Ivy looked. There was a man around their age, holding hands with a little boy of about six, and pushing open the door of the café with the other.

Suddenly, the air was hard to breathe.

He disappeared, with the child, inside the café.

'I was mistaken, Ivy.'

*You were not.*

Something odd was happening to Ivy's legs. They were cold and shaking. She grabbed the top of the passenger door to steady herself.

Jody was oblivious and climbed in. 'Are you getting in or walking home?'

Managing to get into the car without falling, Ivy closed the door and struggled with the seat belt. Her fingers wouldn't work properly and it took a few goes before it clicked into place.

Jody was checking her makeup in the rear-vision mirror. 'There's nothing else you want in town?'

'What?'

'Are you quite okay, Ivy?'

'Home is fine.'

*I'm not going to look. I'm not.*

But as they passed the café, she did. At a window table was a woman whose face she couldn't see, sitting beside the little boy. They were opposite the man. She knew the mop of red-brown hair. The strong jawline. The smile. It was Leo.


*The afternoon of beach volleyball had been the most fun Ivy remembered having.*

*Leo's family and friends were so nice, if loud, and had made her feel welcome. Jody had immediately struck up a friendship with two girls around her own age and in between games was enjoying the picnic they'd brought along. Several people told Ivy to help herself to food but she was self-conscious* for the first time in her life. She didn't want to eat in front of Leo.

There was something about him which made her want to get to know him more. He was self-assured but not cocky. His eyes were kind and smiled as much as his lips. And he had something in his hand to eat every time he wasn't playing or surfing. But she couldn't bring herself to do the same.

As the families began the job of packing up, a few of the younger kids went into the water for a paddle and Ivy found herself in there as well, laughing as they splashed her and happy to give it straight back. She had lots of friends in England but all her own age and none with children yet. Jody was the youngest person she knew well and sisters didn't count, so it was fun hanging out with these bold little people.

'Uncle Leo!' One of the children squealed with joy as Leo joined them. He scooped the child up and perched her upon his shoulders where she grabbed handfuls of his red-brown, almost shoulder-length hair.

'Hold on in case a giant wave gets us.'

She giggled and hung on more tightly as he waded through the waves, which offered little resistance to his movement.

Ivy caught up when he was stomach-deep and the water almost reached her chest.

'My name is Erin.' The little girl announced. 'I like ponies.'

'Hello, Erin. My name is Ivy.'

'What do you like?'

Leo was watching her. 'Yes, Ivy. What do you like?'

At that moment there wasn't a chance she could think clearly because his eyes and his smile were doing weird things to her insides.

'Tell me, Ivy!' Erin demanded.

'Er... writing stories. I like writing stories.'

'Me too! Can I swim now?'

Erin wiggled around and almost lost balance, but Leo's

*hands shot up to steady her. He swung her down and gently lowered her until she was in the water.*

*'Can you race us back?'*

*There was no answer as the child began swimming toward shore.*

*'Is she okay to do that?'*

*Leo grinned. 'Our entire family are water babies. Look at Erin go.'*

*He was right. She was swimming strongly through the water and then stopped long enough to catch a wave all the way back to shore, squealing as she rolled around.*

*'See?'*

*'You have a great family.'*

*'Sure do. What about you? Any other siblings apart from Jody?'*

*A bigger than expected wave caught Ivy by surprise and her footing slipped. Leo grabbed her, steadied her, and kept his hands on her arms. They were so close together she could see little beads of sea water on his chest.*

*Not such a good idea to look.*

*'No. Um, no, just Jody. Unless one of our parents is keeping secrets.'*

*'About another sibling. Do you think so?'*

*'Of course not!' Ivy couldn't believe she'd said such a thing.*

*He looked serious all of a sudden. Had she said something really wrong? His hands moved down her arms to clasp her fingers and electricity shot through her body. How could she feel so alive and yet be unable to breathe?*

*'Do you live here? In Rivers End?'*

*'Sometimes. My home is really in England with my mother but I come here most summers.'*

*'You sound English. But also Australian. I like it.'*

*She didn't know what to say. All she could feel was his skin against hers.*

*A woman waved from the beach.*

*'Looks like Mum's ready to go. How long are you staying?'*

*'A few more weeks.'*

*'Shall we meet up? What about tomorrow?'*

*'I can't. I have to help my dad with something.'*

*'The next day then? Just before sunset? Here. And don't eat first. I have an idea.'*

*'Okay... Yes.'*

*She could feel a blush rising to her cheeks. Oh my goodness, she sounded lame.*

*Did he squeeze her fingers? Just as quickly, he was gone, powering toward the beach.*

'Who is *that*?'

Jody's sudden cry startled Ivy back into the present. They were home, driving down the driveway and in sight of the main house. Jody must have opened and closed the gate herself without interrupting Ivy's memories.

She couldn't see anyone but then, as they reached the corner of the house, there was a flash of movement in the direction of the cottages. A glimpse of someone running.

'Stop the car.'

Almost slamming on the brakes, Jody flung her own door open as the Mini shuddered to a halt. Ivy was out and chasing the intruder and Jody's high heels were clicking behind her.

Whoever it was had a decent head start and Ivy only saw enough to know it was a slender woman. By the time she reached the top of the dunes, the person was on the rocks and in another few seconds, was out of sight. Ivy raced down the slope to the sand but she was too far behind.

'Ivy! They're gone.'

She didn't want to give up but once the person got onto the other side of the cliff, they'd have multiple options to get them off Rivers End beach. Ivy turned and jogged back to where Jody was panting at the edge of the sand.

'Bother. Should we get back in the car and search?'

'They'll be long gone.'

They trudged back, Jody slipping off her heels to walk barefoot. The car's doors were still wide open and the key was in the ignition.

'Good grief. I'd never do that at home! Someone might have stolen you, baby.'

Jody drove the car to its usual spot with Ivy following.

'I'm going to check the outside of the house for anything, if you don't mind looking at some of the other buildings.'

Ivy set off before Jody could argue. They'd checked the cottages on the way up from the beach and nothing seemed out of place. The person might have simply wandered onto the property from the beach and got a fright when they'd come home. It only took a few minutes to assure herself the house hadn't been entered and she went to find Jody.

'The only place is the garage, Ivy.'

Heels back on, Jody had the side door open. 'I put the lights on just now but I'm sure we covered the motorcycle back up.'

The cover was on the ground in a heap.

'We did. Was the door locked?'

'No. But we'd locked it. I remember you doing it, so how has it magically unlocked itself and the cover come off? If it had simply slipped off it would be close by but look how far away it is.'

'Did you get any kind of look at the woman? I only saw her back and that was miles away.' Ivy lifted the cover and replaced it.

'Nope. They were walking up the driveway and when they saw the car they hightailed it. I had no idea you could still run so fast. If you'd had another few metres you might have stopped her.'

Ivy grinned. 'And I'll hurt all over later for that effort.'

Lights off and door closed, Jody locked up and Ivy checked. They decided that for now they would double check everything. But none of this made sense. Who else would have a key? And why go to look at a motorcycle, which was valuable, and then simply wander away? It was time to be proactive rather than wait for Mick Hammond to come up with something.

Ivy and Jody had a phone call with Mary, using the speaker.

'I've only ever had that one set of keys, girls. Did you find them on the kitchen table where I left them, Ivy? Beside the box of cleaning products?'

Ivy lifted the keys. 'Inside it.'

'No. No, I am certain I left them beside the box so you could find them easily. I knew you had a front door key from before but thought you'd need them all.'

Jody bit her lip, eyes worried.

'There's keys to the front, back, and laundry door here, one for each cottage, one for each of the sheds, the skeleton key for the hut, what I guess is a key to the tractor and one for the ride-on mower, and one key for the passenger door of the garage.' Ivy moved each one as she spoke. 'Actually, should there be one for the motorcycle?'

'I'm reading the list I've always had for Fairview and it doesn't match. There should be two keys for the garage so would you check again?' Mary's voice rose a little. 'Never had a motorcycle key.'

Taking the ring from Ivy, Jody went through them all. 'Only one, Mary.'

'Oh my. Oh my, that means whoever broke in through the library window must have taken it off the keyring. I am so dreadfully sorry, girls. Why didn't I just come and meet you when you arrived, Ivy?'

After a few minutes reassuring Mary that none of this was her fault, the conversation ended.

'Poor Mary,' Jody said. 'And we should have described that person to her in case it sounds familiar.'

'Why only take the garage key though?'

'Thought we might not miss one of two? Didn't know it was for the garage? People are more likely to have extra front door keys, and they look similar. Clearly had enough time to wander around and try it, so finding it only opened the garage must have been disappointing.'

Something felt off. More off than an intruder wanting to trash a room. No, whoever was behind that had stolen a key and Ivy would need to talk to the police again. And a locksmith.


Ivy and Jody worked at the kitchen table all afternoon. On the long plane ride from England to Australia, Ivy had set up different spreadsheets and a list of items to add, everything she could think of from the condition of the property and its assets through to the cost of running the property again as a going concern.

'Thank goodness Dad had a decent bookkeeper, because you know he was never any good with money and gave it out to anyone he thought needed a hand,' Jody said. 'Actually, several bookkeepers, because this spans almost forty years. Exactly how did you get hold of all of this?'

'Mr Appleby. The solicitor? He would have sent you all the same information, Jody. Apparently Dad told him to give us full access to anything relating to Fairview. We have an appointment to see him next week.'

'What for?'

'To ask questions and get an understanding of Dad's rights, given he now only owns a third of the property – if we have reached some kind of agreement by then.'

Jody screwed her face up.

'What if you read out the bottom of each profit and loss for me to input and then we'll do the same for the tax returns?'

Over the next couple of hours they created a spreadsheet for the business side of Fairview, compiling years of data into one easy-to-follow document. Neither of them were numbers people but Ivy had begun a business course, including accounting, a few years ago when nursing began to take an emotional toll on her. Before she could finish the course, the world changed overnight with the start of the pandemic and she'd put her plans on hold as demand for front-line workers escalated.

'Looking at this, Dad did a good job running Fairview. But even when I was working alongside him for those couple of years I wasn't given access to this kind of stuff.'

'You sound surprised, Ivy. This was his whole world. I know we mattered but his life revolved around the people who came to stay and all that creative energy.'

'Oh, I know. But I hadn't realised how popular he was as a host, even twenty years or more ago. There were so many repeat visitors and some who booked in for weeks at a time. And there are some interesting names, as in, famous people.'

Jody peered at the spreadsheet open on the financials. 'Am I reading this right? He was only in the red the very first year. Always in the black after that.'

'That's how I'm reading it. He was paying tax and all the bills so I'd say Fairview was profitable. And by giving us a third each, he clearly intended for the retreat to continue and stay that way – or even retire in time and sell as a going concern. We'd then have had proceeds in place of property.'

'Then I say we keep it and build it back up.'

'Will anyone even come?' Ivy frowned. 'So many years have passed and if Dad isn't here then one of the main drawcards for guests is missing. Or maybe not. Those contacts and the huge network he drew on have all turned their backs on him so it would be up to us to start almost from scratch.'

'Well, I'm sure we can come up with ideas. A vision for the future with Fairview repurposed.' Jody pushed herself up. 'And now, I'm going to go and swim.'

# NINE

Although they'd both walked down to the cottages before dusk to make sure each was secure, then to the garage and finally around the outside of the main house, Ivy couldn't help checking inside again after dinner. If the person with the garage key came again tonight then they might very well gain access. The local locksmith had been up in the hills doing a big job but promised to be there first thing in the morning, so Ivy and Jody had piled a kind of booby-trap of boxes close enough behind the door that anyone entering would knock them down and hopefully get a scare and run off.

With nightfall, the sense of isolation was amplified, and what might only be the branch of a tree tapping on the roof could as easily be an intruder climbing the ladder.

*Stop jumping at shadows.*

Ivy had called Mick Hammond again, while Jody was safely out of hearing at the beach. He'd been offhand about the report of the woman running away, suggesting it was a tourist who was lost or else someone curious about people living back at Fairview. Even the unlocked garage door didn't bother him until Ivy mentioned that a key was missing. He took that more seriously and promised to follow up on the fingerprints but warned it would be several days, if not longer, thanks to a backlog. His parting advice was being vigilant but not paranoid. It wasn't a word Ivy expected from a police officer. Then again, this was Mick Hammond, past school bully.

Jody was in the living room with a glass of wine and one of the books they'd purchased today and barely looked up when Ivy rattled each of the windows.

'I'll check upstairs next.'

'Hm? Sure.'

Ivy climbed the stairs and began at the furthest bedroom. There were six in total, and this one belonged to their father. At some point she would need to properly clean it and make it a fresher, more welcoming place for him to come home to.

She'd already been in with Jody but only to take notes about its furniture and the like. One big job ahead was talking to the insurance company who covered home and contents with an updated value. If it burned down right now, they'd receive substantially less than it was worth. As it was, the insurance costs were high, thanks to the place being unoccupied for so long.

This was the largest of all the bedrooms, taking up the full depth of the house. Dad had used half of it as his office. There were three walls with windows and the one facing the sea had been changed decades ago from the typical Georgian style to a sliding door, and a small balcony added outside. That was where Ivy went first, unlocking the door and stepping out into the night air. From here, in daylight or beneath a full moon, one could see the ocean over the cottages and smaller trees. There was a small table and two chairs and in the opposite corner, a surprising find. In a pot was a seaside daisy which flowed over the sides. It was healthy despite what must have been years of neglect. Ivy picked one of the tiny flowers, turning it in her fingers.

'If you could survive all this time, then can Fairview do the same?'

How often had Dad stood here, looking over the retreat he had created? Did he appreciate how successful he'd been when so many small businesses fail? And had he expected to live out his days doing what he loved with such passion?

Ivy sighed and went inside, locking the sliding door behind herself.

She checked each of the other windows, pausing at the desk which faced the sliding door. There were papers left on it. A couple of books of poetry, including one of his, published in the eighties. A coffee cup. Empty and stained. He'd had little notice of his impending incarceration even with his belated admission of guilt. A knock on the door and he'd have walked away from everything he'd built.

Her breath caught in her throat and she hurried out with the coffee cup and flower.

The remainder of the floor was secure and she returned to the kitchen.

The flower went into the narrowest glass she could find and onto the middle of the table. It was tiny and lonely in there. She might pick some other flowers from those growing wild around the grounds. At this time of year there were jonquils, daffodils, hyacinths and crocus all brightening up corners of gardens around the house and cottages.

'All okay?' Jody called from the living room.

'Yes. Yes, fine.'

'Then come and read for a bit.'

There was so much to do and Ivy only knew one way – keep working, keep busy. So much cleaning and planning and working toward decisions which would impact their father, as well as them. Ivy touched the little daisy. It came from a plant which had survived neglect and yet had thrived. There was a lesson there, but Ivy's brain was too tired to work out what.

. . .

An hour or more passed in a flash once Ivy had her head in a book. Wanting pure escapism, she'd picked up a time-travelling novel and was lost in a tale of romance, mystery and intrigue. Legs curled up on the chair and a pillow to rest the paperback on, this was the most relaxed she'd been in days.

Jody was just as engrossed in her book but had got up at one point to pour another glass of wine. A few minutes later, she huffed and snapped the book shut.

'You cannot have finished.' Ivy glanced up. 'Or are you not finishing it?'

With a shake of her head, Jody put the book onto the coffee table and picked up her wine. 'It was fine until the main character decided to leave her family.'

'Go on.'

'She had three children and her husband thought she was happy, but she was miserable, missing the country she grew up in. So she disappeared one day, leaving a note and no forwarding address.'

'But it's only fiction, Jodes.'

Jody rolled her eyes but the underlying sadness was evident in her face.

Ivy closed her own book. 'Mum didn't leave like that and she took us.'

'But she took us away from Dad. Away from here, where we were happy.'

'Do you remember being happy here? You were only three when we moved to London.'

'Maybe not. But then Mum brought us back a few times for Christmas and I do remember having the best fun with all the singing around the piano and a big Christmas dinner, even though Mum kept saying it was silly to roast a whole turkey in the middle of summer.'

Ivy smiled at the memory. 'There were so many guests. People from the town, some who were on their own and Dad loved sharing and making their day a bit better. I think we were together again as a family three times before Mum decided not to come with us again.'

The first time travelling without their mother had been frightening and lonely at first, but as unaccompanied minors it quickly became a world of fun as flight attendants fussed over them. Dad was at the airport to meet them and they spent a night in a hotel in Melbourne to break up the travel before driving to Fairview. And then there were only two or three years they ever missed again.

'Why did she even marry Dad if she didn't like Australia?' Jody finished her glass and held on to it, gazing into its empty depths.

'Love? I've thought about this a lot and it keeps going back to her being so young. She was backpacking around Australia at twenty years of age. Met Dad and within a year, I came along. Then you, the cutest baby in the world.'

Jody's eyes shot up to see if Ivy was being sarcastic, but she wasn't.

'You were adorable. So much golden hair. Big blue eyes and such a smile. I wanted to hold you all the time.' Ivy's mouth lifted at the memory. 'That is, until you'd fill your nappy and then I was quick to hand you back.'

'Ew. Thanks for that.' Jody looked repulsed.

'Pleasure. But going back to our parents... Mum hadn't come to Australia to settle here but to spread her wings. She hated the heat and the distance from any big towns. She'd always planned to be a nurse and couldn't do that living so far out here. You know her heart belongs to London.'

'But Dad loved her.'

'It was a mess. A mistake of sorts but both of them have

done their best to be in our lives. If I don't look at it that way, well, it hurts too much.'

They were silent for a while. Ivy had had enough of reading and bed was beckoning but if Jody wanted to talk then she wasn't going anywhere.

'I always wondered why Dad never remarried,' Ivy said. 'Mum did, even though it took a few years, and she's happy.'

Jody was very quiet. Very still.

'What's wrong?'

'You and I were at Mum's wedding. We didn't put up barriers or decide *her* new husband wasn't good enough.' Jody almost spat the words.

*And here we go.*

'She never said Aaron wasn't good enough, Jodes.'

'No, true. But she projected her own mistakes onto me and I want to know how that is fair? Mum has never even met Aaron yet she had the gall to tell me not to marry a man who is fifteen years older than me. Dad was twice her age when they married! *Twenty* years older.'

'And that's why, sweetie. She was torn, wanting you to be happy but all she could see was how difficult her life had been with Dad.'

'But Aaron isn't Gabe Sutherland and I'm not Brenda Ross.' Jody's face was bright red and the hand not holding the glass was in a tight fist. 'She's English but I am Australian and this country is my home. I married a man I love to the moon and back but my own mother refused to attend my wedding. And so did you.'

Jody got to her feet, having two attempts and swaying a bit once she did.

Ivy jumped up as well.

'Don't play the concerned sister now, Ivy. I didn't expect you to make Mum see sense but I did expect you to be there. At my wedding, Ivy.' Her voice rose. 'But you took her side and now you want to sell Fairview and I won't have you or Dad and I won't have anything left of our childhood. Except that all got taken from me already.'

'Hang on. I'm not trying to take anything from you. Don't walk off.'

It was more a stagger off and when Ivy followed Jody into the kitchen she could see why. There was an almost empty bottle of wine among the full ones.

'Have you drunk all of that tonight?'

'Go away. Leave me alone, along with your judgemental, puritan eyes.'

Jody crossed her arms and leaned against the counter, her lips in a straight line.

Ivy turned and ran up the stairs.


More than an hour of sorting through the books on the library floor had calmed Ivy's frazzled nerves enough to stop her hands shaking. She'd heard Jody come up not long after she had and thought her sister had been outside the door Ivy had closed behind her. But then she'd gone again and her bedroom door had clicked shut.

Whatever had got into Jody tonight – other than alcohol – hit home hard.

Ivy had been put into the middle of the argument over the wedding between her mother and sister and both of them pretty much ended up being angry with her for some reason. The last few comments... about Jody losing her and Dad and Fairview and her childhood and the odd words *except that all got taken from me already* – where had that come from?

It was all such a mess. Here in the library and in their lives, Ivy's and Jody's. Uprooted, travelling across the globe year after year, and living with a mother who said little about their father. And a father who'd always had a sadness beneath the outgoing and flamboyant facade. Ivy would catch him sometimes standing on the grassy dune beneath the big old tree, staring at the sea. He'd smile at her but not say a word and she'd wondered if he was remembering days on the beach when they were a complete family.

'But we were so close once, Dad. I sensed you were sad but never knew why.'

Talking aloud to someone who wasn't present was stupid. She lifted another pile of books onto the reading table along the wall. After he went to prison, Ivy had shut off her emotions. There was too much pain in her heart and closing herself down probably saved her life. It was a terrible chapter and for Jody as well, who had fallen into depression. No wonder Jody was drinking and reactive now that they were back here.

Most of the books weren't damaged by their dreadful experience and Ivy sorted them as she went. Dad used to keep them in order of subject and then by author. It made it simple to walk in and know that if you fancied reading a mystery, there were in one spot. Or poetry, history, or any of dozens of categories.

Unsure if she should attempt to refill the shelves the same way, or just get the books back up off the floor, Ivy decided to get Jody to help tomorrow. All the fallen books were in neat piles on the floor and table and they could separate them in daylight.

What she was curious about – and was becoming a burning question – was the books on the highest shelves, untouched by the intruder.

Ivy reached her hands up as high as she could, on her toes, and couldn't touch the top shelf. Was that the only reason they'd stayed on the shelf? Or was the intruder working their way from the bottom up, looking for something in particular?

*You've read too many mystery novels!*

She left the library and opened the long linen closet further along the hallway. There had to be a stepladder or something here for back when there was a regular cleaner coming in.

Better than that, there were two rolling ladders.

Unable to contain a silly grin about her find, Ivy lifted one out of the closet and carried it back to the library. It hooked perfectly on the rail which ran just under the top shelf. Ivy climbed to the top.

The shelf was separated into six units. She ran her finger along the first few books and sneezed as dust particles lifted into the air. These were the most precious of Dad's collection. First editions and rare copies he'd collected over many, many years. Some were leather bound, or had gold edges to their fine paper. There'd been a plan for her to catalogue these before everything changed, and they should be valued. And for that she did need Jody to help.

Nothing was out of place there so she moved along, up and down the ladder until she reached the last section of the shelf, closest to the window. A few of the books were pushed out a bit and Ivy began to straighten them. One – a fat paperback – refused to go into its place so she pulled it right out to make sure no pages were turned on themselves. Behind it was a thick envelope.

Ivy stared at it.

*Is this what the intruder was after?*

Heart pounding with excitement, Ivy extracted the envelope and then replaced the book.

At the bottom of the steps she drew a quick breath and read the words on the front of the yellowed envelope. Words in her father's handwriting.

*From my one true love. My angel.*

# TEN

Ivy had barely slept and when the first rays of morning sun appeared, she was down on the beach, too restless to stay in the house.

She'd locked the envelope in the safe in the wine cellar and hadn't opened it yet. It was Dad's handwriting, and Ivy was reluctant to intrude on what had to be something private, because why else would he hide it?

She'd always found it funny as a child that Dad had a safe almost large enough for her to walk in but rarely locked it. He kept some of his more expensive bottles of wine in there along with an assortment of papers in boxes and a small statue of an angel, its wings wrapped around its body. He'd never explained it to her, telling her to mind her manners and not ask questions about his private life.

Now it just seemed odd. A sculpture of an angel and an envelope mentioning one.

Dad's old code for the safe had worked but Ivy changed it in case any other intruders broke in. Not that they would know his code. Unless they'd known him. Could it have been someone who'd once worked here? Ivy trusted Mary, but someone else from the small staff over the years? It seemed unlikely.

The half-thoughts of the night were now daytime worries and her mind was in a perpetual loop. If only she could talk to Jody without upsetting her further.

With the rising of the sun came a humid breeze. The day would be hot and sticky and stay that way until a storm cleared the air. Rivers End and the neighbouring regions typically had storms across spring and into summer, some quite savage. It would pay to move Jody's car into the garage once the clouds began to loom from the horizon but right now, the sky was clear.

She wandered along the tideline, letting the water wash over her feet and wishing the waves would whisk her woes back into the sea.

This envelope was a problem. Hidden behind books on the highest shelf, it was there for a reason. But if it needed hiding, why not in the safe? Yesterday she'd chased after a woman along this stretch of beach. Was it the same person who'd broken into the house and trashed the library? If so, were they looking for the envelope?

'Why, though?'

She spoke out loud, startling a nearby seagull.

'What could it possibly be to make it worth stealing?'

Ivy discarded the idea of it being a bundle of cash. It was obvious from going over his accounts yesterday that Dad was careful with money and above board. He'd paid his debts and the tax and keeping a stack of money hidden seemed unlikely. Until the accident, he'd done nothing other than be law-abiding. Except he'd drunk too much one night before getting into his car for reasons known only to himself.

She stopped near the rocks.

There was so much she wasn't clear on and the passage of time made what little she knew cloudier still.

Two years had passed between the crash and his arrest,

which followed him walking into the police station to confess. Until then he'd sworn the car had been stolen by an unknown person. Fairview had been visited by the police several times. All the guests were interviewed. Ivy was interviewed and unable to help because she'd slept through everything until Dad had arrived home with bleeding feet and hands from glass and bits of metal on the road. They'd fingerprinted the garage although Dad said it was pointless as the doors were open and the key in the ignition.

He'd always been careless that way. Too trusting. But why not? Rivers End was hardly a bastion of crime.

A dreadful thought struck her and she gasped aloud. Would he have put money somewhere in case he needed bail? Or to escape justice? Would her father have considered leaving town and starting a new life as a fugitive? Was that why he had the motorcycle? But why would it say on the envelope it was from his one true love? His angel? Had some benefactor given him the means to leave? And was the love nest in the stone hut part of this?

With a shudder, Ivy wrapped her arms around herself and stared at the horizon. It hurt to think back to the chaos and distress after he'd confessed, and she'd dropped the ball entirely by leaving Fairview as soon as she could. Jody had been visiting after auditioning for a new television series in Melbourne. She was the one who'd stayed at Fairview to cancel guests and goodness knows what else while Ivy was on a plane to England.

Ivy noticed how tightly she was holding herself and dropped her arms.

*She* wasn't Dad's angel. The one whose wings were wrapped around its body. But something told Ivy the angel he'd meant, when he wrote on the envelope, wasn't a sculpture. It was a person. Someone completely unknown to Ivy.

· · ·

Right before breakfast, Jody wandered into the kitchen as though no harsh words had been spoken the previous night and made small talk over a meal of yoghurt and fruit.

A car nosed around the front of the house, past the kitchen window.

'Is it the hot-water system?' Jody turned around from putting juice in the fridge. 'Locksmith?'

Ivy and Jody were still using the shower in the cottage and boiling water on the stove for washing up.

With Jody on her heels, Ivy swung the door open to find a young man wearing a suit and carrying a folder. He offered a big smile.

'I wasn't certain I'd catch anyone home,' he said.

Unsure how to answer that, Ivy just said hello and waited. If he was selling religion then she would politely move him on.

'My name is Zac. Zac Bolan. I represent Green Bay Developments and was hoping I might have a few minutes of your time?'

'Not selling,' Jody said. 'Goodbye.'

Zac's smile dropped.

'Jody, come on, we can have a quick chat.'

But Jody had stepped out of view of the visitor and shook her head frantically.

'Zac, was it? Would you mind staying here for a moment? I'll be back.' Ivy didn't wait for an answer, closing the door and grabbing Jody's arm to haul her into the living room.

'Hey, that hurts.'

'Rubbish. Look, I really need for us to be on the same side, Jody. Until we make a firm decision to sell or not to sell, we owe it to Dad and ourselves to consider all options. That includes speaking with developers and real estate agents as well as builders and lawyers. Five minutes won't kill you but might give us more information.'

After rolling her eyes and making a show of rubbing her arm where Ivy had briefly held it, Jody muttered, 'Fine.'

'And be nice.'

'I'm always nice.'

Opening the front door again, Ivy smiled at Zac, who hadn't moved. 'We can give you a few minutes. Would you like to come in? I'm Ivy and my sister is Jody.'

He nodded and began to remove his shoes.

'No, no don't worry. The floors need professional cleaning which we will do later.'

Zac stepped inside and gazed around. 'Quite beautiful in its own way.'

Jody emerged from the living room and stood in the doorway, arms crossed.

'Why don't you come into the kitchen, Zac? Would you like a coffee?'

After a glance at Jody, he shook his head. 'Just had one, but thank you.'

The three of them sat at the table, Jody on the furthest chair and her expression still far from welcoming or friendly.

'I apologise for dropping by unannounced.' Zac opened the folder to remove two business cards which he offered to Ivy and Jody. When Jody didn't move, he put hers onto the table. 'The company I represent is keen to purchase parcels of land in the region. We have clients actively looking for properties such as this.'

'What makes you think Fairview House is for sale?' Jody spoke quickly. 'There isn't a For Sale sign outside, is there?'

'Most of our purchases are by cold calling. I'm only here to introduce myself and answer any questions you may have about a potential sale. Rivers End is rapidly becoming a popular destination for tourists as well as sea-changers and the demand for accommodation and new housing is growing faster than anyone can keep up.'

*Which makes a unique place like Fairview attractive to more than one type of buyer.*

'So, you've been here before? When it was empty?' Ivy was curious about his timing.

He shuffled in his seat. 'No. I've driven past often but was aware the property owner isn't living here.'

'Meaning what?' Jody demanded.

Ivy met her eyes, hoping her sister would let her manage this rather than making it hostile. Jody looked away.

'Zac, what exactly do you know about Fairview and why now? We haven't broadcast our visit.'

'You met my brother, Xavier? He mentioned you have moved in.'

Jody made a humph sound and Ivy felt the same. Small town gossips.

'I see,' Ivy said. 'And did he tell you *why* we visited Rivers End Real Estate?'

Zac's skin flushed red and he shook his head. 'Only that you had questions about the title deeds. He wasn't told what the outcome was of your conversation with John Jones.'

*At least one person in town has ethics!*

Ivy stood. 'Thank you for dropping in but we have quite a full day ahead.'

'Oh, of course.' Zac got to his feet. 'The folder has more about us and also information about Fairview and our estimate of the price range, should you decide to sell.' He shook Ivy's hand and obviously decided it wasn't worth trying with Jody, before heading out of the kitchen.

Once he was outside, he turned to Ivy again. 'If I've upset your sister, I am sorry. Most people in your situation would want to sell quickly and I can make that happen and for an attractive price.'

'Sorry? *Our* situation?'

Zac went down the steps. 'Give me a call if you have questions.'

She did have questions and it took self-restraint not to run after him as he hurried to his car. Ivy forced down a sudden urge to cry. Would the people in town never believe that Gabe alone knew the truth about that night? Would there never be a time when fingers weren't pointed at his daughters?

'We should tell that Xavier person to keep his mouth shut!' Jody was pacing from one end of the hallway to the other. 'It isn't like we even showed him the documents.'

'I guess if we had access to them then we'd be viewed as having the ability to sell Fairview. Only Mr Appleby knows we have equal shares and he won't break that confidence.'

'How do we know that? Maybe the entire population of Rivers End had a meeting to discuss the daughters of Gabe Sutherland, home to sort out his estate so he doesn't have to face the past. Do they not think we have our own lives and aren't here to amuse ourselves?'

As Jody began to turn to stalk away again, Ivy captured her in a hug.

'Let me go, Ivy.'

'Nope. Us being so upset isn't healthy. Stop for a sec.'

Ivy kept her hold firm and after a moment, Jody's body relaxed and she laid her head on Ivy's shoulder. They stayed that way for a little while. Sisters sharing the same need for comfort and support.

'Did we have coffee with breakfast?' Jody mumbled.

'Only one.'

Jody straightened. 'Let's fix that.'

. . .

They took their coffee down to the furthest cottage and sat on the steps, letting the warm wind blow their hair around. Soon it would be too hot to be out here. Hot and humid.

'I imagine that developer turning up here has made you see how much easier it is just to sell the place off. I saw the figure he suggested and it would set Dad up for the rest of his life.' Jody spoke for the first time since they'd left the house. 'I would just put whatever I got into Aaron's charity. And it would give you a decent financial boost, so maybe you wouldn't have to work so hard. Maybe you could even stop nursing and start writing again.'

Tears prickled at the back of Ivy's eyes and she blinked a few times, gazing out over the ocean rather than let her sister see her vulnerability. Jody had never once mentioned Ivy's lost dream. For that matter, nor had Ivy spoken of Jody's. How different their lives would be had they followed their true paths. And she was right. Dad would never need to worry about money again. He could move anywhere – within whatever conditions came with his release – and be unknown in a new community. Logically, it was the best outcome for him. And for Ivy. She'd never have to return to Rivers End. Not even to Australia, unless to visit her sister. Her job would be done and she could move forward.

The image of Leo in the café came unbidden.

'Ivy? Do you still want to sell?'

There was a waver in Jody's voice. Her eyes were sad.

'It's the easy choice.'

'Yes, but is it what your heart wants?'

Out at sea, a yacht was swept along by the increasing wind. So free and unencumbered by the constraints of land.

'My heart wants to be on that yacht.'

Jody followed her eyes. 'Nice thought.'

'Did Dad own a boat or am I imagining it?'

'I remember. It was only a little dinghy or something and I can't recall the last time I saw it. Maybe he sold it,' Jody said.

'When you put the Mini into the garage we might take another look for it. We didn't really look much further than the front part with the motorcycle. And speaking of that... we haven't located a record of its purchase.'

The sound of a motor approached and they looked at each other.

'Hot-water system?' Jody jumped up and stood where she could see the house. 'Yes!'

'Thank goodness. Hot showers in our own bathrooms. Hot water on demand.'

'We'd better hurry in case he thinks we're not home,' Jody grinned. 'Race you.'

# ELEVEN

The locksmith arrived almost at the same time as the plumber and he got to work on changing the garage lock. As soon as the hot-water system was connected and the installer had gone, Jody dived into the bathroom to have a shower. Ivy left her to it and returned to the furthest cottage to collect the small bag of toiletries and a change of clothes she'd left there.

The wind was whipping up the sea and storm clouds were ominously close. This was coming in faster than expected. She locked the cottage and had one last try at pulling down the shutters, but again, they were too stiff from lack of use to move.

After dropping her things at the house, she got the keys to the Mini and the garage. Jody was singing loudly in the shower upstairs, making Ivy giggle because it was a song they'd learned as kids and it was in French. Jody excelled at languages and used to love teasing Ivy in German or Italian – not that Ivy ever knew what she said, being terrible at them.

The garage had two huge doors with an internal lock. They slid apart and were stiff to move, but Ivy pushed and then pulled and finally made a space large enough to drive through. She turned on the headlights as she nosed the Mini in with great care, parking between the tractor and motorcycle. The headlights illuminated the back wall which was a mix of shelving and rows of items, stacked or leaning.

The power had gone off and she left the headlights on to take a better look.

Most of the shelves were empty, apart from a few power tools covered in cobwebs, and a neat line of nails and screws in glass jars.

Long planks of timber leaned against the wall, as did a couple of surfboards. Ivy touched these with a small smile. Dad would take them out into the waves in front of him when they were kids and then he'd taught them to surf as teens. They'd each had their own size-appropriate surfboard but she couldn't see those here. And there certainly wasn't a boat, even a small one. In the corner was a solid and long post which was at an odd angle thanks to half a dozen smaller timber pieces attached at the top, all going in different directions.

It took a minute until Ivy noticed the writing on one piece.

*Rivers End.*

Then another.

*Fairview House.*

'Oh, I remember!'

This was a signpost, last seen halfway between the house and the beach. Dad had made it one summer and the girls helped select the right spot to dig a hole for it. There were distances etched into each name, in miles, as Dad refused to accept metric. He'd say poetry worked with miles but not kilometres and Ivy understood. More romance in the old terms.

'Are you in here, Ivy?'

'Over here in the far corner.'

'I might turn off my headlights. These batteries are a pain to jump start.'

The lights went off, casting the corner into semi-darkness.

'Why isn't the light switch working? Where are you? Hang on.'

Another light appeared to be floating as Jody weaved around the vehicles using the flashlight on her phone.

'Probably just a fuse. The power up here. I'll check soon.'

'You shouldn't play with electricity. Is this the old signpost?'

'Sure is. Can you shine that onto the one at the back? I can't quite read it.'

Jody held the phone higher and read the words. 'Angel's Beach.'

"Huh? Do you remember that one?'

'I don't think so. I wonder if it is up past Rivers End?'

From far too close came a long, low rumble of thunder.

'And that is my cue to go indoors!' Jody took off, with the flashlight.

'Wait for me.'

'Nope. Not waiting for anyone in a storm.'

True to her word, Jody was out of the garage and running in the direction of the house by the time Ivy got to the door.

'Geez, thanks for the help,' Ivy muttered. She opened the fuse box which had a series of switches, one which had flicked off. Finding a new fuse in the bottom of the box, she quickly changed it for the old one and the lights came back on. Jody really should learn some basic skills. She dragged the big doors into place and locked them as a few drops of rain fell.

Unlike her sister, Ivy didn't mind storms – actually, she loved them. It was all she could do to return to the house rather than run to the cottage and watch the sea as the weather closed in.

She stopped at the corner of the house to look at the sky.

'Hurry, Ivy! You'll get hit by lightning!'

Jody peered around the front door, waving with one arm.

*I guess that means you do love me.*

. . .

The storm settled in for the day, moving away and then returning, heavy clouds hanging over the house. The power had gone off for a while then flickered back on and the internet coverage – which was only from their phones – was patchy.

Jody took herself back to the living room to read, picking a new book to start rather than continue with the one from last night.

Ivy was at a loose end.

Her laptop's battery was low so she turned it off. Her phone was fully charged though and she spent a few minutes searching for Angel's Beach. There didn't appear to be such a place within a reasonable distance; well, within the whole state. When the storm passed she'd get Jody to help her drag the signpost back to the spot it used to stand and see if that helped with a direction to look.

Yet again, for the third time since last night, the word 'angel' had appeared. All surrounded Dad. Ivy put down the phone and picked up a pen, dragging her sketchpad closer.

*Angel's Beach. Why is it on the signpost?*

She drew a little picture of the pole with its timber planks pointing in different directions.

*An actual angel sculpture. Who made it? And why was it too important to Dad for him to share its origin with me when I was a kid and asked?*

Another sketch.

*And an envelope. From my one true love. My angel.*

Ivy didn't bother with an image. Instead, she doodled and when that page was filled, began another. She hadn't sketched much in years but had a bit of a flair for it. She drew an angel.

Was it pure coincidence? A beach, a sculpture, and an envelope?

Dad wasn't religious although Ivy knew he had been raised a Catholic. He'd spoken often of being spiritual in nature, a person who saw the beauty and glory in everything but wouldn't follow the teachings made by men. Some of his poems spoke of higher powers and celestial wonders so he may well have believed in angels. That might explain the little statue in the safe.

But to use the term 'my angel' was personal.

*Could it be Mum?*

Putting down the pen, Ivy sat back.

In all the visits back here, Ivy had never seen Dad with anyone special. No girlfriend or dates. So had their mother, Brenda, been his one true love? And had the set-up in the stone hut been for their parents and Dad had left it as last used after his wife had gone?

'Jody? I need to tell you something.'

There was no answer so Ivy went to find her sister.

She was curled up on the armchair under a throw blanket, fast asleep. Her head rested on a cushion and the book was closed, tucked in her hand. With no makeup and her hair still slightly damp from her shower and curling around her features, she might have been in her early twenties. She was so pretty. Always had been and Ivy wished her sister could see herself like this. At peace with the world. Relaxed.

Not wishing to disturb her, Ivy tiptoed out.


Although the rain had slowed to a mere drizzle, the sky still lit up from time to time and Ivy's longing to watch the storm at work won over the more practical job of going through a box of papers to locate the receipt for the motorcycle.

Rather than leave the house with Jody still sleeping, Ivy let herself into her father's bedroom. Up here, the view was spectacular. She opened the sliding door and stepped through, gasping as the glory of the storm battered her senses. The wind was much cooler now and less blustery but carried the salty and thick scent of the sea.

The light rain refreshed her face and she laughed aloud as she pulled her hair back and lifted her eyes to the sky. Directly overhead, the clouds swirled and tumbled in perpetual motion, and now and then they parted briefly to tease with a glimpse of blue sky far above.

But it was the ocean which took her breath.

Huge waves rolled in, pushing each other along to crash high up on the sand, sending sea spray into the air. The colours changed from dark aqua near the beach to steely grey further out and then, along the horizon, the sea was silver. And every so often, lightning zigzagged its way to the surface, hitting with an explosion of water before leaving nothing more than a fading imprint on Ivy's eyes.

She wiped the rain from her face and gripped the railing of the balcony. Her heart was racing with the excitement and majesty.

Exactly how she'd felt all those years ago from a different vantage point, and with Leo by her side.


*Ivy thought she'd made a mistake. Either she'd misunderstood the day or the time... or the place.*

*When Leo had said to meet 'here', had he not meant on the beach?*

*And 'before sunset'? Well, the sun was sinking toward the horizon pretty quickly. It would be gone in a few minutes.*

*He probably had forgotten, or worse, changed his mind. People said all kinds of things on the spur of the moment and because they'd been laughing and having a nice time in the ocean, Leo might have got carried away. And then realised what he'd said and having no way to contact Ivy, simply hadn't turned up.*

*She sat on the edge of the lagoon, feet in the warm water, glaring at her reflection.*

*It didn't matter.*

*Her life was in England and in a few weeks she'd be flying home to start the next phase of it. This was helping her make a decision about which country to live in, so why did she feel so let down?*

'Ivy! I'm so sorry.'

*Her heart leapt.*

*Leo was striding her way from the direction of the tunnel beneath the cliff and alongside the river. He had a carry bag in one hand and a parcel in the other. A white parcel, which smelled fantastic as he got closer.*

*She climbed to her feet and brushed herself down, suddenly shy. How silly. One minute she was lamenting his absence and now it was a struggle to know what to say.*

*But then he was there and his eyes were laughing and his smile was infectious.*

*Not to mention the unmistakable aroma of fish and chips.*

'Would you mind taking this? It is so hot on my arm!'

*Ivy reached for the parcel, almost dropping the lot when she touched his arm and electricity shot through her.*

'You okay? Don't burn yourself. Jetty?'

*She nodded and they headed toward the water.*

'I was worried you might be gone,' Leo said. 'It was so busy at the fish and chip shop and I didn't know whether to run over to let you know I waiting or hold on and hope.'

'Goodness, I hadn't even noticed the time,' she lied. 'What a lovely idea for dinner!'

*He grinned.* 'I hadn't asked what you liked so I ordered a selection.'

*They reached the old jetty and wandered along its timber boards. Beneath their feet, the wood creaked and groaned and there were glimpses of the water through the cracks. Ivy loved it here and at least once each visit to Australia she'd sit on the end and watch the fish, or swim around the pylons below.*

Nobody else was on the beach. Today had been humid, almost uncomfortably so, and along the horizon, heavy clouds flashed with lightning.

'I love storms.' Leo put his bag down and pulled out a picnic blanket. 'We should be right for an hour or so.' His eyes shot to Ivy's. 'Are you okay with stormy weather?'

'Best kind.'

'Whew. Well, we can move to shelter if the rain comes too soon. Would you care to join me?' He took the parcel from Ivy. 'In the bag are some soft drinks and bottled water so help yourself.'

Leo waited for Ivy to sit on the blanket then joined her, opening the paper between them. Steam rose and her mouth watered. Was there anything to match beachside chips with salt and vinegar?

For a while they simply ate – chips, battered fish, potato cakes, and crumbed prawns, with a splash of tomato sauce. Ivy rarely drank soft drinks but washing it all down with a Fanta was nostalgia of the best kind. It was something she and Jody had done with Dad as little kids. She told Leo about it.

'And now you have tonight to add to your memories,' he said.

The words were simple but they touched Ivy. And when he smiled at her she knew she wanted to see his face again. Many times again.

After the last chip was eaten and the rubbish was in the bag, they stayed there, but now their feet dangled off the end of the jetty as they talked. It was dark and the looming storm put on a magnificent display of lightning. They were there for an hour – perhaps more, before the first drops of rain sent them back onto the sand. Thunder was booming and they fled along the beach, hand in hand, laughing as their hair and faces became drenched with the arrival of the storm.

Ivy had thought they might go around the rocks to Fairview, which was only a few minutes under normal condi-

*tions, but waves pounding the edge of the cliff changed her mind.*

*'In here.' Leo tugged at her hand and they threw themselves into the entrance of a cave as lightning struck far too close. It lit the cave for a second or two and they sank onto a couple of boulders where they could watch the storm but stay out of danger.*

*And there they stayed for hours until the storm had long passed and they had talked of their dreams and plans and hopes and wishes. And perhaps even fallen in love.*

The sun burst through a break in the heavy clouds. Ivy drew in a long, shuddering breath and wiped the rain from her eyes. Except it wasn't rain. It was tears.

# TWELVE

The storm returned before Ivy could haul the post out and see if it was possible to set it back in the hole. Unless someone had covered it up, it shouldn't be too hard to find it and scoop out any dirt which might have dropped in. Instead, she'd spent the rest of the day going through the box she'd brought up from the safe.

'Ivy? I might need to go back to Melbourne for a day or two.' Jody flopped onto a chair at the table. 'Did you find anything about the motorcycle?'

There were several stacks of folders on the table.

'No. These are guest files. Looks like Dad kept one for each person who stayed here over the years and there is a photo attached to their financial details. We need to ask Mr Appleby about privacy laws and whether we need to shred these.' Ivy opened the closest one. 'This belongs to a Sam Silverton and is from 1983 through to 1987. He stayed once a year in the dead of winter, for five weeks each time, always in the third cottage. He drank white tea, black coffee with two sugars, and brandy.' She glanced up. 'His food preferences are listed, along with a record of any meal he didn't like and those he enjoyed. And there are comments about his habits, such as usual waking time, the hours he should not be disturbed, places he regularly walked, and a lot about his specialty, which was watercolour seascapes.'

'You're kidding. And it's the same for all the guests over all those years?'

'So far I've got to the end of the eighties which was the entire box, but there are several others in the safe so I imagine so. I just can't believe I never came across these. Why are you going home?'

'Aaron has a big gala event to attend on Saturday starting at midday and I always go with him. Well, normally I do but with being here I kind of hoped he'd be okay going alone. However, he has asked me to attend and if I drive home tomorrow in the morning I'll have time to see my beautician and fix the damage of being here.' She touched her hair with a frown. 'And I probably need new shoes. Then I can have a night's sleep in my own bed before the gala. Anyway, I'll be back Sunday or at the latest, Monday. The day after the day after.'

'The day after the gala or the one after that?'

'After the after.' Jody grinned suddenly. 'I forgot you used to say that. Week after the week after. Remember?'

'Kinda. But you were only little so how do you even recall that?'

'Just came to me. Such a funny way of saying it rather than the day after next, but I guess you picked it up somewhere.'

*A woman with a beautiful face and long hair so dark brown it was almost black.*

Ivy was surprised at the sudden memory. 'It was a guest who used to sing with Dad sometimes. What was her name? Cel? Sal?'

Jody had lost interest and was looking at something on her phone. 'Dunno. Anyhow, I'm going to go upstairs to pack, and I'll phone Aaron and the beauty salon and stuff.'

'Any fancies for dinner? I might as well get it started.'

'Nothing for me.' Jody stood and touched her flat stomach. 'The dress I want to wear is very form-fitting.'

'Avoiding eating between now and then, yet driving a few hours and having a long day, will make you light-headed. You wouldn't want to faint at the gala.' Ivy used her best nurse voice. 'A small salad with some protein. Okay?'

Rolling her eyes, Jody headed for the door. 'Maybe.'

'Give the wine a miss tonight too. That will help.'

Jody turned with a look of mock horror. 'Oh, I might just need to rethink the dress. Salad is fine. With wine with wine.'

'Are you going adapt that little saying to everything?'

'Only if it rhymes. Then it is sublime, sublime.' Jody disappeared up the stairs, her laughter making Ivy smile.


The memory of the lady who'd taught her the funny phrase played on Ivy's mind. After dinner, Jody wanted to read again so Ivy collected another box from the safe.

This one covered the nineties, so Dad must have filed in decades. With so many guests being repeat visitors, it might be that this 'Sal' was a regular. Ivy hadn't noticed her name or photo in the eighties box but it might be in here.

Pot of tea made, Ivy settled into sorting the files into each year of the nineties. Despite Dad's detailed information on each guest, he'd done nothing else other than pile the folders on top of each other in no particular order.

What an incredible wealth of information there was.

It reminded Ivy of creating character profiles for stories she used to write. She was like her father in that respect of being fascinated by details and would spend hours working on the finest points – not only hair colour and build but mannerisms and emotional baggage and deep secrets too. It breathed life into the worlds in her mind and then on paper to the degree of feeling she knew them as a real person.

She got up to pour more tea. Dad had always encouraged Ivy to follow her dream of becoming a novelist. He'd ask his writer guests to let her ask questions and in many cases, she'd get a masterclass, sitting enthralled while a novelist or scriptwriter spoke of structure and characterisation and believing in herself. She chose subjects at school to set her up for a creative arts degree.

*Where would I be had I not given up?*

Instead of sitting again, Ivy took her tea outside.

The rain had stopped and night was closing in. She wandered as far as the little cottage near the beach and stood upon its deck, shrouded in old feelings and lost moments.

It was more than ten years since she'd written creatively. There'd been a long period of shock after Dad's car crash and incarceration when she got through each day with a smile frozen in place and ice water in her veins. She'd begun to write poetry for a while. It wasn't her passion but somehow gave her a way to explore and express the deep sorrow and confusion which threatened to overwhelm her. She had no interest in fiction. Her stories dried up. The ideas were pale shadows of those which once inhabited her life.

With some prompting from her mother – a senior nurse who was still passionate about her career after more than twenty years – Ivy turned to nursing and buried herself in caring for others. But then she and Jody had to come to Australia for the hearing and when she returned to London – without her sister – nothing was the same.

'I've been so lost,' she whispered. 'So lonely.'

The waves were still higher than normal on the sand and the water beyond was choppy but the storm had cleared the humidity from the air, leaving a fresh and pleasantly cool evening. Dusk and dawn were her favourite times of the day and since coming to Fairview, she'd found herself drawn to the sea again. There was a magic about Rivers End and its surrounding areas and resisting the pull of the place was a struggle when her head told her she was only here for a short time and then would never return.

Never.

She forced down a lump in her throat.

Was there a way to get beyond the pain of the past? To forgive Dad for his terrible lapse of judgement and the unthinkable consequences? Selling Fairview made sense. He would be in a position to start over. Jody wouldn't need to worry about driving out here to check on him if he moved closer to her.

'And I can hide in England for the rest of my life.'

'Goodness, don't do that.'

Ivy jumped as Jody stepped onto the deck.

'Sorry. Thinking aloud.'

'Well it sounds like your thinking needs adjusting.' In the near-dark, Jody's eyes were hard to read. 'While I'm away, do us both a favour, Ivy. Walk along the coastline. Swim. Splash in the lagoon, although I'm sure you think you're too old.' She grasped Ivy's arm with both of her hands. 'Think about what it will feel like if you never see Fairview or Rivers End again. Will you do this?'

'Why?'

'Because you never had a real choice about leaving here. This time it is on your terms, so be sure before you turn your back forever.'


Jody left for Melbourne as the sun rose. Ivy rode up in the car as far as the gate to open it, dropped a kiss on her sister's cheek, and told her to stay safe. Then she waved until the yellow Mini was out of sight.

After closing the gate she rested her arms on the top rail,

watching the road. Few cars went by so early but a couple of cyclists streaked past calling out a cheery, 'Morning!'

Over the road, the bushland stretched back as far as she could see through dense undergrowth. Somewhere through it was a disused railway line and abandoned station, left behind when the rail gauge changed many decades ago. The once thriving timber industry which Rivers End was built on came to an end. Losing the transport which had served it for so long came at a time when Patrick Ryan, the last of several generations who ran the timber mills, was ready to retire. His daughters had no interest in continuing the family business and from what Ivy could recall of the stories she'd heard, he and his wife moved to Ireland in the late 1960s.

The town had taken a long time to recover but was now thriving thanks to increasing tourism in the region and some recent developments such as a new assisted living community. Perhaps Fairview had been part of it as well. Decades of bringing business to the little town must count for something.

Her eyes turned to the curve toward Rivers End.

That was where her father, after an evening of social drinking, lost control of his car in wet weather and hit another coming in the opposite direction.

*Rain sleeting. Two cars. One spun around to face the way it came, much of its front crushed in. The other on its side in a ditch. People yelling. Running. Dad was there, pulling on the door of the other car then reaching in through a shattered window. Other people. Cars stopping to help. And Jody... where was Jody?*

Ivy abruptly turned from the gate, her feet slipping on the gravel in her haste. She kept her balance and stalked down the driveway, pushing the pain down. This wasn't her memory. It couldn't be because she'd been in her bedroom. No, this was yet another trick her mind played, gathering snippets of information she'd heard about that night and turning them into a horror movie.

Going back to England and never returning was the sensible choice.

But it wasn't as simple as that. Not now after being here a few days. And not after Jody's plea last night, urging Ivy to revisit the places which were special.

*And if I don't, then Jody will believe I've disregarded her feelings.*

All the way to the house she argued with herself. Whatever she decided would end up causing someone pain. Finding she had only enough coffee left for one more cup had to be a sign and she relented. Into Rivers End she would go.

She forced herself to walk back up the driveway and along the road. Nothing would change if she didn't face her demons and she'd already driven along here the other day. But then she'd had Jody to talk to.

There was nothing to show from the accident. How could there be after more than twelve years? For a moment she thought about visiting the grave of Jean Curry. Leo's great-aunt. Ivy hadn't known her well but remembered a fiercely independent woman in her eighties with a sharp wit and the respect of the extended Webb family. Instead, she kept going and went shopping first.

She'd brought a fabric carry bag with an ice pack inside and only purchased what would fit. Coffee. Some more salad items. A lovely locally made soft cheese and a packet of nice quality thick crackers to have with it. Olives. White grapes. And two chocolate bars. Without Jody to pass judgement, she was going to eat what she wanted.

Slinging the bag over her shoulder, Ivy adjusted her sunhat, put her sunglasses on, and walked in the direction of the river.

As tempting as it was to visit the bookstore again, she decided to wait until Jody was back. Books were one thing that they both enjoyed equally and it mattered a lot to focus on the similarities rather than differences.

At the river, Ivy paused to watch a couple of young girls float beneath the bridge on inflatables. They were laughing and making themselves spin around and it might have been her and Jody years ago. So often they'd done the same.

*I can't lose you from my life, Jodes.*

It was time to stop the gap growing between them.

Ivy wandered along the narrow path which accompanied the river as it flowed to its destination, through the naturally formed tunnel beneath the cliff before pooling into a broad lagoon. From there, only a narrow channel travelled on to the sea.

After removing her runners, Ivy did what Jody suggested. She stepped into the water of the lagoon and as her toes curled into the wet sand, warmth travelled all the way to the top of her head. Not from the temperature of the lagoon; no, this was a beautiful mixture of memories of days in the sun and the sheer pleasure of the sensation of soft water lapping against her legs.

She followed the natural contour of the lagoon, taking her time to savour the feelings. How had she forgotten? Dad had taught her to swim in the lagoon rather than the sea. She'd been fearful of the waves as a young child and although Ivy would watch him surf and paddle in the shallows, she wouldn't go in. So he'd bring her here where there were no waves and the water was always a bit warmer. Over time she'd gained the confidence to swim out of her depth in the ocean.

Ivy climbed out where the channel to the sea began. After the rain yesterday, it was full and rushing to empty the lagoon as the river flowed a bit higher than usual. Other times it would be barely a trickle.

Almost at the jetty, Ivy stopped in disbelief. It was

surrounded by warning signs. The far end, where she and Leo once had their picnic of fish and chips, was gone. Only the pylons were visible, holding fast against the tide. Although the jetty was old, it was sound, so what on earth had brought such destruction? And only at the very end because the walkway was still intact.

*Is this a sign? Jody pushing me and needing coffee sent me here so is this telling me to sell?*

This was a mistake. She'd go around the cliff back to Fairview and keep working on the house. Ivy trudged through the softer sand up from the tideline. At least she could visit the cave in the cliff on the way. A final goodbye to what might have been.

Ivy couldn't believe her eyes.

The entrance to the cave was gone, partly buried beneath rocks, and there were warning signs again, as well as construction site metal and wire fencing.

Her eyes were blurry and she put down the carry bag and ran her hands through her hair. Both special places were gone. The only connection to the best thing which had ever happened to her.

'Lightning. Thank goodness it wasn't the night when we were in there.'

Ivy's heart jumped and she spun around.

His face had barely changed. He was just older. And instead of the ready smile and laughing eyes there was an air of wariness. He gazed at her as if seeing a ghost.

'Hello, Ivy,' Leo said. 'I can't believe it's really you.'

# THIRTEEN

How many times had Ivy dreamed of this moment? The words she would say to Leo had played in her mind over and again. Words of love and regret for leaving the way she had. A plea for Leo to understand what drove her to England and a promise to never leave him again. It would end with his forgiveness and a kiss.

But she was no longer twenty-three and starry-eyed.

True love didn't exist and what they'd once had was a lovely memory but a long way in the past.

Leo had moved on.

So had she.

'Hello, Leo.'

She might have smiled. Had she smiled? It all felt a bit strange.

His guardedness was contagious.

'You said it was lightning. What kind of strike does so much damage?' she asked.

'One of the worst storms in a century.' Leo gestured back in the direction of the jetty. 'Local council still haven't decided what to do about that. Fixable, but some want it completely removed.'

'But why? The jetty has been here forever and people love it. At least, I do.'

His eyes narrowed but then he began to walk toward the cave and Ivy followed. 'Someone was taking refuge inside from the storm and was trapped when the rocks fell.'

'Oh my goodness!'

'All good in the end, but a harrowing experience. And such damage is irreparable.'

They gazed at the fencing and beyond it, the rockpile.

'Hard to imagine after all the...' Ivy couldn't bring herself to speak of their evening. That evening.

Leo had no such reservation. 'All the moments we shared in there? We spoke our hearts, Ivy. Whatever has happened to the cave doesn't change a thing.'

His eyes had turned to her and Ivy had no idea how to respond.

Her perfect words she'd dreamed of saying were lost somewhere and she longed both to run away and to throw herself into his arms.

*Neither are happening. I'm an adult.*

She summoned a polite smile. 'It was nice seeing you, Leo. I have to get home now.' Before she could change her mind, Ivy hitched the shopping bag onto her shoulder and headed toward the rocks around the cliff.

*Don't look back.*

There was no need because Leo caught up and kept pace.

What good was this going to do? Accompanying her as if their lives had merely had a minor bump in the road. A few days apart instead of ten years.

Halfway around the cliff, Ivy stopped and faced Leo.

'What are you doing?' she asked.

'Ten years, Ivy. The last time I saw you was close to this

spot.' He might have been having a conversation about the weather rather than speaking of their painful past. 'You know, I don't make a habit of following people, particularly not around rocks which are going to be swamped by the tide quite soon.'

As though to give weight to his words, a wave splashed over the edge of the rocks.

'Which is why I'm going to keep heading home before I need to wade through the sea.'

'Ah. I understand.' He nodded as if something finally made sense.

'So you should go back. The way will be cut off in a minute.'

He didn't move but kept his eyes on Ivy's face.

'Bye. Again,' she said.

Another wave whooshed uncomfortably close and Ivy hurried away. She was all too aware that Leo was only a few steps behind and as the beach drew closer, panic set in. Having to talk to him was suddenly impossible because how could she explain her abrupt departure from his life? She didn't want to have that conversation. Ivy stepped onto the sand and took off her sandals.

'Where is it?'

'Where is what? I'm confused, Leo.'

He held both arms wide and turned around in a circle, encompassing the beach and sea. 'The portal. The one which you fell into ten years ago. The one which took you away without a word.' Leo stopped being so dramatic and his eyes came to rest on Ivy's as his voice lowered. 'I'm hoping it was a portal because why else would the woman I loved simply disappear overnight and never tell me why? Ivy?'

For a second, something flickered between them. Long-buried feelings. A connection that time and distance hadn't destroyed.

Then he shrugged. 'No answer? Fine. I'll leave you to go

home.' He didn't wait for any response, turning on his heel and striding back the way they'd come.

He wasn't looking back. He wasn't slowing in the hope she'd stop him.

Her lips parted to call to him.

Her feet were ready to run after him.

Ivy clenched her hands as she watched him disappear around the edge of the cliff.


The shopping was unpacked but Ivy didn't remember doing it. She'd left the fridge door open by accident while she'd made coffee and then, when she closed it and went to put the shopping bag away, Ivy found the chocolate bars still inside. Without hesitation she ripped the end off one wrapper and bit chunks, chewing without tasting until it was gone.

She reached for the second and sank onto a chair.

Revisiting the places she loved was a disaster. The jetty and cave destroyed by lightning strikes. Leo finding her. What were the chances of him being on the beach at the same time? Or had he seen her in town and followed?

He'd been so upset. Not outwardly, but she knew him well and had never seen him look as wary or heard such emotion in his voice. At least, she used to know him well.

Ivy removed the wrapper of the second bar of chocolate and then glared at it. Surely not.


*Long after the fish and chips were gone, the taste of vinegar and salt no more than a tang on her tongue, Leo reached into the bag he'd brought and extracted two chocolate bars.*

*'Fancy one?' he'd asked.*

*'Um... chocolate is a bit...'*

*'What? Delicious? Nutty – which is protein and lots of other good stuff. And fruit? A ton of antioxidants and fibre.'*

*Ivy had burst into laughter.*

*'No, really.' Leo was serious. 'Chocolate has feel-good compounds and should form part of everyone's normal diet.'*

*'In that case, yes please.'*

*For the first time in ages, Ivy enjoyed eating chocolate without feeling guilty. How silly that society put such pressure on girls that some would refuse a treat rather than be judged. She'd finished it and smiled at him.*

*And then he'd leaned closer and with a serviette, gently dabbed away a tiny chocolate smudge from the corner of her mouth.*

Ivy touched the corner of her lips. Her heart was playing games with her, fuelled by old memories of a simpler time and a promising future.

This chocolate in her hand was the same kind she'd enjoyed that evening with him. Their first real date. The first of many, even though the terrible car crash had happened the same night and Ivy would have understood if Leo didn't want to see her anymore because the car which killed his great-aunt belonged to her father.

From the minute Gabe said that the car had been stolen and the driver behind the wheel at the time of the accident had vanished, Leo had assured her he'd never blame her father for what happened. Ivy had attended the funeral and been there to comfort Leo when emotions bubbled over. And then for two years they'd grown close enough that everyone expected them to marry.

Her hand was squeezing the chocolate bar so hard it was melting and she got up and threw it in the bin. After scrubbing the chocolate from her skin, she tried to drink her coffee but it was cold and the remainder went down the sink.

*I have to stop spiralling.*

Ivy took several deep breaths. It didn't help.

Oh, how she'd longed to touch Leo's face. Know he was real. And thank goodness she hadn't. The man was married with at least one child. Seeing him through the café window was bad enough, but in the flesh... her heart hurt. Of course he'd have married. He wouldn't have waited around for her, not when she'd left Fairview the same week he'd taken her to look at rings at George Campbell's shop. They weren't engaged. He hadn't proposed. But he had asked her to give him a few ideas of what she liked.

She couldn't help the sudden rush of tears, as much as she hated them. There were tissues in her handbag and she dried her cheeks and told herself to stop being stupid.

There was a message on her phone from Jody. She was back in Melbourne. Ivy replied to say thanks for letting her know and to enjoy the gala event tomorrow.

Something made her scroll through her contact list. Leo's number was still there. She'd sometimes opened his details and started to write a message but always deleted it before sending. She was frozen when it came to him.

Her finger hovered over 'delete'.

There was no logical reason to keep Leo in her contacts. Most likely he'd changed his number in all that time.

He'd made it clear he was angry.

He was married.

*What the heck has logic got to do with love?*

Ivy turned off her phone.


Keeping busy was Ivy's answer to everything and she opened the safe with the intention of sorting through another box of files. The angel stared at her and she picked it up. It was carved from limestone – possibly even from a local source – and was quite pretty, if basic in execution. It was likely a gift from one of Dad's past guests but then raised the question of why was it in the safe? Fairview had a number of pieces of artwork gifted from guests over the years and some were valuable, yet hung on walls in the house. This angel didn't look special.

She laid it on the top of the box and then added the envelope from the library.

All the way to the kitchen she told herself she would take the envelope back unopened, but the minute she set the box down, her hands reached for it.

Her feelings were all over the place from the encounter with Leo and opening this might distract her for a while. She wasn't sure what to expect but it wasn't the thick bundle of writing paper held together with a purple silk ribbon. Ivy slid the bundle out and checked the envelope. No cash, then. A little sigh of relief left her lips. The idea Dad might have hoarded getaway cash had bothered her more than she'd realised.

Ivy undid the ribbon and lifted the top piece of fine paper. Was this poetry Dad had penned and hidden away for some reason? But a glance at the envelope reminded her these were from someone, not to the angel person.

It was a letter, written in neat – if small – cursive handwriting.

*Dear Gabriel,*

*I wonder if you are surprised to receive this letter. Although I told you I would write, you laughed as if I was joking and in hindsight, maybe that is one of the reasons I decided to follow through. Although I enjoy a joke, it is never at the expense of my promises.*

*Letter-writing by hand is an art which is losing its appeal and that is a pity. What better way to communicate than through the thoughts which travel through a pen onto paper? I suppose I could type this instead, but that seems impersonal and besides, the clacking of the typewriter would annoy my family should I use it late at night – when I most wish to write.*

*So here I am, mostly to say thank you for an evening which was as intriguing as it was unexpected.*

*Quite honestly, I expected little from my brother's bonfire on the beach other than rowdy youngsters drinking too much and goodness knows what else. But then I saw you, sitting alone and occasionally looking at me through the crackling fire of driftwood. According to my little brother you were the best teacher he'd ever had. At times you'd get up and talk to the other boys who have graduated now and you were nice. Not stopping them drink or telling them what to do. I heard you'd resigned and that's a pity. The world needs more good teachers.*

*When you slipped away into the night, something took me over. I needed to meet you but had no idea how, not without seeming bold and I've been raised better than that. So I followed for a while and when you stood upon the jetty, I waded in the lagoon, keeping half an eye on you.*

*I got bored waiting and began to sing and then the stars above watched me spin around.*

*And so did you.*

*I have to smile now at the memory, at how brave I felt seeking your attention. You were so serious as though pondering one of life's great mysteries. But then you stepped into the warm, silken water and tossed your sandals onto the sand bank and when I did the same with mine, they flew in different directions and we laughed.*

*When you spoke of your dream to build a haven for artists, a place where painters and writers and sculptors might stay awhile to rest and work and thrive... my heart felt such joy. What a beautiful vision. I couldn't believe that you showed me the place you wished to make this real. Fairview House. I knew of the property because my father has said sometimes how wasted it is with nobody living here. Even he has considered buying it but then he changed his mind. His money, he says, is best spent on another project he is involved in.*

*Well, Gabriel, I think you should buy it.*

*Imagine what you can do with this lovely old home and the land around it. Private and abutting the sea. What better place?*

*We spoke for hours and I didn't want to leave, but although my parents go to bed early, it isn't worth risking being caught coming in so late. I might be twenty but my father considers me his responsibility and would ask a million questions.*

*I'd prefer to ask you more questions about your wonderful plans. Until we meet again,*

*Your angel.*

*December, 1973.*

Oh, it was a sweet letter! A young woman, only twenty years old, taking the time to write to a young man to convey her enjoyment of an evening they'd spent.

Ivy reread it, frowning at the words about Dad having been a teacher.

She'd never known that. A young teacher resigning after what must have been only a year or two in a school. He'd always been so patient and for ages ran workshops for teens interested in pursuing a career in the arts. Why had he resigned?

'So much I don't know about you.' She spoke aloud. 'A teacher. And... this.' Ivy folded the letter and placed it back on top of the little pile of paper. She retied the ribbon and put the pile back inside the envelope.

Who was this young lady and were all of the letters from her? Dad had only been married once, to Ivy's mother, but he'd been close to forty years old on the day of their wedding so it made sense he'd have had a love life before then. That made Ivy a bit queasy and she got up to get a glass of water. As natural as intimacy was, she knew nobody who liked thinking of what their parents might have got up to behind closed doors.

Well, now she had a little mystery to uncover and that had to be better than letting Leo back into her head. And heart.

# FOURTEEN

Later in the afternoon, when the tide was going out, Ivy went for a long-awaited swim. The water was warm enough once she committed to submerging herself rather than the method of gradually walking in. With strong strokes, she swam out past the surf and floated, letting her body and mind drift.

Once Jody was back they should get the surfboards out and relive their older teen days. That's if she still had enough balance to stay upright. Ivy closed her eyes with a smile. She could out-paddle Jody back then, but fell off more in the waves. Those long summer afternoons would merge with even longer evenings and both girls would find themselves having different sleeping patterns than in England. Back at home, with school and household chores – then part-time jobs as they got older – they'd be in bed by mid-evening and up by six. Here, though, the mornings were for sleeping in and breakfast was brunch. Bedtime was whenever someone was tired. It was a lovely, relaxed way to live and it always took a few days to adjust to Mum's stricter rules when they'd go home.

Growing up with parents on opposite sides of the world had its challenges and she had to give them credit for making sure their children had access to both – not equally in time – but certainly in love and experiences.

Ivy didn't really understand why they'd married in the first place, only to separate so quickly. Knowing that her mother had never taken to the Australian weather or lifestyle was one thing. That made sense. But why couldn't she and Dad have found a way to stay together? Couldn't he have come to England?

*Except he only loves Fairview.*

She opened her eyes. The enjoyment of the moment was gone; and no longer in the mood to be out here, Ivy swam to shore and gathered the towel she'd left on the sand. She wrapped it around herself and trudged back to the house.

Why did Gabe have this obsession with the property to the point of refusing to move to England to stay married and be an active part of his children's life? Even the letter she'd read made it clear he was passionate about Fairview all the way back in 1973. He'd poured himself into his grand plans and rarely gone far from the property, let alone visited the other side of the world.

She pushed open the front door with a frown.

Shouldn't she be locking up when she left? There'd been an intruder in the house, the garage had been entered, and they'd chased someone off the place, yet she'd not given it a thought because the beach felt like it belonged to Fairview. But it was a public beach, the same as Rivers End beach was, the difference being the restricted access which forced people to walk around the cliffs or else hike from the other direction along rough terrain. And while she was splashing around in the water, the person who'd broken into the library might have returned.

Perhaps a little more care about safety wouldn't go amiss.

Ivy locked the door behind her and quickly checked the house, although she was unsure what she'd do should she come across an intruder. Nobody was there and Ivy dived into the shower to get the sea water off her hair and skin. She was hungry but had no interest in cooking for herself. If Jody was here she'd make the effort but tonight she might walk back to the town and find somewhere for dinner. Anything to get her out of the house for a while and do something other than dwell on Fairview. And Leo. Despite reading the letter and having gone for a swim, their encounter was still playing about in her mind.


Strolling along the main street in Rivers End with most of the shops closed for the night was oddly relaxing and added a whole new perspective to the little town. She'd done this before, but couldn't recall wandering on her own. When they were teens, she and Jody would sneak out for takeaway to eat on the beach. Then later, Leo would often be with her.

This was nice.

Walking had pushed the hunger down a bit and Ivy took a bit of time to look at the options for dinner. All she remembered was the small but popular Chinese restaurant, which was packed even this early, the fish and chip shop, and the bistro attached to one of the pubs.

But things had changed.

There was a new Italian restaurant and a wine bar. And the bistro had enjoyed a full makeover, certainly from where Ivy stood. Years ago, when she and Jody were kids, Dad would take them there once each visit. He'd make it a special outing with nice clothes and allow the girls to order anything off the menu. As they'd got older and began to visit some of London's restaurants, they hadn't had the heart to tell Dad that his idea of fancy was a long way from theirs. It was all about the family experience.

*And I treasure those memories.*

Ivy couldn't help smiling as she read the menu outside the bistro. She'd forgotten how much she loved Gabe Sutherland –

the one who raised her. He'd been a terrific father and perhaps, with little trips like this down memory lane, she could find a way to separate her feelings for him to before and after the confession. Keeping the love for him as her dad growing up might be enough.

'Is that you, Ivy?'

A woman a little older than Ivy was a few metres away. She was smiling widely and when Ivy smiled in return, closed the distance between them and gave her a hug.

'It is you. How long has it been?'

They stepped back from each other.

'Too long. Hello, Sadie. I heard you were back in Rivers End.'

'Do you remember my mother, Pam?' Sadie reached her hand out to the woman who was with her. 'Mum owns Rivers End Inn.'

'Of course! So nice to see you. Looks like you have some major works happening at the inn?'

Pam rolled her eyes as she half-laughed. 'I had no idea how noisy it was going to be but already I'm getting so many bookings for the summer holidays. Adding a play area and pool is making a difference.'

'Much better than selling to a developer,' Sadie said.

'Mothers are always right, love.'

'Debatable, but I'll let it pass. Are you going in to have dinner? We'd love you to join us, Ivy. Are you alone?'

'Oh. Um. Yes, Jody is away for a couple of days.'

Ivy glanced through the window. The woman – Tessa – who'd acted strangely in the supermarket, was serving a table.

'Thanks for the offer, but I have somewhere else to be.'

'Well, let's catch up another time. I'll give you my card if you and Jody are free for a coffee or something.' Sadie dug around in her handbag. 'There you are.' She handed the card to Ivy and then took Pam's arm. 'Lovely to see you.'

'You too.'

Ivy quickly crossed the road, a bit cross with herself for being such a coward. She had no real idea why Tessa had stared at her and Jody so oddly that day. Assuming she'd recognised them as Gabe's daughters, perhaps she was judging them, as others had. Or, like so many in the town, Tessa might have known Jean Curry. Her reaction might be nothing more than a sudden reminder of the loss of a friend.

*You have to stop imagining the worst.*

Yet how could she blame anyone for thinking that she and Jody had known about their father's crime all along? News of Gabe's confession sent a ripple of shock through the close-knit community and Ivy had been called terrible names by some locals.

She forced herself to stop in the doorway of a closed shop. Her heart was racing and panic was rising enough to make her shaky. Ivy took several measured breaths, pushing the memories away into a little box in her mind.

The people who'd acted so badly were wrong, yet the shame remained, because somehow she should have worked out that Dad was responsible. Too much hadn't added up.

A couple wandered along the street in her direction. They were holding hands and had a golden retriever loose a few steps ahead. Ivy vaguely recognised the man and the dog and instinctively turned her face to look through the window. But a cold nose nudged her hand and she found herself squatting to pet the dog, who'd sat at her side.

'Oh sorry, Randall accosts everyone in the hope of a treat.' The couple stopped nearby and the woman grinned. 'Just tell him no.'

'When has that ever worked, Christie?' The man shook his head but he looked amused. 'Come on, dog.' The couple walked away.

After giving Ivy's cheek a quick lick, Randall padded after his owners.

Ivy straightened. Funny how dogs knew when someone needed their attention. The panic was gone. If all else failed, she could bring a dog into her life, because they weren't judgemental and loved unconditionally. With the panic abating, her hunger returned in force.

The Italian restaurant was fully booked and Ivy took their card so she could plan ahead next time and get Jody to come with her. She moved to the next option.

From outside, Rivers End Food & Wine Co. looked busy and fun. There was a baby grand piano being played by a young man wearing a colourful waistcoat. At first Ivy thought it must be more wine bar than anything because of the large bar with stools around it but then she spied some delicious-looking meals being served at a table by the window. Hoping she'd be lucky enough to get a table without a booking, Ivy pushed the door open.

An immediate sense of welcome enveloped her from the mellow music, delectable aromas and laughter, and Ivy knew she was in for a treat. Whoever had created such a happy space needed congratulating.

A woman a bit younger than Ivy, wearing a similar waistcoat to the pianist's, hurried toward her with a friendly smile. It dropped the minute their eyes met.

*Of all places to choose for dinner.*

This was the same person Ivy had seen through the café window with the little boy and Leo. The one she'd assumed was Leo's wife. But now that Ivy could see her face-on, this woman definitely wasn't married to Leo and even as a ridiculous spark of relief came from nowhere, Ivy was turning to go.

'So you remember me, Ivy.' The woman was very close to her and kept her voice low. Low and furious. 'Do you also remember how we were almost family?'

'I'm sorry, Zara. I'm going.'

Running into Leo's sister was the last thing she'd wanted.

'Well, you've got a nerve waltzing in here. All those years and you think you can just show up as if nothing ever happened.'

Ivy couldn't get outside fast enough but Zara followed and grabbed her arm.

'Do you have any idea what leaving like that did to my brother? *Any?*'

People were staring. People inside the restaurant and others passing by.

'I'm sorry. I have to go.'

Pulling herself free, Ivy about-faced and hurried away, barely able to control herself from breaking into a run. She was almost at the end of the street where she could turn the corner and be safe when a voice rang out behind her.

'Wait! Ivy, hold up!'

But she couldn't face Leo. Not now. Not ever.

Ivy began to run.

# FIFTEEN

She got as far as the bridge before she realised how close Leo was. He was running across the road when she glanced back and something in her just gave up. Ivy slowed to a walk and deviated from the footpath, following a short and narrow track down to the river bank. There, she waited, chest heaving as she drew air into depleted lungs.

If he wanted to tell her off like Zara then he could. Let him say what he needed and she'd listen and apologise no matter what he said. No matter how much guilt and shame he dropped on her. At least then he could get it off his chest.

'What are you doing down here?'

He hardly sounded out of breath and when Ivy turned to face him, something caught in her throat. He looked so handsome, dressed in black pants and a white shirt beneath a black and silver waistcoat. His hair was pulled back in a short ponytail, showing off his cheekbones and forehead. And it made not one bit of sense that he was working at the wine bar. He was a doctor... or at least, he'd been several years into medical studies when Ivy had left.

She lifted her chin. 'Why did you follow me?'

'Why didn't you stop when I called out?'

'I need to go home.'

He raised both eyebrows.

'Please, Leo, just say what you came to say.'

'I came to say sorry.'

Ivy didn't know how to respond. *He* had nothing to be sorry about.

'Zara shouldn't have spoken to you like that. She's protective of me but still, it isn't her place to speak her mind on my behalf. If that makes sense. I'd like for you to come back and have dinner, or a drink... whatever it was you'd planned.'

'I didn't know Zara worked there. Or you. I'd have never just walked in like that... I don't want to cause any more upset... no more sadness.' Ivy's voice faltered. Leo's generosity of spirit was exactly the same as when they'd been together and was one of the reasons she loved him so deeply. Had *once* loved him so deeply.

'We co-own the wine bar. And you are welcome there, tonight or any other time. Zara will be fine.'

*But will you be fine? Will I?*

There was so much Ivy longed to say but now was hardly the right time. If there ever would be a right time.

'Thank you. Maybe another day. I really should go.'

Leo's eyes were dark as the night as he stepped aside to let her pass. Back on the footpath he joined her and she tried to smile but couldn't manage more than a flicker and a subdued, 'Goodnight.'

She quickly crossed the bridge, feeling him watching her.

'Ivy?'

He hadn't moved. She stopped and looked back. It was so quiet. No cars or people in sight and only the flow of the river was a quiet backdrop.

'You can't keep running away. At some point you have to stop and face whatever has you so afraid.'

'I'm not afraid.'

The words were hollow and they both knew it.

Ivy took a step toward Leo but he was already turning away and didn't see.

'Stay safe, Ivy Maeve.'

Tears filled her eyes. Leo was the only person to call her by her first and middle names and it was his little term of endearment. Or it used to be. Because he was a long time past loving her.

The trouble was, Ivy wasn't anywhere past loving him.

The walk home helped clear her head and at the top of the driveway, after closing the gate behind herself, Ivy looked up at the sky.

The moon was rising, a full and bright orb which had lit her way home. How she'd missed the night sky here at Fairview, particularly from the higher ground looking out to the horizon, or lying on her back on the beach. With no light pollution from a city, the stars were a brilliant reminder of how small her life was. Not in a morbid way but to put problems into perspective. Even ones as big as her feelings for Leo and the knowledge that she had single-handedly destroyed their relationship.

She sighed and continued down the winding driveway, careful of the sometimes poor footing. This was something Dad should have fixed decades ago but he'd always said it added to the charm of the place. Breaking an ankle wouldn't add anything other than medical bills.

It was only when she turned on the kitchen light that her stomach growled – quite loudly. The one thing she'd planned to do tonight was eat out and that was a failure. Cheese and crackers and olives and grapes would do. More than do. She made little stacks of the soft cheese on each cracker with half an olive and some of the relish Jody had bought and filled a wine glass with cranberry juice. She toasted the air. 'To makeshift meals and monumental mistakes.'

All that was missing was something to read and halfway to the living room to collect a novel, Ivy changed her mind.

It only took a minute to get the envelope from the safe and she could easily eat with one hand and read with the other. Ivy removed the next three letters and flattened them on top of each other.

*Dear Gabriel,*

*How sweet it was watching you read my first letter.*

*It felt right to hand it to you and anyway, I'm not sure our local post office delivers so far from town. They only come to our street because Father made a bit of a fuss once about important church documents not arriving in a timely manner and he has a way of getting what he wants.*

*You smiled all the way through reading so now I shall continue to bring you a letter each time we meet because I love your smile.*

*One day, I hope I will be visiting you at Fairview House. I believe in your vision of the future, I've never met anyone who knows exactly what they want before being in a position to make it happen. Not like you do. Already you have plans for little cottages so guests have their own special space, do you know I had so much fun pretending to walk through the invisible door to the one you ushered me inside.*

*What fun to decide where the living room would be and the bedroom, both looking out to the sea. I remember what you said:*

*'In here an artist or writer can work without interruption. Or*

*daydream. Or both. There will be seating and tables and a book-case. Only with a few books though because the main house has a glorious library and it will remain open to anyone who stays.'*

*I think I wrote it down as you told me but then I asked about a kitchen and you didn't think it important because Fairview would have plenty of food no matter what time of day. That is a lovely concept but I have been thinking and I disagree about the kitchen. I shall let you know my ideas when I next see you, but to me it seems obvious that a novelist or historian or painter might wish to be solitary for days on end or work well into the night. A small kitchen, perhaps with a kettle and toaster and stove and little fridge, would be perfect for those who lose track of time while creating. I can picture me telling you this now, and you smiling as you see how right I am. And I can picture how Fairview will be in the future, with small elements that have come from my ideas.*

*I am glad we met. You make me think about things outside my usual life and meeting you here on the little beach in the evening is something I never thought I'd do. But Gabriel, I am safe with you.*

*Your angel,*

*December, 1973.*

How wonderful this young woman knew she was safe with Gabe. Her instincts were good because he was a decent person, a man who nurtured and believed in people – which made his lies about the car crash even stranger. Ivy had never known him to keep secrets or be less than honest until that point.

And yet, there were these letters he'd kept hidden for good-ness knows how long.

Ivy read the next one.

*Dear Gabriel,*

*This is becoming a habit, and one I admit to enjoying.*

*Three evenings we've met and each one teaches me something new and intriguing about who you are.*

*I was curious why you became a teacher only to resign after only one year. My brother and his friends liked you a lot. They said you were smart and funny and had a way of making books and writing interesting, even to the boys who weren't readers. But now I understand. I can see you love teaching but struggle with the confines of the education system. And I sympathise because being so bound – even controlled – by the teachings of the church is my reality. You were able to walk away from what restricted you and start over. I fear I don't have that luxury.*

*Tonight we lay on a blanket staring at the night sky and talking. Your hand held mine so gently and I kind of loved the feel of your fingers. They are stronger and larger than mine and I believe no harm could ever come to me when I'm with you. And your dreams, Gabriel! They are so big and powerful and sweep me into them. You light a fire inside me.*

*I pointed at the Southern Cross and asked if you'd ever seen anything so bright and beautiful. And then... I'm almost afraid to write it yet I must... you told me my eyes were brighter and I was more beautiful. The kiss that came next was my first, Gabriel, and it was perfect. There. I said it.*

*Do you remember what you said next? 'When I saw you dancing in the lagoon I was sure you were an angel come to earth.'*

*I love the nickname you have for me. But it makes me wish I was truly an angel. I could bring happiness to everyone I meet. Solve the problems of the world. And stay here, forever, with you.*

*But mostly, it makes me happy, like you do. And brave, like when something took me over and I kissed you. Gabriel, when you lifted me up and spun me around I laughed so hard I thought I might cry. It is impossible not to be with you. But it can only be sometimes and it may not be fair to ask this. There are some things I need to tell you but for now, I shall sleep, and dream of you.*

*Your angel,*

*December, 1973.*

The little meal Ivy had made was all gone and she washed up, her thoughts with the stranger in the letters. She'd been drawn to Gabe, yet something was wrong. She spoke of the constraints in her life, and given that it was 1973 in small-town Australia, a conservative religion would factor heavily in the choices available to a woman of only twenty. It wouldn't be unusual for her to be living at home and following the rules of the family, which were often an extension of the rules of a religion.

Ivy had studied religion at school and found it fascinating and occasionally horrifying, but Dad had told her that a church was only as good or bad as the people within it. Had he been influenced by his 'angel'?

*Dear Gabriel,*

*Tonight you asked me why I don't call you Gabe, and I didn't have a ready answer.*

*Everyone else does. Even your parents back in Melbourne.*

*But I think Gabriel is fitting. You've called me your angel because of my name, but do you know that your own name means 'God is my strength' and is known for the beautiful angel? I think it is no coincidence. We were destined to meet and our lives will forever be entwined.*

*Because I didn't have an answer earlier, I teased you instead about my middle name. You didn't really know how to react when I told you it means nothing more exciting than 'sheep' – or more precisely, a female sheep. Eventually you asked if there was a name I'd rather have had and I told you. It is a name which has several meanings but the one I like is 'intoxicating woman' because it evokes such a carefree and brave person in my mind. Maeve.*

    Ivy dropped the letter in surprise.

    Maeve?

    Her middle name?

    Dad had named her. Mum named Jody.

    Unsure if she liked the way this new information was heading, Ivy picked up the letter to finish it.

*I may not be named Maeve but I had to be brave tonight and tell you the truth of my situation.*

*That spot near the bottom of the hill, going toward the river, is precious to me because it is where we always say goodnight so I can hurry home and sneak in unseen from the gate at the back. I needed the strength from such a place to admit things to you. Thank you for believing that my own wishful dream of becoming an architect wasn't out of my reach. But now you know that it is.*

*I'm an only child but both sets of grandparents share our huge house. All of us belong to a conservative church and I've been raised to follow my father's rules as well as the church's. Having a career is outside those rules. My future will be as a wife and mother and being as involved in church charities as my own mum is.*

*You didn't understand. You told me to break the rules and take control of my own life and suddenly, I saw the chasm of differences between us, dear Gabriel. I began to cry and you held me tight and begged me to say what was wrong.*

*You do have the heart of a poet, of a true dreamer. But my life is different and not my own the way yours is. Father is running for town mayor next year, now he's retired. He also has a project which he is passionate about and for that to happen, he needs to work with another investor.*

*I saw the confusion on your face and you asked what my father's plans had to do with my future. I don't think I explained the next bit clearly through my tears, Gabriel. So let me write it down instead.*

*The investor and my father have similar goals, which include bringing both families even closer together to cement the business relationship. And I'm what is connecting the two families because I'm engaged to be married to the son of the investor. He is a decent young man whom I like being around. I don't love him, but I know that he is my future.*

*I don't wish I'd never met you, Gabriel, and I am sorry for saying so earlier. I just wish it had been before I was engaged.*

*Your angel,*

*December, 1973.*

This young woman had misled Dad. Let him believe she was interested in him, only to break his heart.

*And she dropped news of her engagement on him and ran away.*

Leo's words echoed in Ivy's head. 'You can't keep running away.'

'Well, this is completely different.' Her forceful words echoed in the kitchen.

Ivy folded the three letters and put them into their original order before retying the silk ribbon.

She wouldn't read any more of these until Jody returned. It was unlikely that they had any bearing on their lives or Dad's, but if these were what the intruder wanted, then there had to be a good reason. Too tired to speculate further, Ivy locked the envelope in the safe. She needed sleep, and preferably one without dreams.

# SIXTEEN

After beginning the day with a swim, Ivy had a productive morning going through more of the guest files. She'd finished sorting 2000 to 2009 and continued to be impressed with her father's business sense. He'd worked hard behind the scenes to deliver excellent experiences to his guests so it was no wonder the return bookings were so consistent across so many years. Some names in this batch of files had paperwork going back to the first few years of operation. It made sense to have a person's file kept in the most recent year of visiting Fairview, and this box was considerably fuller than the previous ones.

This was the fourth box she'd gone through and she had a spreadsheet for each decade on her laptop, including the name of the guest, dates of their stays, and the profit and cost of their visit. If nothing else, the data was a good electronic record of the business and it would be easier to cross-reference information in the remote chance the Retreat got up and running again.

*But still no record of the motorcycle.*

This was a puzzle.

Or rather, another puzzle.

Ivy grabbed the keys and locked the house. There had to be

something she and Jody were overlooking. She followed the driveway in the direction of the garage which was on the far side of the house and at least a hundred metres up an increasingly steep climb. Dad had added the garage after buying the property and decided to put it out of sight of the house so as not to spoil the aesthetics.

'Could have been a bit closer!' Ivy grumbled. Her muscles ached after the recent couple of swims and probably the running last night.

How strange she must have appeared, racing around corners and past houses and over roads. Instead of blaming Dad for building the garage so far from the house, she needed to take responsibility for her lack of fitness.

She couldn't keep blaming him for everything wrong in her life.

At the garage, Ivy gazed back the way she'd come. While this building was invisible from most of the house, parts of Fairview were easy to see from here. The roof and chimneys and the very top of two of the windows belonging to Dad's bedroom. She couldn't remember seeing the garage from his room but probably had never had a reason to look. He'd originally said he saw the car leave the garage from his bedroom and ran downstairs to try and stop the thief. But was he even in his bedroom that night?

*Ivy was in the kitchen when Dad's cheerful whistling preceded his appearance. He didn't see her at first as he wiped his forehead with a handkerchief. His hair was covered with raindrops.*

*'Hi Dad. I couldn't find you when I got in.' She scooped ice cream into a bowl.*

*'Oh, Ivy. When was that?'*

*'Not long ago. Before the rain began though. And after the storm.'*

'Where's your sister?' Gabe opened the fridge. 'Already in bed?'

'As if. Jody's playing chess with Mr Carson. Darn, she wanted ice cream too.' Ivy found a second bowl. 'Are you really that hungry?'

Dad had taken an almost-full plate of leftovers out of the fridge and was adding fruit to the side.

'Starving. Forgot to eat dinner.'

'I see.'

He grinned at her. 'You look happy, sweetie pie.'

'Me? I guess. Yes. Can we talk tomorrow? I've worked out where I want to live.'

'Care to drop a hint?'

'Let's just say Mum won't be thrilled.'

He put the plate on the table and gave her a big hug. 'Well I am thrilled. And we'll have breakfast together, okay?'

'Yes please. And by then you might not smell of wine so much.' She wrinkled her nose as she returned the ice cream to the freezer. 'I'm going to go read for a bit, so goodnight.'

That was a real memory from the night of the crash. Ivy knew it was real because she had seen Dad in the kitchen and remembered making plans for breakfast with him. She remembered teasing him about her plans to stay in Australia and how thrilled he'd been. Those were *real* memories. Forgotten, but genuine.

What happened next, though?

Ivy leaned against the wall, eyes squeezed shut, focusing on the kitchen, on the ice cream in the bowl. There was the sound of rain through the open kitchen window. It wasn't a cold evening, just wet. Who left the kitchen first?

The memory ended with her saying goodnight.

His face had been wet. At least, his handkerchief was and he'd been drying his face so he had to have been outside.

And the huge plate of food? Dad might well have missed dinner but he was a light eater and there was enough on there for two...

She opened her eyes and turned them to the narrow track which continued up the slope and around the side of the garage. Further along it was only one destination. The stone hut. Surely that wasn't where Dad had come from? It would explain his wet hair and face though.

Her stomach turned and she dug the keys from her pocket. It didn't matter where Dad really was that night because the result wasn't going to change by Ivy finding out some sordid details he'd left out of his various accounts of the night. She'd rather these memories disappeared again; not only this one but those about Leo too. At this rate she'd need to book in to see her therapist again as soon as she returned home.

The motorcycle wasn't new, but it was in pristine condition. After removing the dust cover, Ivy took photos of it from all angles and then zoomed in on what she thought might be a serial number or similar. Did they even have serial numbers? She knew little about motorcycles but this one, the Triumph Thunderbird, looked exactly like the one Dad had talked about. He'd even had a magazine and circled a couple which he liked. And this was as close to it as Ivy could remember without seeing that old photograph.

There was a key in its ignition. Neither she nor Jody had noticed that and she carefully removed it, wiggling the metal a bit when it stuck. She slid it onto the keyring. Had that woman – the intruder – gone to all the trouble to take the garage key and removed the dust cover, only to leave the motorcycle here? Or had it failed to start?

*You're assuming she wanted to steal it.*

Leo used to ride a motorcycle. Not one this fancy, but he at least would know how to turn it on, which was something Ivy herself wasn't game to try. Well, she wasn't going to ask Leo to help. When Jody returned they could work on the problem together.

Ivy locked up the garage and stood outside while she phoned Mick Hammond. To her surprise, he answered, and offered to come and fingerprint the garage door.

'The garage is up a steep slope. I mean, you could probably drive up but we had the lock changed so is there any point?' Ivy asked.

'Steep? Yeah, nah, can't see the point taking more prints. Not when the backlog is so long. Tell you what though. First thing Monday I'll talk to my regional boss and see if she can make things go faster.'

'I appreciate that and sorry to interrupt your Saturday.'

He chuckled. 'No rest for me. I'm the ears and eyes as well as the law in this town.'

Ivy managed a polite goodbye and once she hung up, burst into laughter. It wasn't to be mean to the man – who was obviously proud of his position – but he sounded more like a sheriff in the wild west than a modern police officer. At least he was taking her concerns seriously.

The lid of the box on, Ivy carried it downstairs to the cellar. The safe was still open from when she'd removed the files and she slid the box back inside. There was only one box to go now which must contain the final couple of years of records.

She reached for it and stopped at a sound above. Was that a footstep?

Instead of removing the final box, she closed the safe and locked it.

Her heart thumped as she tiptoed up the stairs. If the intruder was back then she was going to catch them this time.

Ivy carefully opened the door to the hallway. Just a crack. All was quiet.

She waited. The past few days were making her jumpy. Nobody was in the house. She'd been careful to lock herself in.

But from the kitchen came a definite series of footsteps.

There was nothing she could use as a weapon... not that she'd ever hurt anyone but if she looked serious, she might get the upper hand.

*Stupid idea.*

Her phone was in her pocket and she slid it out.

But who to call? Mick? That made sense but phoning meant having to talk and she might be heard and discovered. There was no inside lock on the cellar door, although there were plenty of bottles of wine she could use to hit someone.

*Also a stupid idea.*

Leo.

The answer felt right in her gut, and before her brain could offer its opinion on this course of action, she sent a message.

> Hi. Sorry. It's Ivy. I'm in the cellar at Fairview and can hear someone in the kitchen.

Almost immediately there was a response.

> Ivy? You still have my number?

> Yes. Sorry.

She had to stop saying sorry all the time. He mustn't have read her message.

> There's been an intruder here before. I'm alone. Except someone is the kitchen. Could you come please?

Why oh why had she messaged Leo, of all people? What

was he going to do with a random cry for help from a woman he probably never wanted to see again? She'd have to try Mick.

The footsteps again. And a scraping sound.

Oh crap. On my way. Stay where you are.

Thank you.

She typed 'sorry for being a bother' and deleted that bit.

Giggles wanted to leave her mouth and she covered her lips with a hand. Standing here was the worst thing. Taking some action would control the hysteria.

Ivy snuck along the wall of the hallway, inch by inch. Just outside the kitchen she turned on the flashlight app on her phone, holding it against her body to avoid the light alerting whoever was in there. She could wait until Leo arrived and use it to dazzle the person in the kitchen if needed.

The front door was ajar.

*I locked it.*

There was the oddest noise from the kitchen. Surely that wasn't someone opening one of Jody's bottles of wine? They had screw lids and it sounded exactly like the crack they made as the metal split.

Taking a deep breath, Ivy turned the phone so that the flashlight faced forward and stepped into the kitchen, holding the phone outstretched as if it was a shield in front of her.

'Stop!'

The expression on Jody's face was comical.

Ivy didn't feel like laughing. Her defences were high and her heart was going at a million miles an hour.

'Are you going to take my photo? Is this because I'm about to day-drink and you want to send an incriminating photo to my husband? If he's even my husband anymore.'

'Jody?' Barely taking in the words, Ivy lowered the phone. 'It's you.'

'Obviously.'

'Aren't you at an event in Melbourne?'

'Clearly not. So if you'll excuse me, I'm going to drink myself to a nice place where I can pretend I'm happy.' Jody had a glass in one hand and the open bottle in another and began to pour wine. 'Turns out I'm a terrible wife who got her dates mixed up and arrived too late to attend the VIP dinner which always precedes the awards.'

'I don't understand.'

'Of course you don't.' The glass was full enough for Jody and she put the bottle onto the kitchen table. 'You just flit here and there when it suits, whereas I have commitments. Or did. Now I might not even have a husband.'

On that note, Jody sank onto a chair and burst into tears.

Against her sister's protests, Ivy allowed Jody only one mouthful of wine before removing the glass and wine bottle and filling the kettle. They were both English enough that tea fixed most things. She pushed a box of tissues in front of Jody and patted her back and made soothing sounds.

'That isn't helping, Ivy.' The sobs were lessening as the used tissues piled up. 'Just let me have my glass of wine back and the whole bottle and I'll be fine in a bit.'

'As if drinking is the way to fix things.'

'It is for me.'

'Then you need to get some help.'

Of course the timing was wrong and resulted in more tears and Jody shrugging Ivy's hand off her shoulder.

Returning to finish making tea, Ivy almost dropped a cup as a car tore past the window and abruptly stopped outside.

'Leo! Oh no.'

'What do you mean, "*Leo. Oh no*"?'

'Oh no.'

'Get a grip. You already said that.'

'Ivy! Ivy, where are you?'

There was no way any words were coming out because it was all Ivy could do to safely put the cup onto the counter. She should have let him know. And now he was here. In Fairview.

'Ivy! I'm coming in.'

The front door banged against the wall and then Leo was at the kitchen door. The sheer worry on his face was enough for Ivy to find her words again.

'It's okay. It was Jody.'

'*Jody?*'

He stepped into the kitchen and glanced at Jody then, running a hand through his hair, turned around, then back again. '*Jody* is your intruder?'

'She's meant to be in Melbourne. I heard footsteps and scraping noises in here and thought the intruder was back and—'

'What intruder? Ivy, you need to explain this to me. I broke the speed limit getting here and almost rang Mick Hammond.' He stopped moving and gazed at Ivy. 'You're okay? You're not hurt?'

The vulnerability and relief in his face and voice made Ivy's heart skip a beat. He cared. He still cared for her. Her feet found their way to him. Closer, anyway.

'I'm so sorry for the false alarm. Someone broke in through the library window just before I arrived here and just after Mary left me a box of supplies and the keys to everything. We found out one of the keys was taken and then Jody and I chased a young woman who was here when we came home one day.'

He blinked. 'Someone broke in. Here? Stole a key. Came back. Have you reported this?'

'Of course she has.' Jody had stopped crying and somehow

got hold of her wine glass. 'All she does is talk to the police as though they are our friends.'

'Hello, Jody. Day-drinking?'

Jody's face reddened even more than from the tears. 'You should try it. Might help you see what's right in front of you.'

'Oh, Jody!' Ivy was shocked. 'Leo, I'm so sorry. She's terribly upset about something and didn't mean to take it out on you.'

'Yes, I did.'

Leo nodded. 'She really did.' Oddly, his voice was calm, and even... amused.

But it was the strange look between Jody and Leo which unsettled Ivy. Something was going on. Or had gone on between them and it wasn't anything good. The way they looked at each other was like seeing enemies come face to face.

# SEVENTEEN

Leo and Ivy stood beside his car after he'd checked the rest of the house... just to be sure nobody else was there.

Jody had gone to freshen up and her absence lightened the atmosphere, but Ivy had no intention of asking Leo about the odd moment between him and her sister.

'I really am sorry for dragging you out here,' Ivy said. 'And all for nothing.'

He opened the driver's door and leaned his arms on the top of it, eyes on Ivy. 'You still have my number.'

'Oh. Yes, I should delete it.'

'That will make it hard to send another message requesting emergency help. Should you need it.'

His face and tone were serious but there was a sparkle in his eyes Ivy remembered and she smiled. Leo had a wonderful sense of humour and an infectious laugh. She'd missed both so much. Missed his eyes when they were amused, like now, or thoughtful when deep in conversation or smouldering with passion... Ivy glanced down. Thinking this way was wrong.

'Ivy?'

'Hmm?' She couldn't bring herself to look at him.

'I'm glad you have my number. And if you feel like talking, just phone or message me. No intruders necessary.'

Now she did meet his eyes. 'Talking? About what?'

'Dunno. The weather.' He grinned. 'The hours of the wine bar, should you, and even Jody, wish to drop in.' Leo climbed into the car and wound the window down. 'Or we could talk about the past. Because I have questions and I also have things to say which you need to hear.'

'There's little anyone can say which is harsher than the way I speak to myself.'

'No harsh words from me. Give it some thought, okay?'

*I never could... What if I break both our hearts again?*

'I'll... think about it.'

He nodded and started the motor. It was only once he was out of sight that Ivy thought about the motorcycle. She could have asked his opinion. Or could that be the reason she might pick up the phone and call him? So much for never.

Ivy started over with a pot of tea and once Jody was back in the kitchen, poured a cup for each of them.

'Before you tell me about Melbourne, what was that thing with you and Leo just now?'

'No idea what you mean.'

'The look between you both. The snarky comments from each of you.'

'I think you are imagining things. And when I suggested you revisit places you loved in order to remind yourself how much Rivers End means to you, I didn't expect you to go straight to hooking up with Leo.'

'I did not hook up with him!'

'You have his number in your phone and he was your first point of call when you thought I was an intruder.' Jody's eyebrows were both raised as she sipped her tea.

'It was nothing more than a chance meeting on the beach yesterday.'

'Nothing more? He didn't stay the night, did he?' Jody suddenly grinned. 'Ivy!'

'No. You've got it wrong.'

'Then why have you turned beet red?'

'It isn't like that.'

Satisfied that she was right, Jody smirked. She'd always enjoyed teasing Ivy but this wasn't comfortable.

The best defence was offence.

'Tell me what happened at home, Jody. All I knew was you were going to be back with enough time to buy new shoes and have your hair done. What went wrong?'

The smirk disappeared and Jody put her cup down.

'I was back in the apartment before midday and phoned Aaron. He was busy but I told him I was going shopping and having a beauty appointment and he told me to enjoy and he was looking forward to seeing me at dinner. I have to admit, being home was a bit weird after being here. Not bad weird but I found myself walking along the river for a while, sorting through some thoughts and feelings.'

'About Dad?'

'Yeah. And Fairview. And you.'

'Me?'

'Yes, you. Anyway, my hair and nails and stuff took longer than I expected and then I couldn't find a dress I liked because I'd changed my mind about wearing the other one. A friend came with me and she arranged a private appointment with an exclusive designer who has a small number of ready-made dresses. We all had some champagne while I tried gowns on and then purchased one. I couldn't wait to show Aaron.'

There was a tremor in Jody's voice which tugged at Ivy's heart and she put her hand over one of her sister's.

'I arrived back at the apartment about seven. My phone had

died during the afternoon and when I plugged it in, there were several missed calls from Aaron. And a message. That was the first time I remembered the VIP dinner and I'd missed it. It was on a boat which had already left dock.' A tear slipped down her face. 'I phoned Aaron straight away, of course. He didn't reply until much later that evening and when he did, it was a text message that he would talk to me in the morning and not to wait up.'

'You must have been so upset. Is he usually like that?'

'Like what? Ivy, he doesn't ask much of me but I always attend any of his important functions and he had every reason to believe I'd be there. I tried to sleep but all I heard were the sounds of the city compared to the last few days out here where the sea is the constant backdrop. It wasn't better or worse, just different. I must have drifted off because I woke suddenly. He'd come home but went into one of the spare bedrooms and closed the door.'

Ivy wanted to hug Jody and take away her pain.

Jody took her hand back and picked up her tea. 'When I finally saw him this morning, he was in a mood. Not angry. He's never angry with me. But disappointed and kind of sad. And I apologised and tried to explain and he brushed it off and told me I need to make some decisions about my future. About our future.'

'Wait... do you think he meant about your marriage?'

'Yes.'

'Because of you missing one event? Which happened right in the middle of you helping sort out our father's estate?'

Now the tears were free-falling and Jody nodded. 'I think I've lost him, Ivy. I think I've lost Aaron.'

Jody wanted to lie down for a while and Ivy encouraged her to have a sleep in her room.

Promising to lock the front door, Ivy borrowed the keys to the Mini to do a bit more shopping. What had seemed a lot of groceries the other day was depleted and she'd eaten the small amount of food from her recent trip to the supermarket.

Before leaving the house, Ivy checked on Jody. Her bedroom door was ajar and Jody was fast asleep, legs tucked up and the evidence of more tears in the shape of used tissues in her hands.

*What is wrong with that man?*

Ivy was fuming inside. She let herself out and locked the front door then headed for the car. She'd never met Aaron but would love to have a conversation with him right now. Jody adored her husband and had driven hours to get back home for him. Making a mistake, forgetting something when she had so much going on with Fairview, was understandable. What kind of person lacked the compassion and love to react without frightening their partner into thinking the relationship was over? But being angry at a man she'd never met wouldn't help her support Jody.

Something made her turn into the car park on the clifftop and for a few minutes, she gazed at the sea while thoughts swirled.

The graveyard was as old as the town and was a history lesson. Generations of the Ryan family were buried here, as was Henry Temple, the man who built Palmerston House. Ivy vaguely recalled seeing the name 'Bardley' on several gravestones and Dad had explained they were the family who built Fairview.

There were two other, smaller graveyards in Rivers End, both attached to churches. The newer of these was deeply traditional and conservative and only members of their flock rested on their grounds. Another day, Ivy might visit and see if she came across anything related to the young woman Dad called his angel. For now, she had one grave in mind to visit and she'd put it off for too long.

Ivy wound her way around plots and little seating nooks. She squatted beside the grave of Jean Curry, pulling out a couple of small weeds and softly apologising for not visiting sooner.

Auntie Jean. That's what everyone called her.

All she'd done was drive up the hill from Rivers End one rainy, late night and been unable to avoid a car on the wrong side of the road. Her loss was keenly felt in the community where much of her extended family lived. The funeral was well attended and Ivy remembered flowers covering the grave for many months to come. She'd brought her own weekly for two years. Sometimes, she and Leo would visit together. And one time she'd found Dad here, tears pouring down his cheeks and repeating the word 'sorry' over and over.

Back on her feet, Ivy returned to the car. How had Dad lived with the guilt for two years? On the surface, he'd been a bit quiet at times but had continued to keep Fairview busy and doing well. And what had happened to make him confess? He'd got away with a terrible crime and Ivy could think of no reason for him to suddenly walk into a police station that day.

Was it possible the letters from that young woman had anything to do with it?

Ivy discarded the silly thought. Dad had simply buckled under guilt. That had to be it.


Shopping took a bit longer than she expected and after packing the bags into the car, she visited the bookstore to buy a couple of new releases Jody had been keen on.

As she made her way back to the Mini, a woman approached from the opposite direction, eyes on a phone in one hand, and eating an ice cream held in the other. It wasn't until she almost drew alongside Ivy that she recognised her.

The woman glanced up.

It was Tessa, and she hesitated. If seemed as if she wanted to speak but then she dropped her head and kept going.

'Wait. Please?' Ivy followed for a few feet then came to a halt. Whatever had got into her? Accosting strangers on the footpath.

But Tessa turned and although she didn't come closer, she stopped.

Ivy offered a smile. 'Do we know each other?'

She was a pretty woman behind a worried look, with lines which told of many smiles over her life. She was older than Ivy – perhaps by ten years or so – and had grey-blue eyes and light brown hair.

Tessa opened her mouth to speak but then she shook her head.

'We don't know each other?' Ivy was getting confused.

'I have to go.'

Dropping the remains of the ice cream into a nearby bin, Tessa hurried away.

Ivy returned to the car and climbed in, not starting the motor but gazing at herself in the rear-vision mirror.

'We must have been friends as kids.'

Saying it aloud made it plausible even with the age difference, because she and Jody had played with other children on Rivers End beach from toddlers to older teens.

Was Tessa offended that Ivy didn't remember? She'd seemed almost afraid to speak to her.

Jody might recall the woman if she described her. And maybe it was time to fill her sister in on the letters. If nothing else, if might keep her mind off her woes.

. . .

Jody was nowhere to be seen but her voice drifted down the stairs as Ivy unpacked the shopping. It was a muted conversation but that had to be a good sign. Ivy assumed her sister was on the phone, hopefully speaking to Aaron and sorting out their relationship.

The day had got away from Ivy, between her morning of working on the files, the visit to the garage, talking to Mick Hammond, and the strange memory. And then all the drama with Jody and Leo and even Tessa. Ivy considered a swim to let her body relax, but knew her mind wouldn't. Not until she'd checked something.

Dad's bedroom wasn't a comfortable place for her to be in but she pushed aside the feelings of being a trespasser and peered through the windows near his bed. These were the ones she'd seen from the garage and even if she stood on her toes, she couldn't see the other building because there were permanent shutters outside, covering the top half. She opened each window and leaned out – quite precariously – to tug on the shutters but like the ones on the cottages, they were firmly in place. More firmly than ten years of no use. These were decades old.

Ivy closed and locked the windows then dropped onto the bed because her legs were shaky.

Dad couldn't have seen the car leave the garage that night.

All it would have taken from the police was a check of this room during the original investigation to know he'd lied. Why hadn't they done so?

He'd been somewhere else and the only place Ivy could think of was the stone hut. But with whom?

'Ivy? What are you doing in here?'

Jody sat down next to Ivy, leaning her head on her shoulder.

'You doing okay?' Ivy asked.

'Better. I may have overreacted by leaving Melbourne so fast,' she said a little sheepishly.

*Oh, thank goodness you're not so stressed now.*

'Never. Not you.'

With a dig in Ivy's ribs, Jody straightened.

'Anyway, why are you in here?'

'I remembered something from the night of the crash. Something to do with Dad and I couldn't make sense of it. The other thing is that I thought we should go through his desk and try to find the receipt for the motorcycle.'

Jody glanced at the desk. 'Good idea. Just not now, okay? Would you like to go for a walk?'

# EIGHTEEN

The sisters wandered along the beach in the opposite direction to Rivers End, stopping at a group of boulders. Both chose one to sit upon, as they had done so many times in their childhoods. The sea was a pretty mix of colours as evening closed in. The sun was still above the horizon, its light on the water and clouds casting shades of pink and gold.

'When I phoned you a few weeks ago, I was in a state of shock at being given a third of Fairview.' Jody sat cross-legged on a flat-topped rock. 'I vaguely remembered you'd said something on your thirtieth birthday about Fairview but quite honestly, I didn't care and I wasn't listening. Three years ago I'd been married for less than a year and your choice to support Mum over me... well, all that time was pretty raw. Chatting to you on your birthday was something I felt I had to do, rather than wanted to.'

'I am so sorry,' Ivy said. 'You are the last person in the world I want to hurt.'

*You and Leo, yet I've caused both of you pain. In volumes.*

Jody shrugged. 'Just giving you some context so don't take anything personally. Please. Anyway, I phoned because I'd had a terrible dream. I'm still unsure if it even was a dream because it happened in broad daylight.'

Ivy adjusted herself to better see her sister's face. Her rock was more rounded and her legs dangled over each side.

'It was from the night of the crash and some of it didn't make sense. I thought I knew everything about what happened yet there was other stuff... things Dad said I had to do... which were a total shock.'

'What things?' Ivy had a sinking feeling. Almost as though the rug was being pulled from under her feet.

But Jody shook her head. 'They faded. And anyway, it made me think about Fairview and Dad and you and how all of this distance and fighting is keeping me miserable. I'm sure you feel the same?'

'So much.'

'We have to fix this, Ivy.' Jody leaned across the short distance between boulders and took Ivy's hands in hers. 'I only have one sister and I love you. But there's been so much crap dropped on us that I feel there's a chasm between us. A huge distance which is so much more than a long-haul flight between Australia and England.'

Out at sea, a yacht cruised along under power, close enough to shore for laughter and music to drift over the water. What a lovely way to enjoy the ocean.

Jody hadn't noticed. 'This thing with Aaron... I could see earlier you think badly of him and that's my fault. You've not met him and don't know him and I got all reactive and emotional and made it sound like he'd done something wrong.'

'Can I be honest? Straightforward?'

'As if I could stop you.' Jody laughed. 'Go ahead.'

'You've changed since I saw you last time. Physically, it is hugely obvious, with your weight loss and hair and makeup and all the things you never used to care about. So yes, I have questioned whether all of the new you is for your husband. And then when you arrive back here and say you think your marriage is over because you missed an event...'

Ivy clenched her fingers into fists as her anger returned.

'Let me tell you a story and then you decide. The week before Dad's last hearing, I stayed in Melbourne. I was totally lost. My acting career was a joke. Over before it began, thanks to so much negative attention as one of Gabe Sutherland's daughters. I was drifting, without any real idea what to do with my life. I even thought about moving back to Fairview and running it until Dad was released. Either as a retreat or even just a guesthouse. But this particular day, I couldn't bear being in the hotel room and followed one, then another narrow street until I realised I was in a dead-end alley. I turned around, not noticing there was a fire-exit door opening from a building and almost got hit by it. I stopped in time and there was Aaron.'

Jody's eyes were happy and she smiled at the memory.

'He was as shocked as me and we laughed and then he bought me coffee and then we had dinner that night. I attended the hearing, said the same words I've repeated ad nauseam for years, and was once again alone when you went back to London. But Aaron was there and less than a week later I moved into his apartment which was in the building through that door in the alley. Three months on we were married.'

'A real whirlwind romance.'

'Aaron is a bit... different. The way his brain is wired and how he functions. He'd not been in a relationship for a long time and had resigned himself to being alone and oddly, he didn't mind. And that's why I panicked.'

'About missing the boat the other day?'

'He isn't very good being out of what is a narrow comfort zone. Poor social skills and he's a serious introvert. My being with him makes a difference. He asks almost nothing of me other than to love him, and knowing I'd messed up and he'd had to manage the event and all those people on his own... it made me feel terrible for forcing him to do that alone, but also made me remember how self-sufficient he is capable of being and that when we met...'

'He'd been happily alone. Oh, sweetie.' Ivy reached across to squeeze Jody's hand. 'But you've been talking?'

'Yes. He says we're fine. I just default to doubting everything and expecting the worst when something goes wrong.'

The pain on Jody's face resonated. Trauma had long-term effects no matter how much therapy one had. Being here was enough to bring up the old bad memories.

'Trust him. It sounds as if you have a sound marriage. A good relationship. Don't let Dad's mess upset you. I'm so proud of you, Jody.'

'Thank you. I want so much for you to meet him so you can see how lucky I am, and Ivy? I just wish you could find your way back to Leo.'

Ivy pushed herself off the rock. 'That boat well and truly sailed. Shall we go back and make some dinner? And then, can I show you something? I found something the other day and it's time you saw it.'

'Forget dinner! I love surprises!'

'You did *what*? Without including me? And how did you even find this envelope and how do you know Dad is the recipient?'

The envelope was in the middle of the table.

'I wasn't trying to exclude you, Jodes. Really. There were all sorts of things which might have been inside. Money. I didn't know and when I did open it you weren't here.'

'My point entirely! You didn't wait for me to be back.'

Despite sounding cross, Jody's eyes kept darting to the envelope.

'Yes, I should have. To answer your questions – I found the envelope in the library, tucked behind a book on the highest

shelf. Before you ask, it was a few days ago and I put the envelope into the safe because I had no idea what to do with it.'

'But... it isn't ours to read, Ivy.'

'I felt that way. I still do but then I wondered... do you think
it possible that whoever broke into the library was looking for
this envelope?'

Jody's eyes widened. 'That makes no sense. It suggests a
person other than Dad knew of its existence and more than that,
had motive to find it. Didn't you say before that these are letters
from decades ago? Before we were born. Who on earth would
be affected by these?'

'But why did an intruder break into the house – into the
library – and pull every book off the shelves apart from those too
high to reach? And then there's the motorcycle, which is
another mystery. And I didn't tell you this yet either, but it had
a key in the ignition.'

'Ooh... and the garage key was stolen and someone
unlocked the door and had the dust cover off the motorcycle.'
Jody got up. 'Is there any dessert?'

'I'm sorry. Who are you in my sister's body?'

Head in the fridge, Jody rummaged around. 'I'm still starving. Oh, can I use the cheese?' She pulled out the remainder of
the soft cheese, more strawberries and some plump cherries Ivy
hadn't been able to resist.

Ivy helped and they took a small platter of the goodies,
along with the crackers and olives, back to the kitchen table.
'Read the first four, Jody. Then if you agree, we can read the
rest together. I bought some freshly made local apple juice if
you'd like a glass?'

Jody was sliding the letters from the envelope. 'Yes, please.
These are old. And such nice quality paper.'

By the time Ivy poured two glasses of the apple juice, Jody
had read the first two letters.

'Sweet. Like a teenager with a crush, really.'

But partway through the fourth, Jody shot a look at Ivy. 'Maeve?'

'I know. How many Maeves have you met in Australia? You know Dad named me and this revelation that his so-called angel wanted that as her name makes this all a bit personal. But read on.'

When Jody folded the letter, she was frowning. She helped herself to some of the platter and ate, still not speaking.

'If we were sleuths it would be fun to solve who this angel is. There are some clues in there. Her first name has some kind of angel or heavenly meaning and her middle name is something about a sheep, so we could narrow down the options using one of those baby-naming websites,' Ivy said. 'Do you think we should keep reading?'

'I think we have to. It makes no sense that she'd drop that on Dad, about being engaged to someone else, yet there are still a heap of letters. Do you want to read, or me?'

*Dear Gabriel,*

*Walking away from you was a terrible mistake and I cannot blame you if you won't speak with me. It is taking all of my courage to bring you this letter, which may well be my last if I've misunderstood our connection.*

*The changing colour of the leaves reminded me there are only a few months of freedom left before I marry and this is the final chance I have to decide whether to go ahead.*

*In the time we've been apart I've thought about you constantly. My heart aches to be with you and I wonder at times how it is that two people meet and fall in love so fast. My feelings for the man I had planned to spend a lifetime with are not even a tiny spark compared to the burning flame I feel for you.*

*Is it possible we can try? The idea of breaking my engagement frightens me. Not only will I hurt a good man, but upset my parents and possibly be ostracised from my family and the church. I've seen it done to other people who wouldn't toe the line.*

*I know you now live at Fairview and wish to buy it. Your dreams are big and beautiful and I hope your heart and mind are willing to explore what we have. Or might have.*

*Your angel,*

*April, 1974*

'And now she's back,' Ivy said. 'She doesn't even love the guy she's engaged to, so was she serious about Dad or just having misgivings about entering a loveless marriage?'

'She's twenty. Instead of worrying about a husband she should be living her life.' Jody folded that letter and picked up another.

*Darling Gabriel,*

*I'm wide awake, although it is almost dawn, and if I don't write my thoughts I shall probably never sleep again.*

*The past two weeks have been the best of my life!*

*We meet every day other than Sundays because as you know, I'm expected to attend the service with my family and then be involved in church activities. By Monday evening I am almost bursting with excitement about seeing you.*

*Just after nine each evening you are waiting for me at the top of the driveway and I can't help but run to you and embrace and kiss and laugh. And after a few hours, which pass all too soon, you kiss me goodnight at the river, not far from my house, and wait until I wave from the back gate before leaving. Saturdays are the best because I spend the entire day with you, and it is fun to help paint walls or draw plans for your cottages.*

*I liked the sheltered spot we found today on the beach. It wasn't too cold for this time of year and the sun was nice on our backs. I asked you whether this little beach has a name. And it was our conversation which has my heart so happy now.*

*'All beaches have names.'*

*You thought you were being funny.*

*'Is it a secret?' I asked.*

*'It is.'*

*That made me laugh and I asked you to share this secret.*

*'Angel's Beach.'*

*'Angels? As in... there are angels on the beach?'*

*'There's one. One angel, so the beach belongs to her. This particular angel is the most beautiful of all of God's creations and so smart. She is kind. Caring. Her soul is ageless and sees into the hearts of men.'*

*I could barely breathe, hearing your beautiful words.*

*'Would the beach not be named after her... her real name?'*

*'But you see, my darling, before I knew your name, I already knew you were an angel sent to earth.'*

*I gestured along the shore. 'This... all of this, you have named after me?'*

*'The wind and the waves did. The full moon sang the name and the last rays of sunset spread it to the rest of the world. My role was to speak it aloud, today.'*

*You truly are a poet, Gabriel. You have a gentle soul and your heart is easy to see into even if I'm not really an angel. I memorised what you said and they have helped me make my decision.*

*I know that you are meeting with the real estate agent tomorrow and hope to finally have news about the purchase of Fairview House. You're worried you won't have enough saved for a deposit or may not be given a loan by the bank but I believe in you. When you put your mind to something, you achieve it.*

*So, when I meet you at the gate tomorrow night, you will have wonderful news to tell me. And then I shall share my news. I'll need you to help me find the right words so I can let my fiancé down gently and explain myself to my family, but I cannot wait to tell you I am ready to start a new life. A new life with you.*

*Your angel, forever.*

*April, 1974.*

'Are you certain Dad wasn't married before?' Jody asked. 'This was written fifteen years or more before he met Mum and the relationship sounds like it was escalating pretty fast. Whoever the angel is, she's besotted with him!'

'Besotted,' Ivy grinned. 'Cute word.'

'I'm a cute person.'

Jody yawned widely.

'Also a tired person.'

'Me too. Bedtime. I'll lock these away again.'

Ivy took the envelope to the safe and when she returned to the kitchen, Jody had washed the platter and glasses. Together they checked Fairview House was locked up.

As Ivy drifted off to sleep a little later, she felt closer to Jody than she had in years.

Coming here was a good thing.

# NINETEEN

Rivers End beach was beautiful any time of the day, but early morning was special. With the sun rising over the cliffs, the sea would begin dark and slowly start to glisten with light and reflect the changes in the sky.

Ivy had woken while it was still dark with more energy than she had in days. Her mind was settled and there weren't any annoying butterflies in her stomach for once. It was their absence which hit home. For too long she'd carried more anxiety than was healthy. She left a note for Jody and donned a pair of runners.

The tide was going out so she cut around the rocks just as the first rays of morning tipped the cliffs.

When she'd lived here full-time, those two years of learning about running Fairview, and writing, and dating Leo, her mornings often began this way. Up before most people. A brisk walk or run or swim and then a little time to sit on the end of the jetty and meditate. Back home to help out with breakfast preparation or any number of tasks.

Almost always, she'd meet Leo here. He'd told her his entire family were water-babies and he more than anyone. Sometimes he'd bring his surfboard to the beach near Fairview and they'd spend time paddling out and racing each other in with fancy twists and turns. But when the tide was low, he'd be out swimming most mornings before his own day began.

It was a wonderful time.

She wasn't here to swim or run. It was enough just to walk along the hard sand and let soft surf cover her feet. Talk to the seagulls and let the sea air do its magic.

Ivy reached the far end of the beach and perched on a rock against the cliff. This cliff wasn't as steep as the one with the stone steps, and had a walking track which zigzagged to the top. When she'd been at her fittest, she'd think nothing of finishing a morning swim with a climb to get one of the best views in the region – all the way to King Island in the far distance if the air was clear enough.

She glanced up and grinned. No big climbs today. If she lived here again then over time her fitness would improve but perhaps not back to those levels.

With daylight came people. It wasn't really tourist season yet, but more and more Melbourne residents also owned holiday homes here as the town became more popular. In a couple of hours the beach would probably be far too busy for her liking.

As she wandered toward the jetty, someone came out of the water. A swimmer she'd not noticed. Her heart did a little jump as Leo waded through the shallows, shaking his head to get rid of the sea.

Ivy waited for him, although it took some quick self-talk about not running away and putting on a friendly and civil face to keep her there. It hadn't occurred to her he might still follow their shared love of early mornings on the beach. Surely his wine bar was open until late and then there'd be all the cleaning up and whatever else happened behind the scenes. It was barely half past six.

'Don't you sleep?' she asked once he was near enough for her to see the trails of seawater on his shoulders. And chest.

*Bad idea.*

He went past her and for half a second she thought he was brushing her off. But then he reached a bag on the sand, and pulling out a towel, dried his face. 'Ah, better. I had half the ocean in my eyes and you were just a blur but to answer your question, I sleep like a baby.'

*Oh.*

Face dry, he rubbed at his hair and then almost as an afterthought, wrapped the towel around his waist. Only then did he properly look at Ivy and it was a long, thoughtful gaze. As she desperately searched for something to say to break the moment before she began to squirm, he scooped up his bag. 'You're heading to Fairview?'

She managed a nod.

'Can we walk together for a bit? At least to the lagoon. I'm living in the apartment behind the wine bar these days.'

*I have so many questions.*

Another nod and they began to trudge through the softer sand. Leo called hello to almost everyone they passed but Ivy kept her head down. He was a local trader and all it would take was one person to recognise her and think they were back together... she couldn't bear for the same kind of lynch-mob mentality she'd experienced to come his way.

'Ivy? Why so quiet?'

'No reason. Was I quiet?'

They were close to the lagoon and Leo suddenly grinned and sat on the bank, dangling his legs into the water and looking up at Ivy like a happy kid. He patted the spot beside him and her misgivings and dark thoughts evaporated.

For a minute or two they sat in silence. Ivy gazed at her feet through the ripples in the otherwise crystal clear water. How often she'd enjoyed the lagoon. Dad teaching her how to swim here. She and Jody playing endless games in the warm and safe water. And she'd once caught a netball almost at this spot.

'Leo, I—'

'Do you remember— Oh, sorry.'

They both laughed and ten years of tension dropped away from Ivy's soul.

'You go first,' she said.

'Can you still catch and throw as well as you used to?'

'Not even to save my life. Although, according to Jody I am strong because I carry heavy things for my work.'

He tilted his head. 'What heavy things? Are you a builder?'

She almost snorted in amusement.

'People. Jody calls them heavy things.'

'Sorry, you carry people? Are you a firefighter?'

'A nurse.'

Leo shook his head. 'Not even possible, because the Ivy I know is a writer.'

'*That* Ivy is long gone.'

'Then the world is poorer.'

The back of her eyes were heavy with a sudden need to cry and she dug her fingers into the sand on either side of herself, willing Leo not to see her reaction. He'd always been able to read her but that was a long time ago.

Some things didn't change. A warm arm came around her shoulders and gently pulled her against him... only for a few seconds. He released her and where they'd touched, her skin blazed.

'Well, since we're sharing... all those years training to be a doctor were for nothing. Turns out when it came to actually treating patients that I have too much empathy.' He laughed shortly. 'It's one thing to care about patient health and another to turn yourself inside out worrying about them.'

'Oh, Leo. I'm sorry. You worked so hard for it.'

'Better I found out before I finished medical school. For a

while I had no clue what to do next and got a job on a cruise ship. Don't laugh.'

'Please don't tell me you were the entertainment.' She managed to keep a straight face. 'Comedian? Exotic dancer, perhaps?'

'Are you assuming I wasn't the captain?'

'I am.'

'I feel judged, Ivy.' His mock sorrow was enough to make her giggle. 'And now you laugh at me.'

She forced herself to at least look serious. 'Sorry. So, what was your role on the cruise ship?'

Leo adjusted his feet in the lagoon, touching hers. Whether he meant to she had no idea but if she moved away, it was yet another form of running and besides, it felt good.

'There's a chef who lives up in the hills, Brock. For a while he was in charge of the menus and kitchens of a European cruise ship line and it was him who suggested I move into hospitality. I spent three years on board two different ships, initially as a kitchen hand then doing some of the cooking and I naturally gravitated to the bar. I love making cocktails, and mocktails.' He gave her a sideways glance. 'Pretty decent ones.'

*You even remember I don't drink alcohol.*

'What made you leave?'

'Homesickness. I missed my family like crazy and when Brock decided to work on a different project, one much closer to Rivers End, I followed. You know me. Once I love someone, it is forever.'

His eyes were impossible to read now. There was no way he meant he still loved her. Not after she abandoned him and didn't do as much as have a final conversation with him.

'I have to go.' Ivy scrambled onto her feet. 'Jody will be worrying about me.'

Leo took his time to stand but once he did, he tossed his bag over his shoulder and adjusted the towel. 'The wine bar's closed today. And tomorrow. If I was to bring a picnic to your beach later... complete with mocktails...' He looked away for a moment.

Ivy held her breath.

When he met her eyes, that same wariness from their first meeting was back in force. Perhaps not wariness. Uncertainty. 'I meant what I said about having questions. But putting those aside, I'd really like to have a meal with you. Lunch? No blame. No harsh words. No expectations.'

*Don't agree. Keep the distance. Protect your heart.*

'What time?'


'Have you heard even one word I've said in the last five minutes?' Jody tapped her teaspoon on her cup as though it were a bell. 'Earth to Ivy!'

'Of course I have. Good grief, you'll break the china if you do that.'

Jody lifted the cup from the saucer. 'Actually, it is a nice piece. Dad managed to find some beautiful things over the years. I wonder if this is valuable?'

'We can get it valued. Along with a ton of other stuff like some of the paintings and the piano.'

'But why the piano – and I know we'd get a good price for it but there's so much sentimental value in it. Don't you remember when we were small and we'd play it with our awful attempts to make music and Dad would sit us on his lap and guide our hands?'

'I remember you screaming at Dad that he wasn't the boss of you.'

Jody burst into laughter.

Ivy continued. 'I doubt if much has changed. You always were Miss Bossy Boots.'

'Never.'

'Always. Particularly with Mum. You'd stalk into the kitchen in our first flat in Walthamstow and demand she make you a Vegemite sandwich. And she'd make it with Marmite because it was hard to get Vegemite and you'd sit on the floor and howl.'

Mouth wide open, Jody slowly shook her head from side to side.

'You did. So, shall I make Vegemite sandwiches for lunch?'

Now, Jody was frowning. 'I vaguely remember the flat. And then we moved into the little house after a while. Mum had finished her nursing degree and was getting regular pay.'

'And Dad sent money. As he should have. There was a day when Mum was really stressed about paying the rent and she opened a letter from Dad. Inside was a cheque and she said it was enough money to cover the rent for six months.'

'I miss her. Ivy, I really do.' Jody's voice was quiet and she screwed her face up as if about to cry. 'Why couldn't she have trusted me to choose the husband I wanted? It's almost like this poor angel person. Having to fight to be with the man she loves against the disapproval of her family.'

Ivy was on her feet in an instant and had her arms around her sister. 'Mum was wrong. Dead wrong. And I was too. You never got the chance to celebrate your wedding with the people who should have been there and I would do anything to change that.'

Jody sighed. 'I know. I wish it as well.'

The kettle began to whistle and Ivy hurried to turn it off. 'More tea? Coffee?'

'Wine? Joking. I know it is the middle of the morning and despite Leo's disapproving throwaway line about day-drinking, I'm not *that* bad.'

'About Leo...'

'What?'

'I'm having lunch with him. Today. Just so we can clear the air and he can say what he needs. And we can part as friends.'

'Bad idea.'

'Most likely. But Jodes, I've told Leo I'll meet him so it's happening. Let's read some more letters and see if we can work out what on earth that intruder wanted to stop us finding out.'

'Fine. Where are we up to?'

*Dear Gabriel,*

*My heart is broken. Shattered. I cannot sleep or eat or think clearly.*

*I'm not going to bring this to you because you made it so clear you no longer wish to see me, but I will find a way to send it. I discovered that the post office will now deliver to Fairview House and I will test that. Of course I have no way of finding out if you receive it, unless by God's grace you have a change of heart and come and find me.*

*But Gabriel... If I am your angel, then how can you abandon me?*

*The very night I came to tell you I'd made my choice – and my choice was you – was the night you crushed me into a million pieces. I was willing to give up everything for you! My engagement. My church. Even – if it came to it – my own family. Do you have any idea what I stood to lose? Not only my parents, but four grandparents, cousins, and aunts and uncles. Every part of my life.*

*For you, Gabe.*

*For you.*

*From the second I first saw you there was a connection between us and you spoke poetically of your love for me and belief in our future.*

*Was it some kind of game?*

*I almost destroyed my life.*

*Are you happy?*

*Did you think I was a toy to enjoy for a while then toss away?*

*I will never, ever, forget your words.*

*'We cannot be together, my angel. Not now. But if you will hold on to our love then the time will come. I promise.'*

*How dare you promise a future when it was offered to you this night? You already had everything you wanted, Gabe.*

*Yes. Gabe. For Gabriel is the man who is above all the pettiness of men.*

*And now you reside beside the worst of them.*

*As furious and hurt and destroyed as I am at this moment, I find relief in God's wisdom. I have prayed so much tonight. And I have my answer.*

*I will be the daughter I am expected to be.*

*The wife.*

*The God-fearing child.*

*And you?*

*Damn you.*

*No longer your angel.*

*April, 1974.*

'Holy crap.'

Ivy couldn't have said it any better and the sisters stared at each other in shared shock.

'I feel like I don't know Dad at all,' Jody said. 'What on earth would make him have such a major change of heart?'

'And she clearly didn't see it coming. Imagine being so young and in love yet pulled in two directions and having such limited time to decide her entire future. I feel sorry for her.' Ivy picked up the remaining pile of letters. 'From the look of things, she kept writing and he kept them all. Do you think he hid them in the library so Mum would never find them?'

'Maybe. Mum was never much of a reader and I can't imagine her on the top of the rolling ladders dusting the top of old tomes,' Jody said. 'But why would he even need to hide them if the relationship with this woman was over?'

'Oh. You're not thinking—'

'I am.' Jody lifted the next letter. 'He'd better not have been cheating on our mother or I'll be selling my share of Fairview.'

# TWENTY

*Dear Gabe,*

*You will be surprised, no doubt, to receive this letter after so long. The months turned so quickly into years, but at long last I feel ready to pick up my pen to write to you. It seems that though our lives moved forward – and apart from each other – I cannot entirely break free of the love we shared. I hope that by writing down my thoughts, it might ease my mind and perhaps show you forgiveness.*

*My love for you lives deep in my heart, where nobody other than God can see and I know that He will judge me for dishonouring my husband with these feelings when the time comes. And Joe is a good man. He treats me well and we have a nice home and life is neither sad nor happy. I see myself more like my mother now and understand her in ways I never did before. Her life revolves around us – her family – and the church. One day, I think I shall be the same.*

*We've not spoken since the night you told me our love couldn't*

*be. So much has happened for me. My wedding was quite beauti-
ful. It was held at the church in Green Bay, because the one
Father helped build wasn't finished. The reception was at Bell
Park and there were so many people and gifts! Yet, as the evening
wound down, I found myself outside for some fresh air and had
the strangest sensation that you were nearby. It was silly, but for
a moment, I remembered dancing in the lagoon that very first
night we met, your eyes on me from afar.*

*It unsettled me but then I asked God for guidance and within a
few seconds my father came out of the house and escorted me
inside for final toasts.*

*This was a powerful message that marrying Joe was the right
thing to do.*

*Even with the love I have for you, I've grown up and know it was
a folly of a young heart. A temptation or test of my beliefs.*

*I hear Fairview is doing so well and I'm proud of you. Perhaps
one day I'll be able to visit and see what you accomplished and
we can then say a proper goodbye and part as friends.*

*C.*

*July, 1978.*

*And we can part as friends. Didn't I just say that to Jody about
lunch with Leo?*

Ivy pushed the thought away. 'So, who is "C"? This might
help find her, so let me get my sketchbook.'

Jody was making a fresh pot of tea when Ivy returned. 'This
is all fascinating but I want to do something else today rather
than read all of these.' She nodded at the letters. 'If you insist on

putting your heart on the chopping block again by seeing Leo then I'd rather not be around.'

'You're not exactly invited to come with us.'

'Might be more sensible if I was. Regardless, I'm going to drive along the coast today. Clear my head and feel the wind in my hair.'

'Sounds nice. Really nice, actually.'

'Then come with me.'

*Not this time.*

Ivy opened the sketchbook. 'What do we know about this woman Dad called his angel? Her first name begins with "C" and has a meaning which fits Dad's nickname for her.'

'Her second name means "sheep". Poor thing, no wonder she considered turning her back on her family. Ooh… then she'd have been the black sheep of the family.'

'Save me from Jody jokes.'

With Jody looking ready to unleash more gems, Ivy returned to writing notes. 'Where is Bell Park? Have you ever come across it?'

'Sounds like a reception centre. If she got married in Green Bay then it's probably there. Does it even matter though?' Tea poured, Jody sat again. 'She sounds as though she's accepted her life as a married woman, and harbouring some old feelings doesn't mean she's about to wreck her life for Dad.'

Jody was probably right. The rest of the letters were probably more of the same ponderings of a woman whose heart still yearned for more than the strict confines of a marriage to someone she'd said she didn't love.

'What if… okay, there has to be a reason why Fairview is so interesting to the person who broke into the library,' Ivy said. She tapped the pen against the table as she thought it through. 'Let's fast forward "C's" life. She has kids. Grandkids even. Her family loves her and she's a valued part of it and presumably, the church.'

'I'm listening.'

'But years and years ago she had a fling and although nobody ever found out, these exist.' Ivy touched the pile of letters.

'She's trying to get them back.'

'Not personally. Someone else is. What if she's hired a thief to retrieve them? Or a trusted child or grandchild. The intruder might be nothing more than a desperate attempt to keep a woman's past a secret.'

Jody scoffed. 'They broke in. And how do you explain the motorcycle?'

'I can't explain it. Or anything really.' Ivy pushed away the sketchbook. 'One more and then we'll give this a break?'

*Dear Gabriel,*

'Wait. Did she really write *Gabriel*? Does this mean they got back together??'

'Jody, shush.'

*And so, my letters begin again.*

*The past week at home was one of turmoil and a new sense of coldness between Joe and me. Without telling me a thing, he applied for a job in Melbourne and was offered the position a few days ago. He was so proud of himself and told my father first! Not his own wife. It isn't that I'd have discouraged him because like my father, he is keen to do well in his career and this new role is one of responsibility and potential. When I asked why he'd not chosen to discuss this before applying though, he gave me a look I have never seen from him before. It chilled me, Gabriel. And he said it was his decision as head of the house and he expected me to support him without interference.*

*I've married a man just like my father.*

*He spent a day packing and I did all that was expected of me. Said the right words. Agreed with his choice of clothing to take for his first week away. For this job requires him to work in the city each week and he has already rented an apartment. I don't even know the address and I'm not going to ask. My parents insisted on taking us out for dinner before Joe left for the trip to Melbourne. He's taking a bus at first until he gets an idea of what he needs.*

*We'd been at the bistro for a while when I felt something which made me look to the corner table near the window. A feeling of being watched.*

*I almost dropped my glass when I saw you.*

*Sitting alone, you had a meal set out in front of you and a glass of beer and I remembered the date. It was your birthday.*

*My husband and father were loudly laughing and I smiled to be polite. My mother's face was the same. And I knew at that moment I had to change something in my life before I completely lost the real me.*

*You didn't stay much longer, leaving a handful of notes on the table with your unfinished dinner before hurrying out.*

*My heart left with you.*

*We all waved goodbye to Joe as the bus pulled out an hour later. My parents dropped me home and Mother fussed about whether I should stay on my own but eventually they left and I changed into running shoes. I couldn't waste another minute, not even to change out of the nice dress from dinner.*

*It must have been close to midnight when I reached Fairview and you wouldn't answer the door. The whole property was deserted with no guests or lights and all I could think about was the spot we always loved to sit beneath the tree on the grassy dune.*

*I stood there alone and was about to give up and go home when I heard you call. A cry. 'God forgive me for asking for too much. I chose a house instead of love.' I saw you in the ocean, standing up to your waist in water, and I had the most frightening feeling you were planning to do harm to yourself. It took only a few seconds to race across the sand and then the water was around my ankles and I called to you.*

*'Gabriel! Come out of the sea!'*

*You laughed.*

*'Gabriel?'*

*'You aren't real. Let my heart break in peace.'*

*Whether you were drunk or distraught, I had to reach you so waded toward you. My dress weighed me down as it soaked through and I'd stupidly left shoes on my feet. But you must have seen it really was me for just as I struggled to stay upright against a wave, your arms lifted me and we kissed.*

*Until it was almost dawn, we talked and made plans, drinking hot chocolate and wrapped in the thick dressing gowns you keep for your guests. My clothes eventually dried and you walked me home, leaving me only a few houses away.*

*We were meant to be together. Fighting it hasn't worked for either of us and now I'm in a marriage with no exit clause. I think God had a hand in Joe's new job because He has a purpose for us. Each weekend I will be a good wife to Joe. And the rest of the time, is for us.*

*Your angel,*

*January, 1979.*

Ivy and Jody stood outside the stone hut, staring at the door as though it would open itself. Or maybe it was a fear that Dad might appear and catch them at the one place expressly forbidden to enter.

'You really think this was for him and his angel?' Jody asked. 'I can't believe you didn't tell me earlier.'

'It was a shock. You go in and tell me it isn't confronting.'

'I guess that's why he made such a deal about us never opening the door or looking through the windows. Remember the time we pushed a wheelbarrow up here and you stood in it and were about to lift me onto your shoulders to try and see in?' Jody peered at the rows of windows which were too high on the wall for anyone to see in without a step. 'Dad came around the corner and gave us a massive fright.'

Ivy snorted. 'My backside remembers.'

'Oh that's right. I remember hearing you squealing.' Jody smirked.

'More like shrieking. Only spanking I ever had and I never tried to look inside here again. Meanwhile, you were long gone.'

'Sorry. Not sorry. You should have run faster.'

Using the skeleton key, Ivy unlocked the door, and Jody

turned on the flashlight they'd brought with them. As before, the air was musty and old.

'It feels kinda creepy in here.' Jody shone the light around. 'Spider webs everywhere. And what's with the bed?'

'Really?'

'I mean, why a four-poster complete with lacy curtains? Was Dad trying to be some great romantic or something? Enough candles to start a fire. Wine. Music. Yet in a horrible old hut.' She shuddered.

'Distance from the house, I guess. What is that at the back of that table?'

Jody turned the light where Ivy pointed. 'Is that an angel? For someone who claimed he wasn't religious, Dad sure like to bring heaven into his life.'

'Lots of people believe in angels without being religious though.' Ivy blew dust off the sculpture. 'Similar to the other one.'

'Other one?'

'In the safe. I meant to show you the other day. It is similar but this one is covering its face with its wings.'

'Don't blame it. I'd do the same if I was stuck in here with those two.'

'Jody!'

The only response was a series of sneezes and then the light disappeared outside as her sister left the hut.

Jody was near the garage, tapping on her phone, when Ivy caught up. 'Best news.' She put the phone away. 'Aaron's charity got a large donation this week. Every bit helps of course, but this was half a million dollars.'

'That is wonderful! What is the charity for?'

'I seriously cannot believe we've not discussed this. It's named after Aaron's mother. The Ruth-Anne Reynard Foundation. She died when he was about fifteen and there was no support for someone his age to deal with it. His father couldn't manage his own grief let alone a teen's. So the foundation offers short breaks for teens and young adults who have lost a parent or carer. They can choose from a few places around Victoria we run and stay for a week or so. We provide an environment where they can chill or talk or play computer games or ride horses even.'

The hairs on Ivy's arm rose. 'What a beautiful charity. I'm so proud of you.'

Jody looked surprised. 'Oh. Well, it mostly is Aaron's doing but I love being CEO, and this new donation will help us a lot. The need is there and we have to expand soon. Anyway, we both have places to be, Ivy, without all these little side trips.'

'One more. Last for now.' Ivy pointed in the direction of Fairview House. 'What do you see?'

'Trees. Can we go?'

'Apart from trees. The windows.'

'Two windows.'

'But from the windows it's impossible to see this spot.'

'*That's* why you were in Dad's room? Ivy!'

'Partly. Yes. Because I remembered after the crash, Dad said he was in his bedroom and saw the car leaving the garage and that's why he followed it.'

Jody's face paled.

'But he couldn't have seen it because of the shutters. So in light of the letters, I thought maybe he was actually back there, in the stone hut, with... her.'

'So what if he was?'

'Why are you getting upset?'

'Why are you dredging this all up again?'

'I have to! I had a memory. It was from that night and I'd made us both ice cream and—'

'Yes, yes, I remember. And then I took my empty bowl to the kitchen and saw Dad running up the driveway in the rain, which is why I followed him.' Jody spun around and strode away.

'Hey, don't take off.' Ivy quickly caught up. 'The reason I raised this is because I've been having other memories, but I don't know if they're real.'

Jody abruptly stopped. 'How can you have memories that aren't real? Isn't that called a daydream?' Her eyes were wide and she swallowed heavily. 'This is pointless, Ivy. It is the past. We can't change what happened.'

'I know. But I need to understand what happened. I'm remembering being at the crash site. Seeing certain people—'

'What people!' Jody grabbed Ivy's arm. 'Who?'

'Calm down. Nobody I know other than Dad. But you weren't there.'

With a big, shuddering breath, Jody released Ivy. 'And that proves you couldn't have been there or you'd have seen me. Sorry, this is upsetting and I'm going to go and get ready to leave for my drive.'

In a minute she was out of sight. Ivy's heart thudded. More than ever she was sure there were gaps in her memory of that night. Even her therapist had said as much and offered to help her through hypnosis but she'd been convinced she knew everything and remembered being asleep in her bed. Jody's desperate need to know who Ivy thought she'd seen changed everything.

She glanced back at the garage. What really happened that night?

# TWENTY-ONE

Ivy almost called Leo to cancel. Twice. She showered and put on a sundress and sandals then changed into pants and a blouse, then back into the sundress. It wasn't just the idea of spending time with Leo which unsettled her, but the interaction with Jody near the garage.

Her sister was still here, in her bedroom, and they'd barely spoken in the hour they'd been back in the house.

When Ivy eventually went downstairs to wait for Leo, Jody followed, going into the kitchen to collect some bottled water.

'You take the house keys. I'll be late.' Jody shot past Ivy and was out of the front door before it was possible to answer.

*Let her go. She'll calm down.*

But what if she didn't? What if she lost concentration and had an accident? What if she felt she couldn't come back to Fairview because she was so upset?

Ivy chased after her.

Jody had tossed a hat and the water into the back seat and glared at Ivy.

'Please be safe.'

'I said I'll see you later, Ivy.'

'Then give me a hug first.'

Instead, Jody walked right around her sister to open the driver's door.

'I love you. I don't want anything happening to you,' Ivy whispered. 'Nothing matters more than you do.'

After rolling her eyes, Jody hugged Ivy. 'I love you too, no matter what your boyfriend says. And he's here.'

'What does that mean? And he isn't my boyfriend.'

'Sure. And I'll be careful, okay.'

Leo stood near the bench beneath the oak tree and Ivy locked the house then went to meet him. Jody had turned the car and was driving out and looked over at them. Leo waved and she shook her head.

'What is going on with you and my sister?' All of these mysteries were beginning to pile up around Ivy and she didn't know if she had the brainpower to solve them all. Or any.

'You look nice, Ivy. Very summery.'

He might have been deliberately changing the subject but it still made her smile. He didn't look half bad himself, with calf-length pants and a white T-shirt with the image of a seagull in flight.

'Did you walk up from the beach?' Ivy asked.

'At great personal risk. The tide is turning faster than I thought and I only made it across the rocks just in time. Do you have a preference where to have our picnic?' He picked up a bag Ivy hadn't noticed in the shade. 'The tree near the beach looked nice today.'

'Sounds perfect.'

As they wandered toward the beach, Ivy glanced at Leo. He was relaxed. It was all coming back to Ivy. How Leo moved. The sound of his voice. The very essence of the man. Nothing was forgotten. Ten years had barely touched him, not physically. His face had a few fine lines she didn't recall. But he was as fit and muscular as ever and she suddenly touched her stomach and looked away. She hadn't looked after herself. Not nearly enough.

'It seems odd to see Fairview again,' he said as they passed the first cottage. 'These are all empty. Instead of a thriving community, it feels a bit... sad. Really.'

'Jody and I are working out what to do with the property.'

'I don't understand.'

'When I turned thirty, I was given a third share in Fairview. And so was Jody, a couple of months ago. We now own the majority of the property and need to make decisions about its future. It's why I'm here, Leo.'

He didn't respond and that worried Ivy. She had hoped they'd be able to find a common ground before blurting out her return was very short term. There were better ways of raising it.

Once they reached the last tree before the beach, Leo opened the bag and drew out a picnic blanket. 'Shall we?' He laid it out and waited for Ivy to sit before joining her. They were facing each other, Leo cross-legged and Ivy tucking hers to one side. In the past they'd have cuddled or held hands but this felt more formal and she had to remember this wasn't an invitation to go back to how things used to be.

'I used to come here sometimes. After you'd gone. After Jody left and the place was empty.' Leo was staring out at the horizon. 'I'd sit and lean against the tree and imagine you in my arms and for a little while, it was easy to pretend you'd come home soon.'

Leo might have told her this morning there'd be no harsh words. No blame. But this was worse, the raw pain in his voice. Ivy's throat constricted. Hurting him had never been her intention and she would do anything to change the past.

'Ivy? Don't cry.'

'I'm not.'

His attention was fully on her. 'Your eyes are shiny. I'm not trying to distress you by telling you that. About me missing you. There's no way forward without honesty. From us both.'

'By forward… I don't understand.'

'It's hard to move on without knowing what happened. Why a relationship I thought was rock-solid fell apart.'

*There's someone else in your life. Of course there is.*

Whatever appetite she'd had disappeared. She summoned a smile. 'As you said earlier, you wanted to talk. I'm happy to talk.'

His eyes narrowed. 'Let's eat.' He opened the bag and pulled out several cardboard takeaway containers. 'Sorry for the packaging. I'd normally bring plates but I couldn't find a proper picnic basket on short notice and wanted to make you something nice to eat.'

Whatever was in there smelled divine and despite herself, Ivy knew she could eat.

'I was lucky and there were some leftover prepped ingredients at work from last night.'

'You made all of this?'

'Don't sound surprised.' He grinned. 'I already told you I've worked in kitchens and had the good fortune to learn from Brock, who is a fine chef. There's rice paper rolls with peanut dipping sauce, two salads, and hopefully these are still hot.' He took out a ball of foil and unwrapped it. 'Warm enough, I think. I just cooked these tempura vegetables and can recommend the sweet chilli sauce alongside.'

Ivy laughed and clapped her hands, stopping when she saw the look in Leo's eyes.

'You used to do that all the time.'

'Well, I haven't in years and I cannot wait to try your food, Leo.'


'Since when are there battery-operated blenders?'

Ivy was holding a mocktail in a real martini glass but gazing at the narrow device Leo had taken from his bag once they'd eaten. Inside had been fat ice cubes, strawberries, cream, and some other ingredients Ivy didn't recognise but they tasted wonderful.

'Very cool, isn't it? Throw everything you need to mix inside and blend when ready. I keep a few at work in case the power goes off. We only recently bought a generator but with some of the big storms when we first opened, we lost power a few times and quickly realised if we could keep serving a mix of drinks then the customers would stay and pay cash rather than venture out into the rain.'

'Clever strategy. Makes the customer feel special and builds the desire to return.'

'So far it seems to be going that way.'

'Why a wine bar? I know you decided not pursue medicine and then did the whole Captain Leo thing on cruise ships, but how did you and Zara end up in business?'

'Captain Leo. I like that a lot. I might keep it.'

Ivy grinned. 'Go right ahead.'

'That's "go right ahead, Captain Leo."'

'Don't push your luck.'

Food had helped her mood. That, and almost two hours of relaxed conversation with no more dissecting of the past.

'I learned on the cruise ships that people are my thing. I like them and get a buzz from different energies and it makes me happy when they are. I guess it was the opposite working with patients.'

'And Zara? Wasn't she doing a business degree?'

'She graduated and the week after that she got married. Two kids in quick succession and then her husband died.'

'Oh no. Oh, I am so sorry.'

'It was dreadful. Heart attack at the age of thirty. It shook up the entire family and brought us closer than we'd ever been. Did I ever tell you I met your father when I was at school?'

Blinking at the sudden change of direction, Ivy shook her head.

'In my last year of school, Gabe was invited to run some classes about art as a career, as well as thinking outside the box, as it were, when it came to carving one's way through life. He was a passionate speaker. Eloquent. Almost poetic. And everything always came back to Fairview House and the joy of creating something from the ground up.'

'I don't know what to say, Leo. This is new information.'

'In a roundabout way, your father influenced me and when Zara began looking at options as the sole support for her family, I remembered his lessons and began to think differently. Zara and I talked a lot about our respective visions of the future and found a middle ground. Our wine bar.'

*My father did that?*

'Zara is the business head of the restaurant as well as working a few shifts each week. Our mum loves being grandma to the children and babysits every chance she gets. And I work with people and make concoctions like this. Win win.'

Ivy carefully put the glass onto a flat piece of ground and stood, acutely aware of Leo watching her with a slightly puzzled expression. A gentle breeze blew off the sea, intensifying the saltiness in the air. Everything felt good. Normal. As if nothing had changed from the last time she and Leo had sat here.

Except... her father was a hero to the family he'd once shattered.

'Ivy?'

*Rain sleeting. Two cars. One on the wrong side of the road, facing the wrong way. The other on its side in a ditch. Noise. Chaos. Screaming. So much screaming. A teenaged girl standing on the side of the road. Shivering. Soaked through. Ivy doesn't know her but she gives her the rain jacket she'd thrown on before she left the house. Dad is there and he's yelling for help, standing on the car on its side. He jumps down and there's a smashing sound and he disappears into the front of the car.*

'Ivy, I need you to talk to me.'

With a jolt, Ivy stopped walking. Her feet were wet. She was knee-deep in the sea and Leo was beside her.

'How did I get here?'

Leo took her hand. 'Come on. Back to the tree, please.'

She went with him, gripping his fingers as if letting go would send her straight back to that awful scene which was still vivid in her mind. At the tree she sank onto the ground and Leo opened a bottle of water and pressed it into her hands, squatting in front of her.

'Why do you look so worried?' she asked.

'Er... because one minute we were talking and then you started to walk straight toward the ocean. Not a word why and you didn't respond to me or deviate. I was about to pick you up when you came back. Has this happened before?'

'A couple of times.'

'Ivy!'

'They are memories which just appear without notice. At least, I think they are. But they can't be because I wasn't there so how can I remember?' Tears began to well in her eyes. 'And I can't talk to you about it.'

'You can talk to me about anything. You've always been able to.' Leo dug around in the bag and found a handful of paper napkins. Taking one, he touched Ivy's cheeks where errant tears had fallen. 'I'm not going to pretend I understand why you left me. We loved each other completely. To the depths of our souls.' He repeated the process with a second napkin. 'I have so many questions. And if you never love me again then I will learn to live with that as well, but for goodness' sake, Ivy, you can talk to me about what just happened now.' He leaned back a bit to inspect his handiwork. 'Even if it is about Gabe. And the crash.'

'What makes you think that?'

'Because you told me from the beginning that you were in bed and slept through the crash. Jody was there. Gabe was there, clearly. But not you. And you just said the memories can't be real because you weren't there. But if they're not your memories then what are they?'

'Oh.'

'Oh. So, are you going to share or do I phone my friend who *is* a doctor and see if she can see you for a check-up?'

While Leo packed up the picnic, Ivy finished drinking the water, her eyes on him the whole time. Had she misheard him say something about if she never loved him again, he would learn to live with it? Why would he even talk about her loving him when he wanted to move on?

'Ready?'

He held out his hand and again, she took it. But once they were walking toward the house, she slipped her fingers out of his. It wasn't right to touch him when there was a world of pain between them. She was being selfish to draw on his strength that way.

'These memories, Ivy. Are they new?'

'Yes. Being back here is difficult on many levels,' she said. 'One being the obvious fallout from the car crash. There's lots of genuine memories about growing up here, and those last two years, even stuff about Dad, and not all is bad.'

'I'd hope not!'

'I wasn't even factoring you into that, but you were the shining light in my life, Leo. The main reason I first decided to stay in Australia. I can't pretend otherwise. I won't pretend otherwise.' Ivy stopped, her head down. 'I shall never forgive myself for leaving the way I did. Not ever.'

'But *I* forgive you.'

Her eyes shot up to meet his. He was being genuine, even though his eyes had worry wrinkles as he gazed at her. 'There's the same look as earlier. Pretty sure I used up all the napkins so if you need to cry, you'll have to use my T-shirt to mop it up.'

Unsure if that was helping or making it worse, Ivy dug deep. The silly crying wasn't her at all. Not on any level. She'd curated her cloak of calmness long ago and had no idea why it was so hard to keep it in place today. Maybe talking would reinstall it.

'Sometimes I don't know where to begin and being back here is messing with my emotions and I hate that. I truly do.'

He smiled, a broad grin, and then his arm was around her shoulders and they were walking again. 'Good thing I'm here. Emotions are a bartender's specialty.'

# TWENTY-TWO

They were in the house for a few minutes so Ivy could freshen up and they could both get more bottled water. She'd shaken her head at her reflection in the bathroom mirror, disappointed with her lack of control, let alone the bizarre flashback, or whatever it was. How could that happen when she was with Leo, of all people?

'Sure you want to walk? We can sit for a while.' Leo still had worry lines.

'I'm fine. Walking will clear my head. As long as you can keep up.'

His response was a muffled chortle.

She locked up again. 'If you hear Jody's car, let me know. I've got the only set of keys. Well, apart from the stolen one.'

'Jody's car will announce itself from its colour. I'd never have picked her as owning a bright yellow Mini.'

'Or having short, silver hair.'

'Not even being far too thin to be healthy.'

Ivy agreed. 'She is. But it's all self-inflicted. I think her default diet consists of kale, yoghurt, and wine. Plenty of the latter. Can we go this way?' Without waiting, she took a left turn from the front of the house.

'Where are we going? And why?'

*Excellent questions. I know the first. No idea about the second.*

'Have you ever seen the whole property? Or as much as can be seen, given the undulations and trees and stuff.'

They walked briskly up the hill, past the garage and then the stone hut. Ivy knew there was a special spot even higher and as the path narrowed and became steep, she powered on. This was one of her favourite parts of Fairview.

The view was stunning, with the ocean expanding out forever beyond the roof of the house. The road to Rivers End was only a few metres behind them but thanks to a boundary of thick bushes, few traffic sounds intruded.

'Wow. This would be a nice place for a bench,' Leo said. 'Imagine sitting up here as the sun sets. Glass of a nice beverage. Nothing but good company and scenery.'

It sounded just about perfect.

'How I've missed the ocean. The Southern Ocean,' Ivy said softly.

'Do you live in London?'

'Walthamstow. It's nice, actually, it's lovely with street markets and easy access to wherever I happen to be working. I used to run a Covid ward but changed direction. Now I work for a nursing agency specialising in elderly patients so get sent all over London. But this? This is where I have always yearned to be. As a child and teen I would grow impatient as the chill of winter turned the days ever shorter, knowing soon Jody and I had our wonderful trip ahead. And we got to have two summers each year.' Ivy swallowed to force down a lump in her throat. This had always been where her heart belonged.

Leo was closer now, their shoulders brushing against each

other, sending sparks of yearning through Ivy. She should move. She didn't.

'Everywhere I look I see the past. I hear the music from the piano and the laughter and singing when a dozen guests and Dad and us girls would be in the living room until the small hours. I see Fairview lit up like it is the fanciest house in the world. I imagine that I'll turn a corner and Dad will have his arms open, ready to welcome me back.'

She drew in a deep sigh and focused on the tension leaving her body as she breathed out. It only helped a bit. 'Are you sure you're not a therapist, the way you've got me talking so much?' Ivy half-laughed. 'It might come in handy at the moment. Between these silly flashbacks and the odd things I've found, I need all the help available.'

'Odd things?'

'The intruder, for one. But there's so much more and I'm doubting what I know about my father. About Fairview. Even about his confession.'

Ivy hadn't meant to say that last bit. She hadn't even realised until it left her mouth that it was on her list of puzzles to solve, but so much wasn't adding up about that night, and the sudden confession from Dad two years later.

'Gabe confessed, Ivy.' Leo got up and wandered a couple of feet away, both hands pushing the hair back from his eyes as he stared at the ocean. 'He had us all believing him, even feeling sorry for him because his car killed my great-aunt and he blamed himself for not locking it up. He was so convincing. And while she lost her life, his kept getting better as Fairview grew in popularity. He had you living with him, which he loved. Friends, guests, money. I got on so well with him. I trusted him, Ivy.'

He turned back and dropped his hands, his words bitter.

'We were all fooled. My family. The town folk. You and Jody. Two years of fooling us, but if he'd been honest from the start, we'd all have begun healing sooner instead of wasting all that time.'

Stomach lurching, Ivy got to her feet. 'And there'd have been no us, would there?'

Leo frowned, confused.

'Had he been honest that night and said he'd been the driver, then you would never have wanted to see me again.'

'Of course I would have.'

'Don't be ridiculous! Look at what happened when he did come clean, Leo. The fury directed at him was deserved. But Jody and I were right in the middle of it all. Particularly me because I'd lived at Fairview the whole time and was known as his manager in training. Do you have any idea what happened?'

Leo stepped forward and Ivy stepped back, her hands up as if to keep a distance between them.

'Word got out even before Dad was arrested. For some reason the police officer didn't hold him after the confession... he was young and probably had no idea what to do. But in the day or two between confession and arrest, the phone rang constantly with media and abusive anonymous callers. The gate was painted with awful words. Overnight, stones and eggs were thrown at the house and we were too afraid to go out and stop them.' Ivy's whole body was shaking and her legs were barely holding her up. 'Then he was arrested and Jody and I were in shock. Our whole world crumbled from under us. We'd trusted him, Leo. He's our father and we'd believed him.'

'Ivy, I've never doubted you.'

'But why not, when everyone else did? There was a news report which interviewed people on the street for their opinion and all of them said I must have known. These were locals, Leo, people I knew. My car was spray-painted with the word "shame" and you know what? It was all I felt. Dad was gone. Fairview Retreat had cancellations coming in hourly. I didn't feel safe and I believed it too, that I should have known Dad was the driver. Of course I felt shame. They were right to use that word.'

Everything was falling apart again. Ivy's heart was breaking afresh.

'So you see, Leo, if even I believed I was almost as guilty as Dad, then why would you have stayed with me?'

There were tears in Leo's eyes and Ivy couldn't bear it any longer. She turned and sprinted away.

Ivy got as far as the first bend before coming to a sudden stop. Running away was all she'd done for the past ten years and it wasn't working out as a long-term solution.

She about-turned and walked back steadily.

Leo hadn't moved.

'See what I mean about messed-up emotions?' She tried and failed to smile. At least her voice was calm again. 'Running away isn't all it's cracked up to be.'

His hand stretched out and Ivy sighed deeply, then took it.

'My turn to talk?'

She nodded, steeling herself not to flee again if she didn't like what he had to say.

'I had no idea it was so bad for you and I'd like to have a few choice words with anyone who behaved so disgracefully toward you and Jody. We'd got news of Gabe's confession before his arrest as well and it came directly from the police officer, who was a terrible gossip and lost his job over the handling of the whole thing, going back to the night of the crash.'

'He did?'

'Our family were in shock, Ivy. Mum in particular as Jean was her auntie and it brought everything back in force. She needed hospitalisation for a few days because it affected her heart. So while the rest of the town was reacting to the news, we were panicking about Mum and taking shifts at the hospital in Green Bay.'

Somehow through all of her outpouring of words and feelings, Ivy's eyes had stayed dry, but now, she burst into tears.

'Oh, Ivy Maeve...'

Leo pulled her against him and held her so tightly she could barely breathe. The familiar scent of him surrounded her and her body relaxed and the tears dried up. He was rubbing her back and making comforting sounds and she never wanted to leave this safe haven.

'Mum recovered. She's actually in good health again and while Zara might take a while to move past her protectiveness of me, Mum says she'd love to see you.'

Surprised, Ivy stepped back, out of his arms. 'She did?'

'She did. But *none* of my family thought for a minute you or Jody knew Gabe was the driver. As soon as Mum was out of danger, I came to Fairview. I'd tried to call both your mobile and the landline from the hospital and got no answer.'

'We stopped answering the landline after the first day. And I turned off my phone once the abusive calls began. It was only when I landed at Heathrow that I turned it on and saw you'd rung a few times and by then it was too late.' Ivy shook her head. 'I did run. I feel there's something I can't remember about the night of the crash but maybe my subconscious knew and that added to the need to leave Australia.'

'Well, you're here now. Are you staying?'

The question was unexpected and Leo's gaze unsettling.

'I... I truly don't know. I intended to be here for a few weeks then go back to my life in England.'

'But?'

'Jody, and Fairview and Rivers End and... other factors, are urging me to reconsider.'

'Then I need to ask something important. I probably should

have asked earlier, in hindsight. Is there a Mister Ivy? Or a potential one?'

With a sudden smile which came from nowhere, she shook her head. 'No Mister Ivy.'

He smiled. His free, joyful, Leo smile.

'Shall we get out of the sun? Your skin is getting quite pink.'

*Not so much from the sun.*

They began down the path and when they reached a little grove of trees overlooking the back of Fairview, Leo stopped them both with a touch of his hand on her shoulder. She turned to him, surprised at the seriousness on his face.

'I don't want to lose you again, Ivy. I'm not asking you to choose me over your life in England or any such thing but I'd like to spend more time with you. While you are here. If that's okay.'

'I'm a different person now.'

'Not in the ways that matter. Would you think about it?'

'Yes.'

There was a subtle change in the air between them, or maybe Ivy's imagination was heightened. But her heart felt a little lighter.

'Whatever is that in the grass?' Leo pointed to the ground behind Fairview.

'Oh. I forgot to put that away. That's the ladder used by whoever broke into the library.'

'And you think it's the same person you saw hanging around?'

'Yes. Oh, can I show you something?'


'I'd say the battery is well and truly dead. Not just flat, but having being left untouched for at least ten years has probably stuffed it.'

Leo had gone over the motorcycle and tried to start it.

'Quite a beauty and in such good shape. Other than the battery. But you know nothing about it?'

'Nothing. Jody and I are going to go through Dad's desk in the hope of finding a receipt or some clue about its origin. I guess we could do a search on the number plate but it hasn't felt like a priority.'

'Get Mick Hammond to do it.'

'I did mention it to him the other day but nothing came of it.'

Leo covered the motorcycle. 'He might take it more seriously if you tell him there's a chance the person who broke in was trying to steal this.'

Ivy locked the garage after them and they walked down to the house. 'There's more than just this mystery though. I found an envelope filled with letters hidden behind a book in the library. On the very top shelf, which was too high to reach without the rolling ladder. They were in a cupboard which the thief didn't find.'

'Hang on... this person climbed a ladder to the library window, broke the glass and lock, came inside, trashed most of the library. They've then gone downstairs where Mary had left a set of keys and removed the only one which was duplicated.'

'Correct.'

'The key belonged to the garage and the same person – we'll assume for now – lets themselves in and tries to steal a motorcycle which has mysteriously appeared sometime in the last ten years?' Leo grinned. 'When you said there were odd things going on, I hadn't expected all of this!'

'The letters? Jody and I began to read them but we haven't finished. They come from a woman from Dad's past. Like, distant past. The 1970s. A love affair while she was engaged then married to someone else.'

'No way!'

'Oh, yes. And our current theory is that those letters are

what this person was looking for in the library, that they are either related to the woman or have been hired by her to remove what might be damaging history. Would you take a look at them? There aren't many names mentioned and she signs herself "your angel" which makes it tricky, but I'd love your take on it all.'

Jody drove in while Leo was reading the fourth or fifth letter. Ivy opened the front door, happy to see her sister more relaxed and smiling, and carrying a shopping bag.

'I found the best little boutique in Port Fairy. So many nice things and even something for you.'

'Thank you! Leo's here.'

'Still? Okay, I'll go upstairs for a bit.'

'Come and have something to drink, please?'

Jody paused at the kitchen doorway, lowering her bag onto the ground as she glared at Leo. 'Why are you reading those?'

He looked up.

'I thought we could get a different perspective with him looking at them. Come and sit, Jody.'

Instead, she stalked in and poured a glass of wine.

'Don't you think we need to get to the bottom of these letters?'

Jody perched on a chair. 'All it will lead to is upset and probably revisiting times which are none of our business. Particularly yours, Leo. Last time I checked you are not part of this family.'

'Jody!' Ivy was shocked. 'Leo is just helping.'

'This is personal, private information. He shouldn't be reading those letters and you should have known better than to bring him into this.'

'Fair enough, Jody. No harm was meant and Ivy only has everyone's best interests at heart.' Leo was calm.

Instead of it defusing the tension, Jody glowered at him.

'You *would* stand up for her. Even after she left without a word, you were endlessly understanding and just about ready to pack up and follow her to England. Ivy needed to deal with her pain her way. And it was clear she didn't want to have contact with you.'

A cold wave washed over Ivy and her eyes moved from Jody to Leo.

His eyes were on Jody. 'Yes, I was prepared to go to England if Ivy needed me to go to her. But as you know I'd already phoned multiple times and if she didn't want to respond to my message as well, then that made it clear she had made up her mind to move on.'

'What... what message?' Ivy's voice came out croaky.

Jody jumped to her feet and grabbed her glass. 'Ancient history, Ivy. I'm going upstairs.'

*Oh no, you don't.*

'What message, Jody?'

After gulping a mouthful of wine, Jody lifted her chin. 'Leo gave me a note to send you because you wouldn't answer his calls. He actually wanted me to phone you and read it but what good would it have done, Ivy? You'd run away because you couldn't deal with what Dad did and nothing mattered but your feelings.' Her voice rose. 'I was left here to cope alone. Leo was left here with his family to care for. How was prolonging his heartache helping either of you?'

Leo dropped his head into his hands.

Ivy's hands were shaking. 'You took it upon yourself to decide not only what was best for me, but for Leo too? Oh, Jody.'

'Oh, Jody, nothing. I'm done with being the one holding on to half-memories and secrets and confidences.' Jody put down the glass. 'Why do you think I drink so much? Pain. Endless pain which is destroying me no matter how hard I try to block it all out. Therapy doesn't work. Nothing works!'

As Ivy stepped toward her, intending to put arms around her despite the anger burning inside, Jody picked up the glass again and threw it at the wall. It smashed and as Jody burst into tears and ran out, the wine streaked down the wall like blood.

# TWENTY-THREE

Caught between the need to throttle her sister or hold her tight until she calmed down again, Ivy did neither. She filled a bucket with water and liquid soap and while Leo used a dustpan to remove the shards of glass, Ivy cleaned the wall. Not a word passed between them as the mess was cleared.

It was only when Ivy poured the water down the sink that her eyes blurred and she gulped hard to stop the rising emotions. How long she stood there, bucket empty and steam around her from rinsing the sink with hot water, she didn't know, but then Leo was behind her, reaching past to turn off the tap then wrapping his arms around her waist. She leaned back against him and he tightened his hold, his chin on her shoulder and the sides of their faces touching.

'She's wrong, Ivy,' he whispered, his breath soft on her cheek. 'You weren't just thinking of yourself. You were protecting yourself and there's a whole world of difference.'

'I never got your message. I never knew.'

*How could she have done that? How could she play God with my life?*

'All this time... Oh Leo, you thought I'd deliberately cut ties to be cruel, turned my back on you. On what we shared. I had no idea you'd tried to reach me again and was so ashamed that I'd convinced myself you were best without me. I am so sorry. So sorry.'

Tears slid down her face and he must have felt them because he turned her in his arms and rocked her gently against him, using soothing sounds and whispering that it wasn't her doing. And yet it was.

'I need you to know.' Her voice was too muffled against him and she leaned back enough to lift her face, tears included, and properly look at him. 'All the way home I mourned leaving you, but I was self-aware enough to know that I desperately needed help dealing with what had happened with Dad. I battled with depression for so long.'

Leo's face was so serious, so sad. He kept brushing the tears away with his fingers as if it would help.

'Then Mum came here to get Jody. I'd abandoned my little sister in the middle of such a mess. No wonder she wouldn't pass anything on. How could I leave her alone like that?'

'Trauma. Flight response. Stop beating yourself up, Ivy.'

Stepping away from Leo to get tissues left her feeling suddenly alone, although he was so close.

'Ivy? I might go home.'

She swung around in the middle of drying her face. 'No. I mean, you don't have to. Not that I blame you because you've been treated so badly by Jody... by me. I'm sorry.'

He picked up his bag. 'Stop worrying about stuff like that. The past is gone and although hearing Jody say she didn't pass on my message was a bit of a shock, I should have worked it out for myself. You two need some time together.'

Leo reached for Ivy's hand and when she gripped his fingers, walked with her to the front door. And then he was disappearing into the night before she could say a word. The words she wanted to say but probably never would vanished with him.

The kettle boiled while Ivy gazed into the fridge. She had no interest in food but the need to comfort herself and stuff the feelings until they were deadened was rising.

'How was the picnic?'

Ivy jumped.

Jody was in the doorway. Her face was pale, other than streaks of mascara, and she didn't seem steady on her feet. Unless she had a stash of wine in her bedroom and had consumed a lot, something was wrong.

'Sit. You look ready to fall.'

'I can come in?'

She wasn't being smart. Her voice was as unsteady as her legs.

'Jody. Come and sit.'

Ivy closed the fridge door and returned to the kettle, which had finished boiling. 'Tea?'

'You don't need to pretend. Or be nice to me.' Jody flopped onto a chair. 'I just ruined your date.'

'It wasn't a date. I was going to bring you some tea and hope it didn't end up being thrown at me.'

Jody's eyes shot to the wall.

Nobody would know it was stained red so recently.

'My temper... sorry, Ivy.'

'Better than at my head, or Leo's.'

'Oh, my dear lord.' Jody crossed her arms on the table and dropped her head onto them. 'Kill me now.'

'Not happening, but a few coherent and honest answers would be good. One being why you haven't changed therapists.' Ivy carried two cups of tea over and placed one near Jody before taking hers to the opposite side of the kitchen table. 'First and most important is why you are so unsteady on your feet. How much have you had to drink?'

Jody straightened. 'Only the one sip before the unfortunate glass came to an untimely end.'

'That's next to nothing. Are you light-headed?'

'More... over-hungry.'

'When did you last eat?'

Jody's forehead wrinkled. 'Not since breakfast.'

'Good grief.'

Ivy hurried to the fridge and pulled out half a dozen ingredients. 'Give me five minutes.'

'I'm not hungry though.'

'You just said you are over-hungry.'

'Well, yes, but I'm kind of past it.'

'Tough. Sit and drink your tea.'

It was closer to fifteen minutes when Ivy put a bowl of stir-fried vegetables and noodles in front of Jody. 'Eat.'

'I don't think I can.'

'You are going to try.' Ivy collected cutlery and sat with her own bowl. 'And you were driving like this? Honestly, no wonder you're shaky and not yourself.'

The last words made Jody grin for a second. 'Nice way of telling me I just acted like a complete idiot in front of your boyfriend.'

'Well, he isn't that but yes, I'm being nice because what's the point of continuing the argument?'

'And I will.'

'Will what?'

'I'll find a new therapist.'

'That's good news. Would you try to eat a little? Please?' Ivy's eyes rested on Jody who picked up a fork.

'Is this how you get patients to do what you want? Stare at them with that nurse face until they crumble?'

'It works, doesn't it?'

Jody had a mouthful of carrot and baby corn so her answer was to roll her eyes.

'Good.'

The food went down quickly for both sisters and after washing up, Ivy scooped up the pile of letters.

'We need to finish this, Jodes. Leo took a look at the motorcycle and if the battery wasn't completely dead, the thief most likely would have taken it the other day.'

'But doesn't that mean stealing the key was the end game? She wanted the motorcycle and the library was a distraction?'

'That's why we're reading the rest of these now. Let's try and narrow down motives.'

They moved into the living room and took opposite ends of the sofa, sitting cross-legged and facing each other. As kids they'd do this when they wanted to talk or read and not be too far apart.

*Darling Gabriel,*

*How could a woman be any prouder?*

*You've given me what Joe couldn't. He always blamed me, saying I didn't pray enough or have faith. For a while I believed him. But after my doctor promised there was no reason I wouldn't conceive, it was clear it was Joe.*

*But none of that matters because Theresa-Louise is living proof of the love we share.*

*Our daughter.*

'Daughter?' Jody and Ivy exclaimed at the same moment and Ivy dropped the letter.

'But how?'

'I'm sure you know the basics, Jody.'

'Okay, so I know *how*, but this angel person is still married to another man. Right?'

'More importantly, Jody, I think we have a sister.'

They gazed at each other and then huge smiles crossed their faces.

'I wonder what she's like.'

'Our big sister.'

'Where is she now?'

'Does she know about us?' Jody asked.

'Probably not. But now we really do have to find out who Dad's angel is.'

*Today I brought her to meet you. Tiny and perfect and beautiful. She gazed at you with eyes so like yours. I still can barely believe she is real and yet this is our daughter. Seeing you hold her so tenderly makes it hard to accept what we agreed at the start.*

*How do I pretend she is Joe's child?*

*I would have named her Maeve Gabriela. Joe and my parents wore me down though, so Theresa-Louise she is, after his and my grandmothers. And I will bring her to see you at least each week. She'll know you as someone special in her life. She is a gift of love and joy.*

*There was no need for you be so generous, either, yet it is a part of you I adore so much and she will be thankful for the trust fund you've set up for her. When you told me it was so she could have the freedom to choose her future, I wept. I promise to raise her strong enough to rise above religion and family expectations.*

*Your angel.*

*August, 1981.*

'A trust fund? I guess Dad couldn't contribute to our sister's upbringing without it becoming public about their real relationship. And I'm glad she got something but it still isn't the same as her having her real dad, or us.' Ivy uncrossed her legs and stretched them out on the sofa and Jody did the same, their legs fitting against each other. 'Remember how our feet would barely reach the middle and we'd shuffle in and giggle our heads off playing footsies.'

'I remember you taking up too much space with all the notebooks you'd carry around.'

'Hang on, what about your books to read and occasional lumps of clay?'

Jody's hand covered her mouth and her eyes sparkled.

'And you'd hide whatever little sculpture you were making if you heard Dad's voice because this room was supposed to stay clean and tidy for the guests.'

'I'd forgotten. How funny though. I think I hid at least a couple somewhere in here which I never retrieved but I can't recall where.'

'We should go on a clay hunt. You didn't by any chance make any angel sculptures?' Ivy teased.

'Lots. My specialty. Let me see... there's the one in the safe which I still haven't seen but has its wings around its body, the one in the stone hut covering its face, there could be one wearing a—'

'I get the picture. Another letter?'

*Darling Gabriel,*

*My world is shattered and I know yours is as well.*

*All because of one word.*

*A word we should have anticipated because our daughter has spent as much time with you as with Joe. She only sees him on the weekends when he's back from his Melbourne job and he plays golf most Saturdays and Sundays are filled with church activities. So we should have seen it coming.*

*Theresa-Louise spoke her first word.*

*She called you 'Dadda'.*

*For a few seconds I was as excited and proud as you. Our little girl was speaking! But then I saw we had a huge problem ahead of us. Theresa-Louise will keep calling you that and once she speaks even more, she'll talk about you. Joe will work it out, sooner or later, and then what will happen?*

*I've never been afraid of him but even if he somehow forgives me, my father will not. I'll be exiled from everything I've known. And Theresa-Louise along with me. Our daughter will suffer terribly. Either Joe will take her from me or else she'll be ostracised from her extended family. And I know you would take us in, even marry me if I was able to divorce Joe under these circumstances, but at what cost?*

*I need to repeat what I said yesterday, while you held her for a while and told her, the way you always do, that you would love her forever. Gabriel, she needs to stay away now. Not grow up confused about who her father really is.*

*I know you think it is a rash decision, based on one word, and I will never forget the tears on your face as you begged me to leave Joe. I was tempted, Gabriel; we could hire the best solicitor money could find to protect me and our little girl.*

*But I have prayed on it.*

*The answer that comes to me is she is one of God's children and it is time for me to return to my marriage, heart, body and mind. I know how much pain this will cause you, I could double over from the loss of you. But we must protect Theresa-Louise. You must let us go.*

*This time I believe it will be forever.*

*This time, it's because I will not lose my daughter.*

C.

*February, 1983.*

'No. Oh, that can't be right!'

Jody took the paper from Ivy and while she read it, Ivy dabbed her eyes.

'Poor Dad.'

'What a cruel woman. How could she do such a terrible thing?' Jody handed the page back. 'I understand her wanting to protect her child's relationship with family and so on, but to completely cut her real father from her life rather than risk answering a few questions? Could she not have made up a reason the child was confused?'

'I guess that's why we've never known about Theresa-Louise. Dad was effectively only a donor to help his angel have the child her husband couldn't give her. The minute it put any heat on her, she fell back on her beliefs,' Ivy said.

'But why the cruel barb about "growing up confused about her real father"? Oh, Ivy.'

About to open the next letter, Ivy glanced up.

'*This* is why someone wants these.'

'I think you're right. There's so much more at stake than an illicit affair. This family seem wealthy, I guess there must be inheritances and reputation at risk.'

Alarm filled Jody's eyes and she jumped up. 'We need to check everything is locked. Come on. I'm putting my car in the garage.'

Everything was done under torchlight as although it was only just after six, low and heavy clouds had turned the sky to night.

Jody locked the Mini in the garage after both of them pulled the doors closed, locking them internally, then leaving through the side door. 'I'm so glad we changed the lock. I admit to feeling a bit nervous.'

Ivy was the same.

'Rivers End is pretty safe. The chances of this thief being here right now are slim, but let's do a quick check of each room and we'll draw all the curtains.'

'Maybe put up some barricades.'

In the gloom it was hard to tell if Jody was joking.

'Would you prefer to move in to the inn? Or we could see if there's space at Palmerston House. Just until we catch this intruder.'

'Hmm. Always wanted to stay in Palmerston House but no. As gorgeous as our Melbourne apartment is, the back fire door of the building opens at the very end of a dark and narrow alley. There is colourful graffiti and uneven cobblestones and on the opposite side of the fire door is a nightclub. One which has a dubious reputation. So I should be fine for a night or two.'

Back in the house, the sisters moved from room to room, checking and double-checking every window and closing curtains. It gave the house an air of privacy which was kind of nice.

'All we need now is a roaring fire.'

'And the piano playing,' Jody added. 'Well, maybe Dad playing because I still can only manage chopsticks. But we could sing.'

'Sing what though?'

'Dunno. Something beautiful. Touching.'

*The fireplace warmed the room and music filled the air. At the piano, Dad swayed back and forward as he did when he played a piece he particularly loved. His eyes were on the guest who'd requested the song. Her hair was long and dark and her voice was pure and strong, singing 'The Air That I Breathe'.*

'You've disappeared again, Ivy.'

'Ouch!'

'Sorry.'

'You are not. Don't pinch me.'

'Then don't go all vacant like that again or I'll book you in to see a doctor.'

Ivy smirked. 'Too late. Leo already offered.'

'Why?'

'I had a memory during our picnic. Of all times. Ended up in the sea with him threatening to carry me out.'

Jody's eyes widened. She actually looked concerned and Ivy took pity on her.

'Look, being back here is definitely sparking off some memories but most of them are pretty inoffensive. That one just now? I saw Dad playing and a woman singing that song, "The Air That I Breathe".'

'Good grief, how old is that?' Jody pulled her phone from a pocket and did a search. 'Of course it is.'

'What?'

'I'm going to have a glass of wine.'

# TWENTY-FOUR

Ivy followed Jody into the kitchen. 'You know I can look it up. My phone is upstairs charging but it will take all of—'

'Fine. 1974.'

'Oh goodness. Close enough to 1973.'

Jody opened the cupboard to get a glass out.

'I'll have one, thanks.'

'Cranberry?'

'Wine.'

*Just for once.*

Although Jody raised her eyebrows, she poured two glasses of red wine and handed one to Ivy. 'Cheers.'

'Oh, I think we need a serious toast. How about... to the 1970s and all the bizarre fallout.'

'Sure.' Jody tapped her glass against Ivy's. 'I'll drink to anything. Are we still reading?'

They settled on the sofa as before and Ivy tasted the wine. She'd tried vodka as a teen at a party, which was enough to put her off drinking for ages, and after Dad's crash lost interest even more. Over the years that changed a little and if she knew there was no chance she'd need to drive, on occasion she'd have a small glass of wine. But nobody really knew that because it was so rare.

'It's nice, Jody. Do you want to read the next one?'

Jody put her own glass onto a coffee table and reached for the pile. 'Oh. This one is different! Look at the paper. Fairview letterhead... and Dad's writing.'

*My angel,*

*Something wonderful has happened. I believe serendipity was involved and so will you, should you read this one day. Or, the day may come in the distant future when you will be a friend rather than my one true love, and sit with me and my own family, with Theresa-Louise acknowledged as mine, and we can speak of the past with fondness.*

*I was on Rivers End beach on a cold and dismal day, walking with my head down, thinking about you and our child. Although I have watched her grow from a distance, my heart is empty from not being in her life. I would still do anything to protect her – and you – but lately I've been aware of loneliness like never before. On this particular day there were no guests at Fairview for once and the lack of company had begun to mess with my head.*

*When I was almost at the far end of the beach, I happened to glance up and I saw her.*

*A young woman, drenched to the bone, splashing in the waves. And it was high tide so every wave was different. Some would cover her toes and others her knees and she'd shriek with laughter and run to the dry sand. Not that anything was dry under the drizzle from a grey sky. She'd left a huge backpack near the cliff and wore, of all things, a pair of shorts and a thick jumper.*

*I began to laugh with her and she noticed me, hesitating at first
but then when I drew closer, she gave me a beautiful smile and I
swear I could feel my heart come alive again in my chest.*

*When she came out of the sea she was shivering, not unexpect-
edly, so I asked where she was staying and offered to carry her
backpack. Would you believe she had nowhere to stay. Her name
is Brenda and she is English and here for an adventure. She was
on a bus and decided that Rivers End sounded like a place she
needed to visit, so alighted with no accommodation or plans.*

*She accepted my offer of a night or two in one of the cottages and
we walked back to Fairview, taking the stone steps to the top of
the cliff and then along the road and down the driveway. I
carried her backpack, which was so heavy that I couldn't believe
such a petite person could manage it, yet she had. All around
Australia. I think she was humouring me about it which was
incredibly cute.*

*That was two weeks ago and she's still here. I refuse her daily
offers of payment and she quietly goes into the kitchen and bakes
extraordinary pastries for my guests. We walk and talk and
although she is so young, her heart is sublime and she's smart. Is
it possible that I've been sent a second angel?*

*Believe me, I will always love you and we are bonded on a level
beyond this dimension. But if I truly cannot share any part of
your life, and that of our daughter, then I refuse to feel guilty
about my feelings for Brenda.*

*Be happy for me. If she will have me, I intend to propose
marriage and at this point in my life, begin again.*

*Gabe. 1990.*

Jody's face was glowing with happiness as she folded the letter. 'He *did* love Mum. He was swept away by her and she was the same and didn't she sound so wonderful?'

'Not at all like the mother I know!' Ivy was smiling. 'She never goes in the sea and it's hard to imagine her backpacking and deliberately being out in the rain.'

'I miss her so much, Ivy.'

'And she misses you. And she's as stubborn as you are so I just hope one of you will make a step toward healing. Look at us, Jody. We haven't got it all right yet but don't you feel like me? That we are finally sisters again?'

The answer was a not-too-gentle kick on her ankle from Jody.

'First pinching and then kicking.'

'Sister stuff.'

'When we find our big sister I'm going to warn her about your toddler tendencies. Good thing you're out of nappies at last.'

Jody had just taken a mouthful of wine and had to swallow fast to avoid spitting it out.

'I rest my case. There's a dribble of wine on your chin if you'd like me to find a bib.' Ivy was having too much fun. 'Or I can get you a straw.'

'Enough. Anyway, there's another one from Dad.'

*My angel,*

*All the good and light and joy in my life is gone forever.*

*Brenda has left me, ended our marriage, and taken Ivy and Jody to live with her in England. My youngest girls. The ones I was able to raise with their mother.*

*Now I have a daughter I am not permitted to call my own and two more who I may never see again.*

*Her leaving is my fault entirely. I didn't see the signs, although in hindsight they were obvious. She longed to visit her family and begged me to make time for us to go to the other side of the world. I promised we would go. I told her I would find a way to leave Fairview for a few weeks in the hands of one of my staff, once I trained them sufficiently. But I let the months slip by without taking any such action.*

*I'd become so comfortable with our marriage. Brenda loved decorating, and planned, then oversaw the refurbishment of the cottages. She was a wonderful baker of bread and sweet goods and always cared for the guests as much as I. So I believed she loved Fairview every bit as much as I do.*

*But she became quiet, withdrawn. I thought she was worried about Ivy beginning school soon. She ran up large phone bills talking to her parents. And when she asked me, once again, when we would visit them, I made more promises.*

*This time was the last time.*

*Until my dying day I will remember her finding me in the kitchen where I was making an early morning coffee. She kissed me. Passionately. And then calmly said that although she loved me, she had lost faith in me and was taking the girls and leaving. I was so surprised that I thought she meant for the holiday. Without me. And my heart lifted because I suddenly realised I'd never wanted to go.*

*I misunderstood. She left a week later with Ivy and Jody, taking the bus into Melbourne. She refused to let me drive them and had*

*already sent several boxes of the children's possessions ahead.
There was nothing I could do. She said she'll bring them for
visits and that I'm welcome to go and see them any time. But will
either of us do that?*

*For months I sank into despair but then I spoke to Ivy and Jody
by phone and they sounded happy. So how could I grieve their
departure?*

*Theresa-Louise came to Fairview just after Christmas. She asked
if Ivy and Jody were home as she'd not seen them on Rivers End
beach for a while. I knew you'd relaxed your stance about her not
meeting my daughters and that they'd played together now and
then. When I explained their mother had returned to England
and taken them, she began to cry. I hadn't realised how close she
was to them and it did occur to me that you might have told her
the truth. That they are her half-sisters. She's almost sixteen now
and I would understand you sharing our secret. But when I
asked her why she cried she said they were like little sisters. Not a
mention of them being her real ones. As much as I wanted to tell
her the truth, I kept the secret.*

*Just as I began to settle into a life without my family and the days
became happier, you shattered my soul.*

*When I saw you wandering along the beach I couldn't believe
my eyes. You must have heard of my great loss and come to renew
our connection. Oh, my angel... you turned and I saw. You are
pregnant, all these years after our daughter was born. And you
told me the child is your husband's, a miracle baby. A gift
from God.*

*I stood in disbelief as you said this was goodbye for good.*

*It isn't in my heart to accept that.*

*Our love will survive every test it encounters.*

*With all my heart,*

*Gabriel, February 1998.*

'And as quickly as he married Mum, she was gone. And us. *And* it was his fault,' Ivy said. 'Not even his angel wanted to be with him.'

'Well, she was pregnant by her husband. And it would have been a bit risky being pregnant because she must have been in her mid-forties, if my calculations are correct,' Jody said.

'She sounds so religious. Did he quote her as saying God had given her a gift? Oh, and what was the bit about Theresa-Louise again?'

Reopening the sheet of paper, Jody glanced down until she found the spot. 'She came looking for us and Dad explained that we'd moved to England. This made her cry and she said we were like little sisters to her.' She looked up. 'Dad wouldn't betray his angel even at the expense of his three daughters.'

It wasn't fair. They had a sister who had loved them and didn't even know they were her siblings.

'What a tangle of lies and deceptions between Dad and this woman. It does seem as though he was faithful to Mum though and for that, I'm grateful,' Ivy said.

'Me too. So is this woman still alive and still keeping secrets? She must be more than seventy, so I can't imagine her shimmying up ladders.'

Ivy smiled at the thought. 'True. But now we know she has two daughters. Theresa-Louise – what a mouthful of a name for a child – was born in 1981, so is a fair bit older than the woman I chased to the beach from what I saw, anyway. But the second child was born in 1998 and is twenty-seven or twenty-eight. She is officially my chief suspect.'

Jody clapped her hands. 'Oh I do love solving a puzzle! Now we just have to find out what her name is and where she lives and then pay her a visit.'

'Er... no. No to the last bit. It is up to the police to talk to her.'

'But then we lose the chance to find out more. Like the name of her mother and sister, who is *our* sister.'

'Seriously, Jody, if this young woman has tried to steal the letters, a key, and maybe the motorcycle, do you think she'll welcome us into her house, make us a cup of tea, and sit down for a good old gossip about her mum?'

'Has anyone told you lately that you are no fun?'

'Only you. Is that the last letter?'

Jody nodded. 'Looks like the angel gets the final word.'

*My darling Gabriel,*

*Life continues to surprise me. Even in my fifties, I am amazed by its twists and turns but for the first time, I doubt God has the influence – or more accurately – the interest, in the small details of our lives the way I used to believe.*

*My God-fearing husband, the one I stayed with out of loyalty for all of these years, more than half of my life, has been cheating on me for decades.*

*His employment in Melbourne ended recently and he decided to retire early. I began to overhear strange phone calls at odd hours. Then a woman stopped me in the street and told me to watch him. She'd heard rumours. I confronted him and he admitted everything. Several long-term lovers beginning during our engagement! Months before you and I met and if only I'd known... but I can't change the past.*

*He didn't love any of them, he says. He calls it a sin of the flesh and that he has certain unusual tastes which he was ashamed to speak of. He begged forgiveness. I was sickened to my soul and ran from the house in the storm last night and came here.*

*Thank you for your kindness last night when you found me soaked through at your front door, I know it is more than I deserve. What if you'd sent me away, dear Gabriel? But without even one question, you ran me a hot bath and brought me a glass of brandy to help me stop shivering. While I warmed up, you lit the fireplace in your bedroom and then wrapped me in your dressing gown.*

*I was torn between disgust and my own guilt. Because we have loved each other forever. We have a daughter. We kept a lie from Joe. But you promised me there is no similarity. What he did was purely carnal. What we have is celestial.*

*There is no more reason for us to not be together. I'll never divorce Joe with Rachel being so young, but now I have a new freedom because if he dares to interfere with our time, I will tell the world what he did. He'll lose his place in the church. And Joe isn't entirely devoid of intelligence.*

*The doubts and fears and worries drained away and we finally spoke of the years we've missed and the ones ahead we refuse to miss.*

*And so here we are. Us again.*

*Your angel, forever.*

*October, 2001.*

Ivy and Jody finished their wine and then looked at each. The letters were between them, all read.

'It's kind of sad, really. A genuine love story but one punctuated by roadblocks and detours when all along, had she known about Joe's true nature, Dad might have married her at the beginning.'

Jody turned to put her feet on the ground. 'There'd be no us in that case. Not three sisters, plus our sister's sister. Rachel – did you pick up that's her name?'

'I did. But I'm confused, do you think they split up yet again? Because we'd have met her, surely. Unless she just stayed away each summer holidays? There are no more letters so we need to find another way to fill in the years between 2001 and 2012.'

'Are you sure you don't know her?' Jody stood and collected both wine glasses. 'When you lived here for two years she'd have to have made an appearance if they were together. Even sneaking up to the stone hut would have been noticeable at some point!'

*The kitchen late in the evening.*

*Dad appeared, wiping his forehead with a handkerchief. His hair was covered with raindrops.*

*He made small talk and took a plate of leftovers out of the fridge then added fruit.*

*He said he was starving but he would never eat so much in one meal.*

*When Ivy was going up the stairs she glanced back when she heard the front door close. The kitchen light was off.*

'Would we have noticed though? Think about that summer in 2012, Jodes. We spent a lot of time away from the house. That was when we knew Sadie and her friends as well as met Leo and his family. And the following two years I was so busy.

Three days a week I was attending classes for my arts degree, and I was learning about running Fairview, and seeing Leo almost every day. I guess if someone wants to hide something enough, they'll find a way.' Ivy picked up the pile of letters. 'Case in point.'

Jody yawned and a moment later, so did Ivy.

'On that note, I'm going to go to bed, big sis – although now you are middle sister. How funny. Shall we revisit this tomorrow?'

*Or set the letters alight.*

At the top of the stairs, Ivy and Jody headed for their respective bedrooms and then, without a word, both turned and embraced each other. The hug was long and warm and overdue and when they parted, each smiling, some of the cloud had lifted.

# TWENTY-FIVE

Once again, Ivy was up before dawn but this time she was in the garage rather than walking along a beach.

Sleep hadn't come easily. Partly because of the roller-coaster of emotions from the day, and partly because her mind wouldn't stop going over the letters. It was as though she and Jody were on the edge of a huge discovery but there was a sheer drop between them and the final clue.

She'd opened both the big doors and as the sky slowly lightened she was dragging the signpost out, after finding a pair of gloves to avoid splinters. It was a bit tricky getting it past the tractor then the motorcycle and Mini, but once she was outside things got easier. The end with the signs wasn't as heavy as she'd imagined but still, by the time she reached the spot where she thought it once stood, Ivy was panting.

For a while she poked around the ground with her feet then returned to the garage for a shovel. That proved more successful and she cleared a small area around a narrow concrete hole.

The signpost had stood here for as long as Ivy could recall but she couldn't remember when she'd last seen it. Certainly she hadn't been around when it was removed and hidden away in the garage.

Ivy manoeuvred the base of the post until it touched the concrete hole, then tried to lift the end with the signage. It was long and bulky and difficult to manage and impossible on her own and she gave up after a few attempts. The sun wasn't far away now, with the sky behind the house a pretty mix of light pink and dark blue. There was just enough light to read each of the signs.

*Fairview House*

*Rivers End*

*Melbourne*

*Warrnambool*

*Darwin*

*Tasmania*

*Angel's Beach*

The inclusion of Darwin, the capital of the Northern Territory close to four thousand kilometres away, and Tasmania, less than five hundred but across a vast stretch of ocean, were a source of amusement for visitors. Warrnambool – which was a major town in the region and an easy enough drive away – was understandable, as were Melbourne and Rivers End.

'So this *is* Angel's Beach?' Ivy thought the sign pointed in the direction of the sea but until Jody helped her get the post into position it was a guess.

She returned the shovel to the garage and closed and locked

the doors. As the first rays of sun touched the top of the house, her eyes turned to the path leading toward the stone hut.

Another mystery. Dad had created a private place to be with the woman in the letters. His angel. C. There'd been music from 1973 – the year they'd met. Candles. Wine. A romantic four-poster bed.

Ivy suddenly shivered and abruptly walked in the opposite direction. Thinking about one's parent in a... romantic situation... wasn't pleasant. There was no logic behind her reaction. She was a nurse. And not altogether inexperienced with men but her heart always blocked the potential of a relationship. No, this was purely a knee-jerk response which most people had if they thought too much about whatever might have gone on between their parents.

At the front door she paused before going inside. Maybe she had this all wrong. The stone hut could have been a private place for her own parents to spend time away from the day-to-day life of running the artists' retreat and having two little girls hanging around. This might have nothing to do with an illicit affair between Gabe and a married woman.

Deep down, Ivy knew it wasn't true. Dad's angel was the love of his life. The same way Leo was the love of hers.


Jody cooked breakfast, insisting Ivy sit and talk to her rather than help. The envelope with the letters was on the table next to the angel from the safe. There wasn't much conversation as Jody was intent on poaching the eggs perfectly, sautéing English spinach, and whisking up a hollandaise sauce. Ivy watched with initial surprise and then admiration of the confident cook her sister had become. She even toasted some sourdough bread and then presented café quality Eggs Florentine.

'This looks delicious.'

'I hope so! A couple of years ago Aaron asked what I

wanted for a birthday and when I said cooking classes, he hooked me up with one of Melbourne's best chefs. Got to work alongside him in a hatted restaurant in Southbank for a few days but it was getting a handle on breakfasts which was the most fun.'

*How much money do you have?*

The meal was every bit as scrumptious as it looked, and silence reigned until both plates were empty.

'Thank you, Jody. I haven't eaten such a nice breakfast in ages.'

Jody's smile was wide and genuine and reminded Ivy how much praise meant to her little sister.

'You could do that professionally.'

'Nah. Not my thing. It isn't like I cook a lot but once a week, Aaron and I try to have a day together, no matter what else is going on. I'll do breakfast. We go out for lunch. Then he cooks dinner. In between a day of eating whatever food we fancy – including carbs – we catch up and talk and visit a museum or similar and dance around the apartment to music, and... well, you know.'

Jody blushed and she got up and collected the plates.

'If I lived in any city other than London, it would be Melbourne and I would probably love the eateries and laneways as much as you. But being here again reminds me how much I love the country life,' Ivy said.

'I really am sorry for being so unkind last night, particularly saying Leo wasn't family because he really is, in his own way. Not passing his message on was a terrible thing and I can't excuse it. But I wish I had told you because then you might not have been so sad and lonely for all these years.' Tears glistened in Jody's eyes. 'Stay here in Rivers End. If there's any chance to be with Leo then take it, because the two of you are made for each other and always were.'

Ivy had no words. Not about Leo or staying here. Her brain

hurt every time she tried to think about the possibilities and it was better left alone. At least for now.

'I forgive you. Honestly, I was so determined to run from Rivers End that I might not even have reached out if you had passed on his message. And I love you, Jody. Sisters matter and I don't ever want anything to come between us again.'

'Before we plan the day, would you mind helping me to get the signpost into the ground again?'

'I could use some exercise after that big breakfast. Give me a min and I'll put on better shoes.'

Ivy grinned as Jody's feet pounded up the stairs. Even as a kid she'd sounded like a herd of elephants running up and down them and somehow managed to find every creak and groan in the old boards.

She located the gloves she'd worn earlier and wandered outside into the sunshine.

'There you are!' Jody burst out of the house and caught up. 'As much as I hate the idea, shall we look for that motorcycle receipt today?'

'I'd like that. And a swim?'

Jody slipped an arm through Ivy's. 'And I would like *that*.'

Getting the post upright almost undid their good moods, with Jody at first refusing to lift the post even with the gloves but happy to boss her sister around with directions which weren't working. Eventually they set the post upright and then slid it into the concrete hole without resorting to calling each other names.

'Is it the right way?' Jody squinted at the signs, the sun in her eyes.

'No. There's the one pointing to the house so if we turn it a bit more... there we are.'

'But it's leaning, Ivy.'

'Only a tiny bit.'

'Lots.' Jody pushed it and it leaned the other way. 'For goodness' sake!'

Ivy had to laugh and it didn't help when Jody crossed her arms and pretended to stamp her foot, before grinning.

'It needs some more concrete or a shovel of dirt,' Ivy said. 'Easy to fix. But look.'

The sign saying *Angel's Beach* pointed directly to the sand only a couple of hundred metres away.

'I never heard it called anything. It was always just called the beach,' Jody frowned.

'Well, it doesn't have an official name, just the one Dad gave it in honour of his angel. Remember, in the letter she wrote?'

'I remember. But we might be wrong. What if it is somewhere on an island out there?'

Ivy pulled out her phone and brought up a map of the region. 'Not unless it is one of those magical moving islands.' She showed Jody an expanse of ocean. 'Next stop Antarctica. It points too far to the right to be on King Island or Tasmania.'

They started walking toward the house.

Near the bench, Jody stopped and faced Ivy. 'Do you think it's possible to forget stuff in only ten years? Because the longer I'm here, the more little things come back to me and not all of it makes sense.'

Ivy nodded. 'I hadn't realised how much I'd forgotten, and you've seen me have these kind of blackouts which accompany a flashback, but I have to be remembering things which aren't even real. Probably hearing about some things gave me fake memories. Trauma. At least that's what my therapist said.'

'Yeah. Mine too. Coffee?'

'Lots of it. Did you leave the front door wide open?'

Jody frowned. 'No. It clicked shut after me. I didn't lock it though. Oh. Crap.' She grabbed Ivy's arm and dragged her a few steps away to whisper. 'What if the intruder's back?'

'In the house?' Ivy whispered back. 'Then we confront them.'

'Are you kidding? What if they're armed?'

'I'll call the police.'

'Nope. Nope you don't. We'll check. Carefully.'

Ivy's heartrate skyrocketed.

'I'll go around the back,' Jody whispered.

'We should go in together.'

The front door slammed shut.

'Go round the back!' Ivy yelled as she raced toward the closed door.

She heard Jody take off and in a few seconds had the front door open again. There, she paused, listening.

Silence.

Ivy inched along the hallway and peered into the kitchen. The envelope with the letters was gone.


There was a sound toward the back of the house, a key turning in a lock and then the familiar creak of the back door. The key turned again. It had to be Jody locking them in. All of them. After checking the living room, she moved back to the hallway and stood, listening. Not even a sound from Jody, so she sent her a text.

> They're somewhere in the house.

Her phone vibrated almost immediately.

> Where are you?

> Hallway. Can you see if the laundry door is locked?

She could have sworn she heard Jody groan and then hesitant footsteps in the direction of the laundry, which was the only other room with a door leading outside. Ivy messaged Leo.

> Hi. Sorry. We seem to have cornered the intruder. Maybe.
>
> Can you phone the police for me? Not in danger but trying to be quiet.

Except maybe they were in danger. A message from Jody.

> Locked. Shall I come to you?

> Yes. Check rooms as you do.

A minute later, Jody appeared around the side of the staircase. She held a closed umbrella in an attack-ready pose which would have made Ivy burst into laughter if things weren't so serious. Too many spy movies.

Leo messaged.

> Police coming. I'm on my way.
>
> Leave the house. Please.

> We're safe. Leaving now. Thanks.

With no time to consider if fibbing about the situation was a good plan, Ivy would deal with it later. For now she had a thief to find. Gesturing for Jody to follow her, Ivy moved to the kitchen door and when her sister caught up, she put her fingers to her lips in a 'shh' motion and then pointed to the table.

Jody's eyes widened as she registered the missing envelope and she clapped a hand over her mouth.

'We have to get them back,' Ivy whispered. 'Leo and police are coming, this is serious.'

'Then let's find them first. We need that envelope.'

'Shall we split up?'

'Not a chance,' Jody whispered.

'Go up or check the basement?'

A sudden creak directly above them decided the answer. Their eyes shot upwards and as one, Ivy and Jody took the stairs. Ivy knew which spots to avoid but Jody was oblivious and they weren't even halfway up when footsteps, running toward the far end of the top floor, galvanised them into a mutual burst of speed.

Reaching the top of the stairs first, Ivy glimpsed a figure slipping through the partly open door to Dad's bedroom. She raced along the hallway between the bedrooms and library and sitting areas and flung the door wide. Jody was close behind and together they rushed inside.

There was nobody in sight. Not near the bed or the wardrobe or the desk or cupboards.

Jody nudged her. The sliding door was open. 'If they're on the balcony there's nowhere for them to go.' She kept her voice low as they took slow steps forward.

A sudden flurry of movement on the balcony startled them both.

'They're climbing over!' Ivy surged forward through the door, grabbing at the person as they stepped over the railing.

It was a young woman wearing a baseball cap and active wear and running shoes and she was out of Ivy's reach as she hung by both hands from the bottom rail. How she'd managed to keep hold to lower herself was a feat on its own.

'I'm going down!' Jody was gone.

Ivy leaned over, hands outstretched. 'Let me help you.'

There was only a few feet between them and at last, the woman's face was visible. Fine features and dark brown eyes – angry eyes – stared back. The envelope was tucked down her top, as precarious as the woman's situation.

Dropping to her knees, Ivy slid her arms through the gaps and managed to grip the woman's wrists.

'Let... go.'

'I don't want you falling! Rachel?'

The woman twisted her body and the envelope began to slide. She tried to pull her hand down to secure it but Ivy held fast although her arms and shoulders were burning.

'Why have you stolen that?' Ivy demanded. 'Are you Rachel?'

With a grunt, the woman started to swing her legs. The drop to the ground wasn't far enough to hurt her unless she landed badly and she was clearly willing to take that chance. Jody appeared below and in the distance, a siren wailed.

*Please hurry.*

Ivy was losing her grip. The angle was horrible with all the pressure on her back and knees.

As the woman kicked madly in the air, the envelope fell out of her top and straight into the waiting hands of Jody.

'No!' With a final yank, she freed herself from Ivy's grasp and dropped onto the ground near Jody.

'Run, Jodes!'

Ivy watched in horror as the woman flew at her sister.


It was over in seconds. Jody might be stick-thin but she was agile and quick and as the police car – lights flashing and sirens blaring – screeched to a stop near the front of the house, she ran around it to use it as a barrier.

The woman hesitated and glanced up at Ivy with a hiss. 'Destroy them. Do the right thing.' Then she was bolting for the beach.

Ivy pushed herself to her feet and got downstairs in time to see Leo jump from another car and give chase. Senior Constable Hammond was lumbering in the same direction but stopped when Leo passed him. Jody ran to Ivy and they hugged.

'I thought she was going to hurt you.' Ivy didn't want to let go.

'Ha. She never had a chance. Most fun in ages.' Jody stepped back. 'I'm putting these in the safe, okay? Nobody gets their hands on them.' She glanced behind Ivy. 'I might stay with them until he goes.'

In the second it took Ivy to look to see that 'he' was Mick Hammond, Jody was out of sight.

*Ninja sister.*

Mick stopped to catch his breath.

'Shouldn't you drive around to Rivers End beach or the car park near the graveyard? She's going in that direction,' Ivy said.

'Nah. She's long gone. Leo won't catch up either.'

'But if you don't even look for her...'

What was the point of even asking. The police officer didn't care enough and he shrugged. 'Too many ways off the beach.'

'Well, did you recognise her?'

'Barely saw her. That sister of yours ran right in front of me.'

'She did not.'

Ivy turned her back on him as Leo jogged back alone. He shook his head as he reached her. 'Sorry. Too big a head start.'

'Thanks for trying. Thanks for being here and phoning for help.'

'You okay? Both of you?'

They walked toward the house. Mick was at the back of his patrol car with the boot open.

'We are. Do you know her? We think her name might be Rachel.'

Leo glanced at Mick who was lifting a case out. 'She looked familiar. Maybe she's been a customer or something but I'm going to ask around. Rachel? I reckon she's maybe mid or late twenties?'

'Agree. She'd stolen the envelope and dropped it straight into Jody's hands, believe it or not.'

He grinned. 'Well, she did tell me once that she's a better catcher than you.'

'You remember that? Anyway, she'd gone to lock it in the safe and I don't want—' she lowered her voice, '*him* touching it. A lot's happened since last night.'

'I'll need to take a statement and dust for prints so what did she touch?' Mick was still huffing a bit from his short excursion. 'And where's your sister?'

'The best place to dust... um, the only place I saw her touch was the balcony railing.'

Mick gazed up. 'Why is it every time I come here you want me to climb those stairs?'


Ivy opened the cellar door and called down. 'Safe to come up. Bring the letters, Jody.'

'Are you alone?'

'Leo is making us coffee.'

'I'm actually fine down here.'

Ivy went down a couple of steps. 'He won't bite and I think we could use an outside opinion. Come on.'

After a moment, Jody emerged from the darkness, the envelope in her hand. 'Did the police find anything? Can we find out who she is?'

'He's dusted and taken a statement from me. He wants you to go to the station tomorrow to do one but I kind of told him you weren't feeling well and it might not happen immediately.'

Jody's expression softened with relief. 'Thanks.'

*Why do you get so stressed about the police?*

The aroma of coffee welcomed them to the kitchen and three mugs were steaming on the table. Leo leaned against a counter. 'You need a coffee machine.'

'True. But it's pointless for just a short stay,' Ivy said. She hadn't meant it to sound like that, as if she was about to leave.

Jody had paused in the doorway, her eyes on Leo, who now looked at her. Lifting her chin, she quickly walked across the kitchen and stopped just in front of him. 'I need to apologise to you for last night. I also apologise for not passing your message to Ivy. It was wrong and I regret it so much.'

Rarely had Ivy been as proud of her sister as this moment. The genuine and humble words and tone of voice were a sign of how much had changed. A pang of something uncomfortable... a kind of grief, forced Ivy to swallow hard. If she returned to England to live she'd miss more than Leo. Her own sister would again be half a world away and it might as well be the distance of the moon.

'I accept both apologies, Jody. Please forgive yourself about the message, both of you were under extreme pressure.'

Jody nodded, then suddenly threw her arms around Leo and kissed his cheek. She let go just as fast and dropped onto a chair. 'Even without a machine this is still much-needed coffee.' She put the envelope back into the middle of the table. The angel was gone, so Jody must have taken it back to the safe earlier.

As much as Ivy wanted to kiss Leo herself – properly – she joined Jody at the table. Leo followed. And they all stared at the envelope.

# TWENTY-SIX

'I agree with Jody's comment last night – the spirit of it – that these are private letters.' Leo's eyes were bright with interest after Ivy and Jody had filled him in on some of the details. 'It would be a lie to say I'm not curious. Gabe is a unique personality and talented in ways most can't imagine and to know he had this entire other life before meeting your mother is so intriguing.'

'And afterwards. The thing is that Jody and I are too close to be entirely objective. There's been some emotional moments—'

'Like your middle name being the one his mistress wished she'd been called,' Jody interrupted. 'Don't give me that look. It was a shock.'

'Is calling her his mistress appropriate? All we know is she was married and he couldn't let go of his belief they'd be together. And it turned out neither could she.'

'Mistress is nicer than some terms I could use.'

'Seriously, Jody.'

Leo was grinning.

Ivy and Jody both turned to him with 'what?' at the same time.

Then all three laughed.

After exchanging a quick glance with Jody, Ivy pushed the envelope toward Leo. 'If you'd like to read the ones you haven't seen yet, I'll get you a notepad for anything which jumps out at you.'

She dashed to the downstairs bathroom to wash her face and take some deep breaths. This morning had been eventful and she was still feeling the effects of the shock of it all. The young woman's face was etched in her mind. And her words.

*Destroy them. Do the right thing.*

Ivy hurried back with a notepad and her sketchbook.

Leo and Jody were laughing about something, which was a relief. Them getting on mattered a lot to Ivy. 'Sorry about that.'

'Do English people say sorry a lot?' Leo asked.

Ivy and Jody nodded in unison.

'It doesn't always mean "sorry" as such,' Jody said. 'Mum is a shocker for it. Every second word sometimes.'

'I don't think I ever met your mother.'

'She's... interesting,' Jody said. 'Great mum to us. Good example of how to work hard to care for your family.'

'It still amazes me that when we went to England as kids, she had to start over with only a bit of help from her mother and sister. She trained as a nurse and worked night shifts for ages so she could be around for us during the day.'

'And you're a nurse as well.'

'I admit it wasn't my first choice,' Ivy smiled. 'Mum was pretty persuasive, and who could argue, seeing how passionate she still is about her job.'

Jody was staring at Leo.

'What's up?' he asked.

'Aren't you a doctor?'

'Change of plans, Jody. Zara and I own the new wine bar in town.'

Her mouth formed an 'O'.

'And you both should come and have dinner soon. My younger brother even plays piano there most nights.'

*A woman sang while Dad played piano. Her hair was long and dark and when she leaned over his shoulder to turn the page of the music sheet, they shared a smile.*

The memory was fading and Ivy opened the sketchbook.

'Ivy?'

'Two secs, Jody.'

She began to draw, focusing on the vision which had filled her mind for only a moment. When there was nothing to add, she turned it for Jody and Leo to see and they peered at the page.

'I had no idea you were so talented,' Leo said.

'I'm really not. Just well trained by Dad and some of his guests. But I had a sudden memory and before it completely disappeared I wanted to capture it.'

'Why do I know her?' Jody pulled the sketchpad closer. 'I can't see much of her face, just the smile and jawline, but it is familiar. Her hair as well. Didn't you say something the other day about a woman who used to visit?'

'You said that funny saying about the day after the day after or something and... yes, it was this woman who taught me that. She had a way with words and was always so kind to us.' Ivy took back the sketchbook. 'Why don't I remember more about her? If this is Dad's angel, she was around when we were teenagers, so was it all the way through his marriage to Mum too?'

'I just don't think he'd go that far and the dates of the letters indicate not. It doesn't mean she never came to Fairview though.'

'Well I think this is her. Sal. I'm sure her name was Sal... or Cel.'

'Short for Celestial? Surely nobody has that as a real name

but Dad uses it a couple of times. Celeste? Celine? Celia? An angelic meaning, anyway.'

'And you both have a sister you never knew about... that's kind of wonderful.'

Ivy nodded. 'One good thing which came from their affair. You'll read in the letters how her own husband blamed her lack of faith for the lack of a baby. She probably feared he'd leave her if there wasn't a child.'

'My mother's dear friend never had a child although she wanted one with all her heart. Her husband was infertile and told her he understood if she needed to divorce him and start over while she could,' Leo said. 'They didn't have the money or will to go through IVF.'

'What an incredible gesture.'

'She didn't want to have a family without him, so they became foster parents. It doesn't take much to do good for others.'

Ivy gazed at Leo. He was inherently good. Decent. There was nothing hidden or fake about him. His love of other humans and his default of seeing the best in them was at his core.

And he wanted them to have the chance to be together, at least to get to know each other again. Ivy's heart was being torn in two and suddenly she couldn't bear it any longer. Making some excuse about needing some fresh air, she headed for the front door, intending to step outside for a moment to gather her thoughts. Instead, her feet took her away from the house, only at a brisk walk, but she found herself unable to stop or turn around.


The sand under her feet was hot and Ivy made a beeline for the sea. There, she stopped and doubled over to catch her breath. The water around her ankles was cooling and calming as it gently whooshed in small waves.

*What am I doing?*

She had to manage these emotions. The feelings were so powerful that they threatened to overwhelm her. Every new day at Fairview loosened the tight hold she'd had on them for a long time but reading those letters, discovering things about Dad which didn't make sense, and having these odd memories all contributed to her state of mind. And then all the stuff with Jody, even the good parts, was exhausting. On top of that was the intruder and her peculiar words about destroying the letters.

In the middle of this swirling, difficult whirlwind, was Leo.

Ivy burst into tears and sat down.

The water was only just above her hips this close to shore during low tide and it didn't matter that her shorts were sopping wet.

She wept for the little girl she'd once been whose parents had split up. And for the sister she'd left to cope alone under terrible circumstances. For the loss of the will to become a writer. The shame of her father's actions. And losing him as her dad. Mostly, Ivy's sobs were for ten years without the love of her life and not being able to see a way for them to be together now.

After a while the tears dried up and little fish swam around her legs and made her giggle like a child. It was too hot today to sit out here much longer and when she knew there were no more tears left to cry, Ivy got to her feet and headed back.

Her logic kicked in. She was good at mentally filing problems in order of importance, probably from having to juggle competing needs when nursing.

Leo had asked for time with her. Was it only three days since they'd reconnected? They'd packed so much in *and* he'd dropped everything twice to come to her aid. She owed it to him, to them, to give him that chance. So, she made his file, in her mind, as 'Pending'. And that included thinking about moving back here.

It seemed as though Jody had sorted her marital problems

out and today was the best day they'd had so far, even with the intruder. Jody didn't get a file name because everything to do with her was ongoing.

As for the young woman... the police might come up with something from the fingerprints Mick lifted or Leo might be able to help with clues from the letters. More so, there were now other clues worth following and she and Jody had yet to search Dad's office. Ivy filed solving the clues as 'Highest Priority'.

Ivy stopped at the first cottage, stepping on its decking. This, of all the accommodation, was her favourite, with a sense of tranquillity which lent itself to creative pursuits. If she put a nice chair here perhaps she would write again as the rest of the world faded away, leaving the sound of the ocean and rustling of the trees. And maybe she would give that some serious consideration once the other priorities were dealt with.

Leo was partway through the letters when Ivy came back but while she was having a quick shower, he left to attend to some interviews for new staff at the wine bar.

'He'll be back in a couple of hours and I've locked the letters away. Why on earth did you dash out like that before?' Jody was flicking through the sketchbook, stopping to read notes and look at drawings. 'You've done a lot more thinking about all of this than me.'

'I'm a natural worrier.'

'You are a natural talent. Nice sketches. Are we going to get this thing out of the way?' Jody looked up. 'Dad's office?'

# TWENTY-SEVEN

'Did you ever use Dad's desk? When you were working here?'

The sisters stood a few feet from the desk in question, neither wanting to be the first to touch it.

'Never. Although he did set up a little table for me. One that folded up. That way if he was working on menu-planning or bookings or whatever, I'd be able to sit close enough to see his processes. Mostly, though, we weren't in here all that much and I feel Dad used the desk to work on his poetry.'

'But I'm sure he told me he would write wherever inspiration struck. He always carried a notebook; in fact, didn't he use those fancy ones?'

'Like this one?' Ivy stepped forward and picked up the top of a small pile of leather-bound notebooks. They were of excellent quality and different colours. 'And you're correct. He didn't write poems in here, but he did edit and refine them. And he would write to his publisher and even respond to fan letters.' Ivy grinned. 'Does poetry attract many fans?'

Jody pulled out his chair and sat. 'He wasn't exactly famous. I have a theory that as much as he has the heart of a poet, he's also practical, and decided long ago he needed to find another way to pay the bills and live the life he wanted.'

'Agree. Isn't it odd though that he stumbled across Fairview and as a young man with very few means, managed to buy it?'

'For a dollar, no less.'

Ivy pushed the chair, with Jody on it, to one side. 'I'd forgotten about the deeds to the house.' She opened the shallow drawer in the desk's centre. 'Do you remember what the receipt said? About the arrangement being concluded or something?'

Jody nudged herself closer again and peered into the drawer. 'It was weird. Are those all fountain pens?'

'Every one of them. And nothing else of interest. Instead of sitting there, why don't you search the left and I'll search the right?'

'Now who's Miss Bossy Boots?'

'According to quite a few junior nurses, me.'

'Can't quite see you as a nurse. Apart from the death stare you use sometimes.'

'How do you see me, Jodes?'

*If you say overweight and frumpy I'll stab you with a fountain pen.*

'You are the most beautiful person I know. Inside and out.'

Certain she'd misheard, Ivy knelt to start going through her side.

'I have always wanted to be like you, Ivy. So smart. And pretty. And you were always kind, even when I was being a brat.'

*That hasn't changed.*

'Nobody has ever said anything as nice, Jody.' Ivy reached over and hugged her sister. 'You're pretty special to me as well.'

Ivy's side had a drawer and a cupboard. The former had the usual bits one keeps in a desk drawer but nothing resembling a receipt or registration certificate. When she opened the cupboard door, a heap of files slid out, scattering across the floor.

'You are also my messiest sister,' Jody observed. 'Actually, we don't know that. Theresa-Louise might outdo you.'

The files were ones about Fairview and Ivy sorted as she went.

'This one has decades of land rates. All paid, by the look of them. And my goodness, Jody, the valuations they include on the property are insane. The early ones are all five figures but the last one – this is before Dad went to prison – is almost seven figures.'

'Here, let me see,' Jody moved closer. 'So when a developer comes along with a seven figure offer, they actually know what they're talking about.'

'Like the one from that young guy... Zac?'

'Exactly. This is going to sound like a stupid question and it is, because it has never occurred to me before now, but who has been paying the rates all this time?'

'Mr Appleby. Same as with the insurance and so on. And the money must have come from whatever savings Dad had but... something isn't right.' Ivy opened another file which was bank statements for the business. 'The account is still open, according to the information we were both sent, and there's a statement here from the quarter before he confessed, so I imagine the solicitor has the more current ones. There doesn't seem to be enough to have covered ten years of annual payments and cover any of the legal fees.'

'From his personal account, then?'

'He told me numerous times he paid himself a small salary and that was all that went into his personal account. Oh, hang on.' Ivy closed the file. 'Remember me saying Dad hated online anything, which is why he kept all the guest records on paper? All the time we've been here I didn't give it a thought, because the shares in Fairview you and I now have are for the property. Not the business, which isn't active now. But just because there's only paper statements here doesn't mean a thing. I tried to get Dad to learn online banking and had got as far as it being set up.' She scrambled to her feet. 'I still remember my password.'

Ivy's laptop was open on the floor between them and while she was on the phone updating her credentials, Jody finished searching the drawers. She shook her head as she closed the last one.

'Lovely, thanks so much for that. Cheers.' Ivy hung up. 'I can get in now.'

'How do you remember a password from ten years ago? I can't remember one by the time I finish typing it.'

Ivy grinned. 'IvyLeo2012!'

The page opened to the current transactions and both women gasped. There was a balance of more than half a million dollars.

'Where on earth did this come from?'

'Let's find out.'

It took searching through ten years of archived statements to do that.

A single deposit of seven hundred and fifty thousand dollars came from W. Bell in 2012, less than a month after Dad's confession.

'What's in the back of the cupboard?' Ivy peered into the depths. 'Jodes, can you turn on your flashlight? I think it's a safe.'

'Does this help?' Jody's hand, holding her phone upright with the light on, squeezed past Ivy's head. 'When did your head get so big?'

'Lucky I'm in here. It is a safe and it's bolted directly onto the floor. Looks like the bottom of the cupboard has been removed. There's a panel with the alphabet and five spots to fill.'

*What's with all the cloak and dagger, Dad?*

'Five? Not his name, or Fairview, or us. Ah, try angel.'

'Makes sense.' Ivy pressed the letters and the safe made a beep. Not the right kind of beep. 'Beach?'

The result was the same.

'How many tries do you get, Ivy?'

'I'm not an expert on safes.'

'We have two at home and they both allow three tries.'

'And then what happens?'

'They self-destruct. Haven't you seen *Mission Impossible?*'

'Jody!'

'Alright, alright. Five letters. Oh. Maeve.'

Ivy tried to look back at Jody but got light in her eyes instead. 'Are you sure?'

'No, silly. But it was the name the angel wished she'd had and it is your middle name, so unless you have another idea?'

M A E V E

This time the bolts moved and the door clicked open.

'I was right!'

'Can you keep still, please. There's stuff in here.'

Ivy rummaged around and then slid backwards.

Jody turned off the light as Ivy sorted through the handful of items.

A photo album.

A large, fat yellow envelope.

And another of Dad's smaller envelopes, like the one holding the letters. On this was just one word, in his writing. *Destroy.*


'Is it too early for wine?' Jody gazed longingly at the remaining bottle. 'Time to go shopping soon, seeing as you are drinking me out of house and home.'

Ivy was too stressed to respond. Each had their own way of dealing with this.

They'd returned to the kitchen, both having had enough of the desk and its outpouring of bizarre information. The three items were lined up on the table while they made coffee. It wasn't as simple as just ripping them all open. Whatever was in them was going to be life-changing. Ivy knew it in her soul.

'Which one first?' Jody asked, when they sat. 'Photos?'

'You choose. We don't have context on any of this but I am a bit afraid to open the one saying "destroy". Is that a line we shouldn't cross?'

'As much as I still love Dad, he crossed a terrible line and if he didn't dispose of it himself, then that's tough.'

Ivy couldn't help smiling at Jody's fierce tone and reached over to squeeze her hand.

'Let's start with the photo album, then.'

It was a small one with a handful of pages, each with just one image. The first was a young woman of perhaps twenty, sitting beneath the tree on the grass near the beach. She had dark hair going down her back and a beautiful face with fine features. She smiled at the camera.

'She looks so like the thief. I saw her close up and they both have the same-shaped eyes and mouth. This has to be Dad's angel. And our thief is definitely Rachel, her daughter.'

'I've seen her before.'

'At Fairview?' Ivy asked.

Jody's face was screwed up in thought. 'It would have to be.' She didn't sound convinced.

There were several more which were similar and then one of the same woman, older, holding a baby.

'Do you think—'

'Could that be?'

'Oh she's gorgeous. Look, Ivy, she is as divine as me at that age.'

'I agree she's gorgeous, but she isn't blonde and throwing things, so it's definitely not you.'

They pored over the photo and three more, all showing the child at different stages until about two years old.

After that were photographs of Ivy and Jody, together and alone, and a couple of Brenda.

'Mum doesn't have these. It should be okay for us to get copies made?'

Jody began taking photos of each image with her phone. 'Better than nothing but of course we'll get copies.'

There were only two more images.

One was taken near the lagoon on Rivers End beach. There were three children. Ivy aged about five, Jody was only a toddler, and both sat on either side of a teenager. A girl of maybe fifteen. All three were laughing.

'Theresa-Louise. It must be, Ivy. Didn't Dad's letter say something about us playing with her there sometimes? Oh... that's our... sister.' Jody's voice broke and she began to cry, her finger tracing the teenager's face.

Ivy moved her chair closer and took Jody into her arms, rocking her back and forth as she blinked away her own tears.

'Sorry. Better now than when we meet her.' Jody went in search of tissues. 'And we will find her. Show me the last photo.'

Gabe's face smiled at them. He was just as Ivy remembered him when she was little. She realised she was smiling back.


The big yellow envelope provided much-needed answers about the motorcycle. As well as more questions.

'Look at this, Jody. It was registered in Dad's name three months after the car crash. But there's no receipt to show he purchased it. And I never saw it here. Not ever. Dad never drove again after that night... and we know why. I had a small hatchback here for a bit and would run him around as needed but he refused to replace his own car.'

The contents of the envelope were spread out. Most of it had been loose inside and Jody was helping match up documents.

'Here's a receipt from Green Bay Storage Units. Um... for two years, paid monthly, for one motorcycle.'

'Huh? He bought it then stored it?'

'Except the receipts are made out to a Mrs Markham.'

'Well, well. Who is Mrs Markham?'

'Ivy, is this a birth certificate?'

It was and they sat in silence, reading and rereading the details.

Theresa-Louise Markham. Born in Green Bay hospital in 1981.

Her mother was Celia Rachel Markham and her father Joseph Markham, both of Rivers End.

'Celia. We almost had it right. Ivy, open your laptop. Let's do a search for her. And this Mr Bell person.'

Ivy and Jody sat close together in front of the laptop.

'The Markhams lived along Temple River.' Jody had taken over the search because Ivy's hands kept shaking. 'This is from a newspaper article in 1979 about the opening of a new church. Joseph Markham Snr and Walter Bell were the driving force behind its construction, which took several years and came about when the two families became related through marriage.'

'Wait on... *Walter* Bell? I'll be right back.'

She ran upstairs and collected her printed files. It finally felt as if pieces were coming together in this puzzle.

At the table again, Ivy opened the file she kept on Fairview and flicked through the pages. 'Here it is.'

'What?'

'The deeds. Remember what John told us at the real estate

agency?'

'That Fairview House might be eligible for heritage listing which would stop it being destroyed.'

'Well, yes. But also about this exchange of contracts.' Ivy pointed. 'Here, where there is a one-dollar payment it says "transaction complete after satisfactory completion of agreed terms". I'd assumed it was for a loan to help buy the house but—'

'But Dad broke up with Celia out of the blue. Do you remember? I'm sure she made the comment about Dad now owning Fairview and her not understanding why he'd sent her away. She'd just decided to choose him over her family.'

'Oh my goodness. What if her father found out about them?'

'And he gave Dad an ultimatum. That offer would have been irresistible to him.'

Ivy's feet tapped on the ground in excitement. 'The letter when Celia found Dad on his birthday? I'm sure she wrote that he was crying out to God about choosing a house over love!'

'Holy...' Jody tapped on the laptop. 'We'd better confirm Celia *is* Walter Bell's daughter.'

Both of them peered at the screen as Jody's fingers flew across it to search for Celia Rachel Bell. It didn't take long. Jody clicked onto an old newspaper article which included a handful of photographs, beginning with a wedding on the steps of a church.

At Celia's side was a man about the same age. He was nothing out of the ordinary, with a broad smile and bulky frame.

The next photograph was a formal one of the bride and groom and their parents. 'Is that Walter Bell?' Ivy almost touched the screen as she jabbed at the face of the older man standing beside Celia. He was bald, close to sixty, and had an unpleasant smirk on his face. 'I don't like him.'

Jody read the line beneath it. 'Bringing the Bell and

Markham families together is the marriage of Joseph to Celia. 1974.'

There was another entry. 'This is her obituary, Ivy. She died four years ago.'

'I wonder if... would Dad know?'

How heartbreaking to love someone for a lifetime yet never have the life with them which was so longed for.

'Would you search for Walter Bell please?'

'Do we really want to see more of him? Okay, okay. Here we go.'

There was an obituary from 2011. Walter Bell had died at home from natural causes in his nineties. There was mention of his work with the church and the historical society. His wife had died a few years earlier.

'Celia is dead and so are her parents. Whatever their secrets, they've taken them to their graves,' Ivy said. 'What's left to look at from Dad's desk, Jodes?'

The final surprise was a letter in an official-looking envelope. It came from a legal firm in Melbourne, dated 1981.

Jody took out several folded pages and opened them so they could both read.

'Oh... this is about our sister!' Ivy scanned the first page, which was a brief letter to Dad from the firm. 'Teresa-Louise Markham – details of her trust fund.'

'It says it would mature and access be provided to her on her thirtieth birthday. Same as us except we got shares in Fairview. Ivy, if she has received this money she must know where it came from.'

'And in turn, why she had it. At some point she'd have discovered Gabriel Sutherland is her biological father and we are more than the girls she thought of as little sisters.' Ivy drew in a long breath. 'All we can hope is that she does want to meet us.'

*Now we really have to find our sister.*

# TWENTY-EIGHT

The search for their sister was put on hold after Jody had a call from her personal assistant.

'I'm going to have to do a couple of Zoom calls, Ivy. This is about that big donation and I can't afford for us to lose it.'

Deciding to give Jody a quiet house for her calls, Ivy walked up to the graveyard with some flowers she picked at Fairview. She sat at Jean's grave, talking to her and telling her about how much she was missed. But her thoughts drifted to the accident.

Had Celia been at the house – or the stone hut – the night of the crash? Was it possible she felt guilty about Dad drink-driving because they'd been drinking together in their love nest? Her family had money. Maybe money was a way to reduce guilt and goodness knows, there was a lot in their collective family to feel ashamed of.

'You didn't belong to their church, Auntie Jean?'

The question wasn't logical. If she had been, she'd be buried at the church graveyard.

Ivy got to her feet and said goodbye but rather than going home, she wandered to the edge of the graveyard, where she could look over the sea. Another yacht – or perhaps the same one from the other day – was under spinnaker in the distance. She'd never have the money to own such a lovely boat. Jody did, but wasn't interested in yachts.

*Close to half a million dollars in the business account would buy one.*

With the excitement of finding details about their sister, the huge deposit from Walter Bell had been pushed to one side. The man had something to do with Dad in the early days of Fairview – possibly concerning Celia – virtually giving away a valuable property. Then only weeks after Dad was arrested, a vast amount of money landed in his business account from Bell.

Was it guilt-money?

Something to do with Celia being at Fairview that night?

If she'd been there that night... then why had Dad left? Driving off in the pouring rain with wine in his system. This was a man who never drove if he'd had even a sip of alcohol.

Was he taking her home?

Ivy started walking back to Fairview, her mind racing.

Jody had insisted from the beginning that Dad's car was empty when she arrived on the scene of the crash. Their father was trying to help Jean and his car door was open but there was no occupant.

*What if you aren't remembering everything? Same as me?*

Her phone buzzed with a message from Leo.

> Got delayed. One more interview. Will phone
> before I leave to see if you still want me
> there. X.

X? Ivy grinned. He'd always signed off that way.

> All good. Have news about sister. Talk later.

She needed to talk to him about more than the letters now. He'd been through so much.

*And yet, I think he still might love me.*

Jody had finished her calls and taken herself to the beach for a swim. Ivy wandered down and paddled in the shallows. Once this was all sorted, all the puzzles solved and decisions made, she'd spend at least a week just swimming and lying on the sand. It was a rare promise to nurture herself and was one which made her feel good.

While Jody was so keen to meet their sister – once they found her – Ivy had doubts. She couldn't help them, despite a deep longing to know her. But if Theresa-Louise didn't know she had two sisters, how would she react on finding out from them? Being ten years older than Ivy, it was likely she'd have her own family and there was no information on the brief search they'd done which showed her up as an adult. Was it even fair to drop this into a stranger's lap?

'You look pensive.'

Jody was wrapped in a towel, hair dripping, and looking more relaxed than Ivy had seen her in ages.

'Pondering life.'

'Can you ponder up a coffee for us while I shower?' Jody grinned as she walked past.

Ivy caught up. 'What if Theresa-Louise doesn't want to know about us?'

'Of course she will. Look at what she'll gain. A fantastic youngest sister who is a fashion queen and well connected. A middle sister who is... well, a nice enough person. Yeah, maybe we'll tell her you are adopted.'

Not in the mood for joking, Ivy dug house keys from a pocket. It was doubtful the intruder – Rachel Markham – would risk another visit after coming so close to being caught, but they weren't taking chances.

'How will we tell Mum?'

'Jeez, Ivy, what is going on? Mum can find out later. This isn't about Fairview, is it?' Jody followed Ivy inside. 'Are you worried she'll have a claim on it?'

'Of course not. If she's our half-sister then she has probably does have rights to Fairview but let's not speak as though Dad isn't alive! And we've just seen that she had a trust account, so I'm hardly worried.'

'Hold the thought because I'm making the floor wet. Five minutes and we can have a proper talk about it. And coffee. Please?'

Making coffee helped Ivy calm down.

*Once I return home I'll make an appointment to see my therapist about all of this.*

The boiling water she was pouring into a cup splashed over her hand and she whimpered, somehow not dropping the cup and quickly putting her hand under cold water from the tap. Tears filled her eyes and she let them fall. Nobody would see. Her hand hurt and she was cross with herself for being careless. As a nurse, she'd seen too many burns to make such a silly mistake. But the tears had nothing to do with the boiling water and everything to do with the default internal dialogue about returning to England.

Why was it so difficult to choose love?

Heavy footsteps on the stairs warned of Jody's approach and Ivy grabbed some paper towel, first to dry her face and then to gently dab her hand.

'Are you okay?'

'So silly. Managed to get some boiling water on my hand but it's fine.'

Jody ran outside without a word.

Was it that scary looking at a mild burn?

Ivy finished making coffee, a bit more carefully, and put the cups on the table. Jody had dropped her laptop there and as Ivy sat, she returned, carrying a short, thick piece of aloe vera.

'Hand.' Jody snapped the aloe in two.

It was cooling as Ivy held the piece onto the burn.

'I had no idea you knew about that.'

'Might not have fancy medical training like you and Mum, but Dad was always banging on about the plants and they live forever.'

Jody sipped coffee, her eyes on Ivy.

'Really, I'm fine. And this is helping.'

'Would you rather we leave finding her for another time?'

Ivy shook her head. 'I guess I'd rather know I had sisters if I was her.'

With a big smile, Jody nodded. 'Where do we start looking, then?'

Leo was the key.

He phoned while Ivy and Jody were quibbling about what to have for dinner.

'I'm still happy to drive up. Just had one of those days.'

'Did you find someone for the job?' Ivy asked.

'We did.'

Ivy decided against talking over the phone about the day's finds, but there was one thing she could ask.

'Have you ever met anyone in Rivers End called Theresa-Louise Markham? She's older than us.'

He chuckled. 'She'd be horrified if you call her that. How many people do you think have that mouthful of a first name?'

'I know her.'

'Hang on… what?' asked Jody. 'You *know* Theresa-Louise?'

Ivy held out her arm which was covered in goosebumps.

'Impressive. So, who is she?'

But Ivy's mind was going a million miles an hour and she was on her feet in an instant.

'Where are you going now?'

Ivy picked up her handbag. 'Are you coming? It'll be faster if we drive.'

All the way to town, Jody asked questions.

'All I know is I've come across her a couple of times. Leo doesn't know her history, just that she arrived in Rivers End a couple of years ago after a long absence.'

'This really is doing my head in.'

Jody was driving and when Ivy pointed out a parking spot, was in it in a second. And Ivy was out of the car almost as fast.

'Seriously, Ivy, you can't drag me down here and not tell me why. I didn't even put proper makeup on after my shower and my hair is all over the place and people will see me!'

Jody had a point. Standing outside the bistro, which wasn't open, staring through the windows, was getting them a few odd looks.

'What is the time?'

'Don't nurses carry a watch twenty-four-seven to randomly take pulses?'

'You won't have a pulse in a minute.'

'Scary sister!' Jody glanced at her watch. 'Just after five. And the sign here clearly states not open Mondays so nobody is home. Same as in your brain. Nobody is home, Ivy.'

'Then how will I find her?'

She must have sounded desperate because Jody stopped teasing and patted her arm.

The door to the bistro opened and a middle-aged man stepped out. 'We're not open today. The Italian restaurant is your best bet on a Monday.'

'Thank you, but we're actually hoping to speak with Tessa. Is she here?'

'Tessa?' Jody murmured.

'Day off. Probably at home. Can I take a message?'

'Thank you but no. Sorry to bother you,' Ivy said.

'No bother. Come back and have dinner sometime.'

As soon as he closed the door again, Ivy held her hand out. 'Keys.'

'Huh?'

'You navigate better so I'm driving.'

*What if I'm wrong? I can't get Jody's hopes up yet.*

Grumbling beneath her breath, Jody handed the keys over and followed Ivy to the Mini. 'Who is Tessa?'

'You almost ran her over with a trolley the first time we were at the supermarket. Hurry up and get in.' Ivy slid behind the wheel. She adjusted the rear-vision mirror to look into it. How had she missed the clues? Tessa's eyes were the same colour as hers.

'Where am I navigating to? And if it's too far we'll need some fuel first.'

'Not far. I don't know the address so you'll need to do some searching.'

'I know I said I like puzzles but a bit more information wouldn't go amiss.'

Ivy started the engine. If she was right, they were about to meet their sister for the first time in decades.

# TWENTY-NINE

The narrow, uneven road was at odds with the beautiful estates lining its length. Following Jody's instructions, Ivy had driven back past Rivers End Inn and turned left. After half a kilometre or so, she took a right onto Ryan Road and almost immediately, another right, effectively heading back toward town.

'Are you sure?' Ivy had asked but when the first of the big homes appeared on their left, she knew Jody was correct.

'It should be the third along. I remember us walking on the other side of the river as kids and being in awe of these places. So are you telling me our sister lives this close and we should have known this all along?'

'What if I'm wrong, Jody?'

'I don't see how. Tessa might easily be shortened from Theresa. While I don't remember seeing her at the supermarket, your description of her age fits. And anyway, Leo said it's her. Go left here.'

Bell Park was one of twenty or so small acreages backing onto the river and most included long-established large homes, with a handful being closer in size to small mansions. This was one of the latter, a box-shaped two-storey white building with balconies around the top level and a lot of floor-to-ceiling windows on the lower one. The driveway was lined with English box hedges which grew with unruly abandon, and weeds poked through garden beds filled with standard roses and camellias.

'Not quite as perfect as one would expect,' Jody noted. 'I wonder who else lives here.'

'Hopefully Rachel.'

'Ooh! Then we can have that nice cup of tea and gossip about her mother.'

Ivy parked behind an older SUV. 'Unless she can offer a compelling reason why not, I'll be reporting her to Mick Hammond.'

'Seriously, don't involve the police.'

'Why? For that matter, what is it with you and the police? Have you had a run-in with them?'

Jody turned deathly white and let herself out of the car.

*Well, that went well.*

By the time Ivy locked the Mini and met Jody near the front door, her sister was back to her normal colour. But as Ivy lifted her hand to knock, her courage drained away and she lowered her arm.

'What?' Jody asked.

'This is... huge. If Tessa is our sister, then what happens next?' Ivy's legs were shaky and her stomach began to churn.

Jody though seemed unconcerned and tapped on the door a few times. But as footsteps approached, she reached for Ivy's hand and squeezed it.

The door swung open.

Tessa gazed at Ivy, then Jody, then Ivy again. Her mouth was slightly open and she was still. Very still. Waiting.

'Hi, Tessa. I'm Ivy. And this is Jody.'

'I know.' The words were spoken softly.

Jody took a small step forward. 'And you are Theresa-Louise? We think... well, we know you're our sister.'

With a deep, shuddering sigh, Tessa managed a nod and she moved to one side. 'Please come in. We have a lot to talk about.'


Being inside the home where Dad's angel – Celia – grew up – was strange to say the least. Ivy and Jody followed Tessa through a vast foyer with a curved staircase, past formal living and dining rooms, to the kitchen.

'Coffee? Tea? Sparkling water? I have apple juice.'

The kitchen was big with black and white floor tiles and marble counters. It was spotless but what was noticeable was a lack of appliances, other than a coffee machine and kettle. There was a row of stools along a counter.

'Please sit. What would you both like?' Tessa bustled about filling the kettle. 'Would you like something to eat? I have some quiche in the fridge. A salad. Would you prefer to sit outside under the pergola?'

'Tessa—'

'Yes, we should go outside. At least then we're out of this horrible house and...' Tessa's words faded as she stopped moving from side of the kitchen to the other and instead, her face kind of crumpled and tears began streaming down her cheeks. Water bubbled out of the spout of the kettle and Jody got to it just before Tessa's fingers loosened enough for it to fall.

Then Ivy and Jody embraced their sister and Tessa held on to them as though she'd never let go. She fitted with them. It was perfect.

'Come and sit. We'll make a drink later,' Ivy finally said.

Tessa grabbed a handful of tissues from a box on the way to a door leading outside, blowing her nose and trying to stifle the flow of tears, with limited success. They sat around a wrought-iron table beneath a covered pergola, Ivy and Jody on either side of their new sister. For a while there was silence while Tessa gathered herself and Ivy had to wipe a couple of tears from her own eyes. Jody though had a wide smile and kept looking from Ivy to Tessa.

As with the front garden, the area around the pergola was overgrown and needed some attention.

'Do you live here alone?' Jody asked.

'Oh, um, no. And yes. I have a small flat above the bistro. Rachel is supposed to be living here. She *insists* on living here because she believes the house is entirely hers but then spends weeks or months away for work. I come here a few times when she's away, just on days off. Usually overnight because then I can try to sort the gardens during the day and the house at night.' She bit her lip.

'With nobody to help? Goodness, that's a huge job.'

'But isn't that what you are doing at Fairview, Ivy?' Tessa asked. 'I'm going to be totally honest with you both. Since I came back to Rivers End two years ago, I've gone to your father's... *our* father's property every month. Just to connect to the past and think about you two. And I've been sad seeing the disrepair and slow deterioration of such an iconic and vibrant house.' She shrugged. 'There was nothing I could do. As far as I knew, I wasn't wanted in your family so how could I try and tidy the grounds, let alone make the house lovely again?'

Ivy and Jody each reached for Tessa's hands at the same moment and all three giggled. It broke the ice and all of them began to talk and ask questions and for a while there was everything being said and nobody hearing anything other than snippets. But then Tessa's phone beeped and she checked a message.

'That was Rachel. She knows she did the wrong thing by breaking into Fairview and I have a whole phone full of similar messages, but she won't discuss it in person.' Tessa put the phone, face down, on the table. 'The thing is that she's terrified you will tell the world about it all.'

'It *all*?' Ivy asked.

'Me. Mum. Even her father. My pretend father. And all the rest of it.'

*The rain made it so hard to see things clearly but there were two cars. One was Dad's and the other was all smashed up in a ditch. Dad was partly inside that car and he yelled for Ivy to help. Get blankets. Call an ambulance. But she'd already done that at the house so why wasn't anyone here to help yet?*

Ivy jumped. The others were staring at her. Concerned. Her heart was beating so fast she almost panicked.

*Slow down. Breathe. It isn't your memory.*

It couldn't be.

She'd been asleep in her bedroom the whole time.

She'd got home from leaving Leo partway along the rocks, her heart singing and her thoughts racing about their next date. Already she knew without doubt that he was her soulmate. They'd connected on a level she'd never experienced. Their minds were aligned, as were their principles and outlook on life. Rivers End was where she wanted to spend the rest of her life and she needed to talk to Mum to let her know. They were young, but sometimes people just knew. And she knew.

'Ivy? What's going on?'

Jody was beside her. When did she move? And where was Tessa?

'Say something. You kind of zoned out and your eyes closed and your hands were shaking. Actually, they still are shaking. Tessa is getting water but I think you need a shot of brandy.'

'No. No, I'm fine, Jodes. What are you going on about?'

But remnants of the memory remained and far clearer than previous ones. It was unsettling and distressing and made no sense because she hadn't left her bedroom. Not until Dad arrived home, crying and covered in blood.

'Here's water. And some brandy.'

'Good woman!' Jody grinned and pushed the brandy closer to Ivy. 'This will help.'

'Really, I'm okay.'

'Surely as a nurse you know this is medicinal?'

'I just had a kind of flashback. To the night of the car crash. Sorry.'

Ivy picked up the glass of water and sipped slowly. Her nerves were still jangling but at least she could breathe properly. Tessa was gone again and Jody's hand on her back, gently rubbing in circles, was comforting. The fog cleared and she put the glass down.

'When we get home, can we talk about that night? I've been having such weird memories but I don't think they're mine.'

'I think you need brandy if you believe you can read other people's minds. But okay. If it matters so much then perhaps it's time to get it out in the open. Let the cards fall where they will.' Jody wouldn't meet Ivy's eyes and she moved back to her original seat as Tessa returned.

*What does that mean? Let the cards fall where they will?*

'This is probably not the time,' began Tessa. 'Or maybe it is. But I know about the letters. The ones our father wrote to my mother? She posted them back to him just after the car crash, according to Rachel. Mother stupidly told Rachel about them, and worse, about the ones she'd written to him over many years. And that they contained deeply personal reflections as well as information which might be harmful to her.'

'To Celia?'

'No. To Rachel. And she refuses to tell me what on earth it is. At first I wondered if she wrongly assumed you both might have a stake in Bell Park, being my half-sisters, but she's made it very clear she'll fight anyone who tries to take it from her.' Tessa's forehead was creased. 'She can have it. I left home the year after your mother returned to England. There was so much fighting between Mum and Joe and during one argument I over-heard Gabe Sutherland named as my real father. I couldn't bear living in this house and moved in with a friend who wasn't part of the church to finish school.'

Jody's eyes were wide. 'Does Dad know that you know?'

'He told me. Mind you, I was twenty-five and had been working at the pub for years because I wanted to be around for Rachel. I had a vague idea about saving up to do a decent management course but hadn't made much headway. Gabe used to come in for a drink and we'd chat and then, out of the blue, he told me the truth.'

'At your job?' Jody asked.

Tessa rolled her eyes. 'Thank goodness nobody overheard and at least I knew so it wasn't a total shock.'

'Did he explain why he'd taken so long?'

'It was a short conversation, Ivy. Long enough to tell me that in five years I'd be getting a trust fund worth more than enough for me to kickstart my dreams. And he handed me an envelope with a few thousand dollars to get started. He said he loved me and was sorry and it had to stay secret.'

'Oh, Tessa,' Ivy said. 'We had no idea.'

With a shrug, Tessa took something from a pocket. A thin envelope. 'After a while I left Victoria and then when Mum died, I finally felt I could come home again. This time, it was on my terms and I took over the bistro and put my training and experience to good use.' She put the envelope on the table. 'I found this in Mum's things and I'm sorry but I have read it – but only since seeing you back in Rivers End. And it makes almost no sense to me but perhaps you two will understand what she is going on about.'

'But if it's private, we shouldn't,' Ivy said. As desperate as she was to rip it open, the newfound relationship with Tessa meant far more than any words from a woman who had lived a life of lies. She sat back and glanced at Jody, who merely raised her eyebrows.

'It might affect you both. And our father,' Tessa said. 'Would you prefer I read it aloud?'

*Beloved Gabriel,*

*I'm lost about where to begin or what to say and have spent days going back and forth in my mind. At this point there are no police at the front door of either of our homes but my dreams are filled with fear and my conscience cannot abide keeping the secret.*

*What was lost that awful night was more than a car but as you know, I arranged delivery of a new motorcycle – the one you always admired and spoke of one day buying to go exploring. It hurt me a bit that you immediately put it into storage and I couldn't bear you paying for that, so took over the payments. But that's old news, since you've been getting the receipts for almost two years rather than have them come to my house. What you don't know is that I've cancelled the storage and the motorcycle will arrive at Fairview this week. Do with it as you wish.*

*As for that poor woman... a sizeable donation was anonymously sent to her family and I pray for her soul every day.*

*My guilt is overwhelming. None of this would have happened had I not been with you that evening, sharing our love and food and wine in our special place. It was I who encouraged you to open the second bottle and for that I will never forgive myself.*

*What I'm trying to say is that night was our last ever time together. My prayers and lamentations have brought clarity. Our love was a sin and this terrible incident was punishment. My husband already knows about Theresa-Louise being your child and has for many years. Rachel does not deserve to be pulled into this in any way, as she is the only innocent one. So I shall atone by confessing about my part in this.*

*We had something rare, Gabriel. But it wasn't real.*

*Reading this back to myself I'm realising you need to hear me say these words face to face. I need to tell you that I'm going to go to the police and explain the real events of that night. Nobody knew I was at Fairview. We've kept that secret and you seem to have moved on from the accident while I sink further into depression the longer we hide the truth.*

*Whatever I have to say to the police is not to hurt you, although I know our lives will be forever changed. It is time for Jean Curry's family to have proper closure and for us to be judged by the law.*

*The angel statues I gave you over the years were meant to keep you safe. Your lack of faith in your own church has blinkered you to their power.*

*Be strong, Gabriel. What will come soon is for the best.*

*Celia.*

Tessa tossed the letter onto the table and rubbed her eyes. 'My own mother believed Rachel was the only innocent party. What about me? I didn't ask for her to go outside her marriage.' She dropped her hands and sighed. 'Like I said, most of this makes no sense.'

Jody's face was red with fury. 'She sent a donation to the family of the deceased and a motorcycle to the man who killed her? Because she had religious guilt over her affair?'

'Sorry, Tessa. I know Celia was your mother but that letter...
you said you found it among her things? She never posted it?'

'It doesn't have any address on it. Nothing. I assume she
went to see him like she mentioned and it didn't end well so the
letter was never sent. And she could have simply handed it to
him. Unless he read and returned it, but I see no point endlessly
speculating.'

'She was going to the police to tell them there was no thief.
That Dad was the driver. But he decided to confess first in
order to keep her name out of it,' Ivy said.

Tessa was quiet. Her eyes were on the envelope.

'Sorry to sound so angry.' Jody touched Tessa's arm.
'Meeting you is one of the best things ever to happen in my life.'

Ivy nodded. 'Me too. I just can't believe we didn't know you
existed and I am so sorry for Dad's part in that! And the couple
of times we've met? I had the strongest sense of knowing you
but my memories are all over the place and I figured you were a
friend of ours. A big sister type of friend.'

When Tessa looked up, the tears were back but so was a
beautiful smile. 'I thought of you both as little sisters and then
one day you were gone and I cried when your— our father told
me. There's so much I don't know and understand but I do
think he loved my mother completely and would do anything to
protect her. That's a rare kind of devotion.'

# THIRTY

'Why are you kneeling on my bed with your head out the window?' Jody asked from the doorway of her bedroom. 'Is there someone down there?'

Ivy turned and sat and Jody joined her.

'The memories are ganging up on me a bit,' Ivy said. 'I was walking past here and suddenly remembered sitting on what was my bed back then, eating ice cream and thinking about Leo.'

'Oh. That night.'

'That night. Do you remember me bringing you ice cream? You were playing chess with Mr Carson.'

'I'd just beaten him. He asked if I could make him a pot of tea and I needed to take my empty ice-cream bowl in anyway and then I saw Dad through the window. He was running up the driveway.'

'So that's what made you chase after him. And later, there was a lot of yelling. Actually, it was me yelling at him.'

'No.'

'Yes, Jody.' Ivy screwed her face up thinking. 'Somewhere in my head is a long conversation and me yelling at him. I'm so certain it was that night or the next day. Or both.'

'But how?' Jody frowned. 'I know you talked to him in the kitchen that night but that was before the accident, wasn't it? You weren't at the scene.'

'I was.'

A shiver ran down Ivy's spine and she leaned back to peer out the window again.

*There'd been noise outside. A car. That made Ivy look into the night, cupping her face with both hands against the window to see. Nobody should be driving out. The guests were still downstairs or else settled in their cottages already. She could hear but not see the car but then Dad was there, running up the driveway. Ivy pulled shoes on and looked again. Now it was Jody who was tearing along at a great rate.*

*And then there was a terrible sound from the road. Screeching tyres and a loud bang.*

*She raced down the stairs and grabbed a raincoat from a hook and yelled into the living room for someone to call an ambulance and police. Outside, the rain was getting worse and her hair was quickly soaked through. The driveway was so muddy and slippery but there was no turning back because something was terribly wrong.*

*The road was deserted and Ivy stopped, looking both ways.*

*But then she heard screaming.*

'Ivy! For goodness' sake, come back to me!'

Her whole body shuddered as Ivy looked around.

'How? Why are we here?'

They stood in the middle of the road, at the crash site.

'We ran. Good grief, Ivy. You can't just take off like that.'

Jody was panting and then, as a car approached, she pulled Ivy to the side of the road. 'Do you have your phone on you?'

She did and handed it to her sister, still trying to clear her head. How had she not known she'd left the house and come all the way here? Ivy had no memory of it and the shock of it all was messing with her sense of self. This wasn't her. She was calm and logical and had an excellent memory. Except for that night.

'Are you okay to go home?' Jody still had her phone. She'd just finished tapping on it and slid it into a pocket. 'The house is unlocked and who knows if Rachel is lurking around.'


*Why was there a girl out here in the rain? Had she come from one of the cars? It couldn't be from Dad's car. But Dad hadn't driven it. Had she stolen it?*

*Ivy went to her. There's no way she'd been driving. She must have been thirteen or fourteen and was tiny. Skinny and not even up to Ivy's shoulder and Ivy could only just see over Dad's steering wheel, his being one of those old, huge boxes of a car.*

*The girl was shivering and her eyes were staring at the car, which was on its side. Dad stood near it, screaming for help. Ivy took off her raincoat and put it over the girl's shoulders. 'What happened?'*

*There was no answer, so Ivy gently turned her to face away from the awful sight. 'Tell me what happened?'*

*'I think Mum killed someone.'*

*Had she heard right? Ivy leaned closer.*

*'Was your mum driving my dad's car?'*

*'I saw her in the stone hut. She was naked on the bed. The door was a bit open and I pushed it right open and she called out something.'*

*How could this be? A woman in the stone hut in a bed?*

*'I ran but she'd seen it was me.'*

*Ivy looked over her shoulder. Dad had something metal in his hand and was hitting the windscreen of the car which was in the ditch.*

*'But where is she?'*

*The girl stopped talking and held the raincoat closer. Ivy ran to help but she didn't know how. Dad was half inside the car and as he pulled back he was gripping someone's arms. He saw Ivy.*

*'Go. Get help now.'*

*Ivy noticed the boot of Dad's car open and found a blanket. Sirens were blaring and cars were stopping and all of a sudden there were people everywhere.*

*The girl was gone, the raincoat left on the ground.*

*After picking it up, Ivy sank onto the sodden ground, not bothering to cover herself from the rain. It seemed ages, but Dad joined her. His bare feet were bleeding, and his hands, but he put his arms around Ivy. He was crying and Ivy was just cold inside. She'd worked out who the woman was because it all made sense now. A woman who'd visited Fairview so often, who sang like an angel...*

*'It was an accident, sweetie pie. Someone stole the car.'*

*'Celia.'*

*He released her as though stung.*

*'No.'*

*'I spoke to her daughter. She told me everything.'*

*'Ivy, she's mistaken. You can't tell a soul. You have to promise not to repeat any of it to anyone.'*

*The blood turned to ice in her veins.*

'I remember everything.' Ivy and Jody sat at the top of the stone steps overlooking Rivers End beach. They'd gone there rather than home after Ivy's memory ended and she'd returned to the present.

'And I never forgot.' Jody held her hand. 'But I didn't see the same things that you did.'

'It was Celia all along who was the driver. Goodness knows why Rachel was there, but Rachel saw enough to make her believe it.'

Jody suddenly gasped. 'I didn't know who Celia was.'

'I don't understand?'

'You just said you saw me running after Dad.'

'So where were you? Dad kept telling me, over and over, that you'd seen the crash and were frightened and I should go home and find you. And I kind of remember you being in bed when I got back.'

'I walked to the river with Celia and waited until she was out of sight near her house. Except I didn't know it was called Bell Park or who she was. Just a visitor now and then. She was standing near Dad's car when I got there. He told me to help her get home. That she'd tried to help. That someone had stolen the car. And that I could never, ever tell a soul about her because she would get in terrible trouble from her husband for being out alone late at night.'

'Oh, Jody.'

'All this time I thought I was helping a woman who was scared of her husband. How did I not work out she'd been the driver? I could have told the police and—'

'No, you don't blame yourself for any of this, Jodes. Two adults made dreadful choices at the site of the crash and we got dragged into it.'

Leo's car pulled up in the car park behind them.

'Why is Leo here?'

Jody handed the phone back.

'Why did you text him?'

'You were running down the middle of a road and who knows what next.'

'Sorry.'

'You should be. Gave me a heck of a scare.'

But Jody kissed Ivy's cheek.

'Hello, you two.' Leo sat behind Ivy, slipping his legs around hers so she could lean back against his chest and was encased in his arms. 'Care to share?'

Jody quickly updated him on their visit with Tessa and the revelations about Celia being the driver of the car that night.

'She cared so much about stopping Rachel telling anyone about herself and your father that she took his car, late at night, in the rain, and having drunk a lot of wine,' he said. 'And then in his need to protect Celia, your dad lied about the car being stolen, and told you what he wanted you to believe.'

'Pretty much.'

'So why did he confess two years later?'

Ivy shuffled a bit so she could look at Leo. 'There are some letters at home we found but haven't read yet. They say to destroy them but I think need to read them. We might never know, but my guess is that Celia told Dad she was going to confess and he panicked. He probably realised Jody would be dragged into Celia's confession because she'd been the one who'd walked her home and then repeatedly told the police that there had been no driver at the scene. He would rather go to jail for something he didn't do than let that happen.' Her eyes shot to Jody. 'That's why the thing with the police? Oh, Jodes.'

'I've been in fear my entire adult life. I had to be there for Dad's hearing four years ago and I had to rattle off the same crap. And he thanked me for believing in him and apologised for his lie. And now I know the lies were so much worse and I was in the middle of them.'

Jody's brave face finally fell and she nestled against Ivy and wept.

## THIRTY-ONE

The sun was slowly sinking as Ivy and Leo wandered across the rocks toward Rivers End beach. Almost a month had passed since they'd first reunited near the cave, and in the time since Ivy and Jody had met with Tessa, rarely had a day passed without them spending some hours together.

'I had a Zoom consultation with my therapist in London,' Ivy said. 'He believes now I've had some dissociative amnesia from the trauma of the crash and the way Dad kept telling a different story from my memories.'

'Any long-term effects?'

'He thinks not. Jody and I both have a lot of work to do, but it's healing work rather than trying to puzzle out details. And although Dad made plenty of terrible choices, I'm not as angry with him anymore.'

If anything, Ivy was sad for him. He'd thrown away ten years of his life, far from his home and even further from his own three daughters.

They settled on the side of the lagoon, bare feet dangling in warm water. Summer was almost here and the days were both longer and progressively hotter. Ivy loved this time of year and had no intention of ever missing it again.

'Jody and I opencd the envelope marked "destroy" because we spoke to Dad and he said to go right ahead. He wants no more secrets.'

The first phone call was the hardest. But now there'd been three, each becoming easier, more natural. There was a lot going on in the background with his barrister and solicitor to have him freed now that so much new information had come to light.

'So you finally read whatever was inside? And you don't need to share the details, Ivy.'

She smiled and took a folder letter from her pocket. 'If you don't mind, I'd like to read this one. There were four letters, one for me, one for Jody, one for Tessa.'

Leo turned his body a little to better look at Ivy. 'Of course you can. Has Tessa read hers?'

'We all have now. It's quite touching because Dad expresses how much he longed to be her father in every regard but had to respect Celia's wishes. He tells her a few funny stories from when she was very little, before Celia stopped bringing her to visit, and also about the day he gave her the money.' Ivy took a deep breath. 'Apparently, walking away from her that day was one of the hardest things he ever did.'

'So why would he want that letter destroyed?'

She shrugged. 'I haven't asked him, but I wonder if he wrote them more for himself, because it was the day he confessed, and then panicked in case the contents reached the wrong people. Maybe the police arrived to arrest him before he could safely dispose of them and he locked them in the safe.'

'You said there was a letter for each sister. That's three. Was the fourth one to Celia?'

'No. And I had to think for a while before talking to you because it is really sad in parts. Leo... he wrote it to Jean.'

Leo inhaled sharply, his eyes widening.

'Or I can leave it with you to read when you're ready. If you want it, that is.'

'Please, read it to me.'

*Dear Jean,*

*I only had the pleasure of meeting you a few times and remember a fiercely independent person who looked people in the eye and always had a ready laugh and a kind word.*

*You deserved so much more than what happened that night – and after it.*

*Even now I'm being less than honest with everyone else but at least there will be some closure for your loved ones. My daughters, the young women who are my world, will always see me as a monster who took the life of a good woman and then lied to protect myself.*

*Perhaps even by confessing to driving my car that night – a lie – I am protecting that part of me which couldn't live with seeing Celia behind bars. For most of my life, she has been my guiding light and great love and she is also the mother of my eldest daughter. She chased her younger daughter that night out of desperation. You see, Celia is blinkered by her beliefs in many ways and thought if she could stop Rachel there'd be a way to explain what the child saw.*

*I saw the crash. The impact of my car on the wrong side of the road which sent your car into a roll. I didn't know it was your car at first. My first thought was that Celia must have been killed in such an impact but when I pulled her out there was barely a scratch on her. I've heard it said that drunk drivers are often the ones who survive.*

*When I looked inside your car I knew it was you and I was equally certain your beautiful life force had left your body. My heart broke for you, Jean.*

*So much of it is a blur. There was so much rain. So many questions. And both Ivy and Jody were caught up in the aftermath through no fault of their own. And my lies just made it worse for them.*

*Now I hope to make amends, even if it still isn't the whole truth. At least one person will be behind bars for your death. And I am at fault because I left the car with its keys inside and both Celia and I had drunk far more than we should.*

*I'm going to plead guilty to drink driving. I'm not going to hide that the driver was drunk. You were faultless.*

*I shall never forget you.*

*And I shall never forgive Celia, or myself.*

*Gabe Sutherland.*

Leo was gazing into the lagoon and Ivy touched his cheek.

'I'm sorry. I just thought you needed to know...' She'd done the wrong thing.

His hand reached for hers and they sat in silence for a few minutes, until darkness was almost upon them. Then he sighed and climbed out of the lagoon, Ivy close behind. He held her against him.

'She lives in my heart, Ivy. And he might not forgive himself, but I do. And Auntie Jean would have. He was right about her looking people in the eye and she couldn't bear lies, but she was a kind person and used to say life is here to be lived, not regretted.'

'I like that.'

When Leo released her, his face was still sad but there was a glint of something else in his eyes. 'I like it as well and I have no intention of regretting anything else.'

*And I feel the same.*

'What is that smile for?' Leo asked.

'I came back to Fairview House feeling alone and lost. Jody and I were at odds. Dad was someone I never wanted to think about. And I believed you were long gone from my life.'

'And now?'

'Now, I have two sisters! And Rachel, although I think she has a lot of growing up and learning to do before we can all become friends. But we will.'

'And Fairview is looking wonderful. Your Dad is likely to get released soon. And then, there's me.' He grinned and kissed the tip of Ivy's nose. 'Not long gone at all.'

They walked for a while. It was nice. No pressure.

'Ivy? Are you staying?'

Some pressure.

'Let's get Dad home and I'll see what happens.'

'With him? Selling Fairview or otherwise?'

'Actually, Jody and I have some ideas about Fairview's future. I just need to work out how to unravel my commitments in England and explain to Mum that I am seriously considering moving back here.'

'Considering?' Leo lifted her hand and kissed her fingers.

'This time I have to make the right decisions. The right ones for me.'

'And I'm here, no matter what you decide.'

The final ray of light faded from the sky but Ivy was not in the dark. She leaned against Leo's shoulder. Rivers End and Fairview were where she belonged. And the man at her side? He truly was her home.

# EPILOGUE

The bus drove away from where it had stopped to let Gabe Sutherland off. In minutes it would reach Rivers End then go onto Driftwood Bay and eventually, Warrnambool.

Gabe picked up the small suitcase which carried all his belongings from the past ten years and hobbled through the open gate. Sitting in a bus for so long played havoc with his knees but the further he went down the driveway, the less his joints complained.

He inhaled deeply and as the sea air filled his lungs a sense of homecoming finally began to edge out the belief that he'd never see Fairview again. Never see the ocean again. And never speak to his daughters again.

The last was the most important of all.

Everything was bearable, but the loss of his children had almost crushed his soul.

As the roof of Fairview House came into view, Gabe halted and put down the suitcase. This precious place was still standing.

But what of the future?

Gabe was as afraid to see Ivy as not see her. And Jody,

should she be here. He couldn't bear to think about Theresa-Louise, the forgotten child.

Both Ivy and Jody had spoken to him by phone, following a letter from Jody. It took him a week to find the courage to open it but his heart had lifted as he'd read. She'd said she was happily married and she and Ivy were closer than ever and that she hoped his release would happen soon. He'd cried quietly in his bunk that night but from joy.

The day had come when the doors had opened and he'd left a free man. No parole. No conditions. Much of what he'd done was forgiven and new charges of obstructing justice and so on were considered time served. He'd spent days at a cheap motel, acclimatising himself to the world he'd turned his back on. Showering alone. Sleeping. So much sleep. And shopping, but only for the clothes on his back so that he presented himself as a normal human who had not spent more than a decade behind bars.

Picking up the suitcase, Gabe continued toward the house.

He deserved those years imprisoned. What he'd put his daughters through was criminal, and all for love. But not love of them. Misguided love of a woman who'd owned his heart and mind for so many years and at the end, when he'd needed her to be the best version of herself, she had hidden behind her beliefs. The same beliefs drummed into her by an overbearing father.

Gabe sighed. Now was not the time.

With every step toward Fairview, Gabe's heart lightened.

His belief in himself as a young man might be viewed now as egotistical or arrogant or absurd but it was pure. For reasons still unknown, he and Fairview were connected. And for a long time, he'd misunderstood his purpose and believed Celia, his angel, was the factor which bound them all together.

He was at the bottom of the driveway and Gabe gazed back the way he'd come.

No longer could he run up and down the driveway with

ease. His days of running were long gone. However, his mind was sharp and his creativity had never died. Only been paused. For a long time.

For ages he'd worked on his best- and worst-case scenarios.

The worst was being alone, without his family, for the rest of his life, and left without Fairview House. Should this happen he would find a little cottage somewhere, bring a cat or two – rescue moggies – into his life, and write poetry.

The best? Living out his days at the only home he'd known and loved for decades. Spending time with his daughters. Walking the beach. Swimming – oh, how he longed to swim in the Southern Ocean again. Gabe didn't believe for one minute he'd be able to resurrect the retreat, but just perhaps there would be people who enjoyed evenings of music and laughter and food.

He was smiling as he turned the corner and went to the front door.

There was a bright yellow Mini parked close by, as well as an expensive Lexus and an older SUV.

There was a wreath on the door. It was made of ivy and Gabe laughed softly. How he loved the name and the plant and the child who become one of the great loves of his life.

But what was on the other side of the door?

Gabe's courage failed him.

How could anyone forgive him?

He wasn't worthy.

Gabe turned from the door.

He made it as far as the bench beneath the old tree when the door opened.

'Dad?'

'Daddy?'

Gabe turned.

His girls were coming toward him. Three girls. All beautiful, grown women and all with smiles.

Behind them was young Leo, and a tall, serious man. Jody's Aaron, perhaps?

In a moment he was surrounded and hugged and fussed over and then they were all inside Fairview, which was decorated for Christmas and the most wonderful thing he'd ever seen.

Gabe stood on the beach at dawn. The water was warm on his bare feet as he let it lap over them. This was what he'd dreamed of so often and missed so terribly. The healing power of the Southern Ocean.

It was Christmas Day.

Fifty-one years since his first here at Fairview.

And without doubt, this would be the best one ever.

His daughters had not only welcomed him home but made it clear that he was forgiven. Jody had said that his years in jail was more than enough time taken away from them all and that whatever was left was precious.

It was a dream. But real.

Celia was gone. He hadn't known until yesterday but Theresa-Louise – Tessa – drove him to see her grave and left him in peace to talk to her for a while. It was a short conversation because he'd said all he had to say when she'd come to Fairview before he'd confessed. And while he didn't regret one minute of their time together, he had come to see their love as something less than celestial and more human than before.

'Dad?'

Ivy was there.

They hadn't spoken as much but her eyes had followed him all the time.

'I guess I understand,' she said. 'I lost Leo for so long but he was always in my heart and I'm so very lucky to find him again.'

It wasn't the same. What he'd had with Celia was

extraordinary and rare but it was based on dishonesty. Ivy and Leo were the real thing.

He held out his arms and Ivy snuggled against his chest just like she used to as a child. Then they turned to watch the sun rise over Fairview House.

*A year on.*

Ivy and Leo had taken the driveway, stopping to admire the new sign beside the gate.

*Ruth-Anne Reynard Foundation, Rivers End.*

In a few days, the first group of teens would arrive to stay in what was now a selection of eight cottages. There was a new tennis court and the garage had been converted into a welcoming space with all-weather games, creative corners, and a general hang-out area complete with juke box and small kitchen.

Dad was set to run some small workshops as well as teach again. All the stuff he used to do and love. Ivy was the manager and a year expanding her training into counselling would be put to good use. Jody would be here a few times a month and Aaron had arranged one of his team to attend each intake and offer classes around information technology.

'You should be proud,' Leo said.

'We all should. Being able to put Fairview to such good use matters. Tessa's generosity made a big difference as well when she and Rachel sold Bell Park and donated a sizeable chunk to the Foundation. We're so lucky.'

Leo took her hand and they began walking again. They walked down the hill and along the river until it became the lagoon, and past that toward the sea.

As they neared the jetty, Ivy squealed. 'I can't believe it!'

The old structure was almost completely rebuilt.

'Still a few days away but it should be open again soon for picnics and sunsets and lots of kisses.'

Ivy giggled but then Leo dropped her hand and took a few steps away.

'What?'

'A bit more than thirteen years ago we met on this beach and my life changed forever. You see, Ivy, I fell in love. Head over heels in love and what's more, I knew I'd found my soulmate.'

Tears prickled at the back of Ivy's eyes and she blinked quickly.

'Then after you finally came home, I asked you for time together again. To see what happened.'

She opened her mouth to speak but he shook his head and moved closer to take both her hands in his.

'What your father did by letting you and Jody and your mum leave because he refused to be flexible was an error of judgement and I'm sure he regrets it on some levels. Seeing the impact on you both made me look deep into my heart.'

All of a sudden there was a vulnerability in Leo's eyes and his fingers tightened.

'Please hear me out. I've never been one to roam too far from Rivers End but I made the decision that if you returned to England, I would ask if I could go with you. To be with you mattered more than where I lived. I saw your struggle about where to be and which life to choose. I know you are settled here getting Fairview running again, but if you ever change your mind...'

Now, Ivy shook her head.

'No, Leo.'

'No?' His voice was barely a whisper.

'Oh. Oh, I didn't mean no to us. And that is the most beautiful offer I could imagine. But Leo, my soulmate, there's no chance I'm going anywhere.'

Even as he sighed in relief his whole body seemed to relax but then he was getting lower and he was on one knee on the sand.

A shiver of pure delight flooded Ivy.

His eyes were shining. 'I really didn't think this through and there's no ring, but George Campbell is ready and willing to make you the most perfect engagement and wedding rings. That is, if you say yes.'

Ivy whispered. 'Yes.'

'But I haven't asked.'

'Yes.' This was louder.

'Ivy? Will you marry me?' Leo rushed the words.

'Yes, yes, yes!'

And then Ivy was on her knees on the sand and Leo was kissing her and the whole world was the way it was meant to be.

# A LETTER FROM THE AUTHOR

Many thanks for reading *The House at Angel's Beach*. I hope you enjoyed visiting Fairview and being part of Ivy and Jody's sometimes tumultuous journey. If you'd like to join other readers in hearing all about my new releases and bonus content, you can sign up for my newsletter.

www.stormpublishing.co/phillipa-nefri-clark

If you enjoyed this book and could spare a few moments to leave a review, that would be hugely appreciated. Even a short review can make all the difference in encouraging a reader to discover my books for the first time. Thank you so much.

This story came about after a chance encounter on a beach on Australia's Mornington Peninsula. Although quite a distance from where the book is set, it is still a beautiful area which is not much different from how I see Rivers End and surrounds.

I was staying in the area to attend an evening book signing event. During the afternoon I was drawn to the beach and wandered along the jetty, then back to head to the hotel. Back on the sand, a man approached me and asked if I'd take a photo of him and his brand new fiancée! Of course I took quite a few and even encouraged them to re-enact the proposal for a keepsake.

We got chatting and Matt told me that the proposal came thirty years after he met Amanda on this very beach. I had goosebumps and still do when I think about it. As they left, I watched the couple holding hands, their love so evident. And there began an idea. A scene where there's a proposal on the same beach where a couple met. And while it didn't turn out to be thirty years but thirteen, Amanda and Matt are the inspiration behind Ivy and Leo.

How wonderful if one day they come across *The House at Angel's Beach* and see the dedication. And isn't inspiration an amazing thing?

Thanks again for being part of this incredible journey with me and I hope you'll stay in touch – I have so many more stories and ideas to entertain you with! From my heart to yours.

Phillipa

www.phillipaclark.com

facebook.com/PhillipaNefriClark

x.com/PhillipaNClark

instagram.com/phillipanefriclark

tiktok.com/@PhillipaNefriClark

# ACKNOWLEDGEMENTS

First and foremost I have to express my sincere gratitude and appreciation for my gorgeous editor at Storm Publishing. Emily Gowers has gone above and beyond for me with this book. At every step she has been my rock and guided me to write the very best book I could, even though we needed to make some major changes for that to happen. With each book I write for Storm, I learn more about myself as a writer and that is an incredible gift.

As always I also thank the entire team who look after all the things which make a story into a book. This includes but isn't limited to Oliver Rhodes, a man so passionate about publishing that he has created this amazing place I call my home; Alexandra, Elke, Anna, Naomi, and everyone involved in the process. The cover designs are always so gorgeous and the fabulous narration of the audiobooks in this series by Brigid Lohrey are beautiful.

A special mention to the authors of Storm, who are such a supportive and friendly group, as well as my incredible network of authors here in Australia and overseas who always are there if I need them.

Not least, my family and dear friends who always believe in me.

Thank you all.

Printed in Great Britain
by Amazon

41773754R00169